JUMPING THE GUN

Sam heard Teddy Bonsell shriek behind the roar of the rifle shot, throwing both hands up as if hit by a sudden attack of hornets. Sam levered a fresh round into the Winchester even as Bonsell's holster, Colt and all, fell to the ground at his feet. The startled outlaw's rifle flew from his hands as Sam's rifle sights swung to Jake Cleary and he fired again. Cleary jerked back against the rock behind him, then staggered forward bowed at the waist.

The Ranger quickly levered another round as he saw Bonsell sidestep and reach down for his rifle in the dirt. Aiming for the rifle stock, Sam fired again. But this time instead of hitting the rifle stock, his shot sliced two of Bonsell's fingertips off at the top knuckles and sent the bloody inch-long nubs flying up into the outlaw's face. Cutthroat Teddy let out another shriek, this one louder, longer.

"Don't shoot . . . !" Bonsell shouted.

"[Cotton's] works incorporate . . . pace and plot in a language that ranges from lyric beauty to macabre descriptions of bestial savagery."

—Wade Hall, *The Louisville Courier-Journal*

"Gun-smoked believability . . . a hard hand to beat."

—Terry Johnston

GOLDEN RIDERS

Ralph Cotton

A SIGNET BOOK

SIGNET
Published by the Penguin Group
Penguin Group (USA) LLC, 375 Hudson Street,
New York, New York 10014

USA | Canada | UK | Ireland | Australia | New Zealand | India | South Africa | China
penguin.com
A Penguin Random House Company

First published by Signet, an imprint of New American Library,
a division of Penguin Group (USA) LLC

First Printing, October 2014

Copyright © Ralph Cotton, 2014

 REGISTERED TRADEMARK—MARCA REGISTRADA

ISBN 978-0-451-46594-8

Printed in the United States of America
10 9 8 7 6 5 4 3 2 1

For Mary Lynn, of course . . .

PART 1

Chapter 1

———————

The Badlands, Arizona Territory

Arizona Ranger Sam Burrack rode a thin, steep game trail up through a maze of large squat boulders and tall standing chimney rock. At the top of the trail there would be four gunmen waiting for him. He was certain of it. There had been five gunmen starting out last week, but yesterday he had reduced their numbers by one when he put a well-placed bullet squarely in the back of Cordell Kane—right between the shoulder blades. It was the best shot he could get, so he'd taken it, knowing that one fewer gun to face in the end could make the difference between dying or staying alive.

Now for the other four . . .

Two of the gunmen waiting up ahead for him were bank robbers Cutthroat Teddy Bonsell and an old ex-lawman turned outlaw, Jake Cleary. The other two were brothers by the name of Cundiff, Willie and Joe Cundiff. They would all be waiting with guns in hand, and this part of his hunt would be over—here atop a rocky hillside in the blazing sun. This was where their trail had brought him, Sam told himself, looking all around. Here was where their lawlessness would stop.

Beneath him, the barb, a coppery black-point dun took the trail at an easy walk, raising its muzzle now and then and sniffing the air up ahead. Sam thought it reasonable to believe that as long as he and the dun had been trailing these two miscreants, the horse had come to know their scent as well as it knew the scent of a bear, a coyote. It was just a notion he'd come to consider, knowing that horses were not always given credit for being as smart or as crafty as, say, a dog, a wolf or a mountain cat. Yet, he reminded himself, it had to be noted that the equine species had managed to survive among its many hungry predators for long ages past. That had to speak well for these fine fleet animals. *Doesn't it?* he asked himself.

Of course it does. . . .

He patted a hand on the dun's neck; the horse sawed its head a little and blew out a breath, as if in some silent agreement with him. They rode on another three hundred yards through twists and sharp turns around land-stuck boulders, and now and then past a lank and sparsely clad pine whose very presence implied that God had a strange sense of humor. Finally the top of the trail revealed itself against a blue cloudless sky. There the Ranger brought the dun to a halt and stepped down from his saddle, rifle in hand.

"Here's as far as you go, Copper," he said to the dun. The barb took a sidestep away from him as if to protest his decision and continue on in pursuit. But Sam held the reins firm-handed and rubbed the horse's nose.

"You think so now, but what if it doesn't come out to suit us?"

The horse chuffed and slung its sweaty head a little, but then settled under such sage reasoning.

"That's what I thought," Sam said, cradling his Winchester in the crook of his elbow.

He led the horse a few feet to a lank pine where he loosened the cinch and dropped his saddle from the horse's back. He slipped the bit from the horse's mouth and spun one of the reins around a stub of a pine limb and tied it in a loose slip hitch that the horse could easily pull free if it needed to.

The coppery dun stared at him almost warily, Sam thought, as he peeled the trail glove from his right hand and shoved it down behind his gun belt.

"Don't start being a worrier on me," he said with a trace of a wry smile. He raised his big Colt from his holster, checked it and let it hang down his side, his thumb over the hammer. "I plan on coming back for you."

At the top of the trail, Cutthroat Teddy Bonsell eased down behind the hot boulder he'd been lying on. His shirt glistened wet, covered with sweat from the heat of the boulder standing exposed with no shade on its sides or face. He pulled his shirt free from being stuck against his wet chest and fanned it back and forth as if to cool himself.

"Man!" he said to Jake Cleary sitting on the ground beside him in the boulder's shade. "If hell's any hotter than that, I pity the devil."

"The devil ain't in hell," said Cleary, idly scratching

his salt-and-pepper-colored beard. "He's smart enough he's laying somewhere in a cool stream. Did you see the lawman?"

"I saw him; he's headed up," said Cutthroat. "He's riding slow, watching the ground." He gave a thin grin. "Riding right into our laps."

Cleary shook his head.

"What's he still watching our tracks for? Where else could we be but here?"

"Ask him that when he gets up here," said Cutthroat, levering a round into his rifle chamber. He looked along a line of rock where the brothers leaned, waiting, watching him, all four tired horses standing on their other side. Cutthroat Teddy raised his arm and swung it back and forth and pointed toward the trail on the far side of the boulder.

"No hurry yet," said Cleary, seeing Teddy and the Cundiffs quickly preparing to meet the Ranger. "The way I figure, he'll leave his horse down there a-ways and ease up the rest of the trail on foot."

"The way *you figure* . . . ," Cutthroat said flatly. He gathered the front of his shirt and squeezed sweat from it. "Let me tell you something, Jake. I'm the one who laid up there on my belly watching for him. We're going by what I figure. He'll be riding up here any minute. You'd best be ready to tell him hello."

"I am ready," Jake Cleary said, jiggling his rifle in the crook of his arm. He spat and wiped his hand across his mouth. "You never seen me when I was *un*ready."

Teddy settled a little.

"Riding, walking, I don't care how he gets here. I

just want the man dead and off our backsides." He raised his hat and wiped sweat from his forehead. "I figured killing Cordy would have been good enough for him, the way these lawmen are," he added in disgust.

Cleary just looked at him.

"How are they?" he asked.

Teddy shrugged, leveled his hat back atop his head.

"You know what I mean," he said. "I figured he'd got himself a dead outlaw to show all the folks in Nogales. That's all he cares about."

Jake Cleary looked bemused, cocked his head curiously and gazed coolly at him.

"Are you sure you've ever heard of Ranger Sam Burrack?" he said quietly.

"Yes, I heard of him," said Cutthroat Teddy. "He killed Junior Lake, a couple of other second-rate saddle bums. So what?" He gave a shrug. "It ain't going to get me all wrought up and worried inside." He gave a lopsided grin. "Come on," he said, "let's get around this boulder, be ready for him when he gets up here." His grin widened. "Maybe he'll tell you the story of how he killed Junior Lake and his gang of desperados."

"I ain't making him no bigger than he is," Cleary grumbled, following Teddy around the large boulder.

"Hell, old man, *everybody* makes him bigger than he is," said Cutthroat Teddy. "I expect I just ain't as easily impressed as the rest of yas." The two stopped on the other side of the boulder and waited as the Cundiff brothers walked over closer to them.

"I never said I was impressed with him," Cleary said in a gruff tone. "I'm just saying what I know. He's a tough nut, and a man ought to keep that in mind before trying to kill him."

"Duly noted, Jake," said Teddy with a smug grin. "However tough he is wouldn't have meant spit once Brax found out he killed his brother Cordy." He tapped his forehead proudly. "See, I figure we're doing Brax a favor when we kill this fool."

"You mean *if* we kill him," Cleary put in grimly.

"Don't cast doubt on me, old man," Teddy warned. "I will split your gullet like a Christmas goose."

Cleary grumbled under his breath, but he turned away and watched the trail the Ranger would be coming up. Teddy turned to the Cundiffs. As the two drew closer he waved them to a halt.

"What the hell are you doing coming over here?" he said in a harsh whisper. "This ain't no church gathering! I need you both spread out, over there, the other side of the trail."

Without even stopping, Joe and Willie Cundiff turned a tight circle and walked away toward the other side of the trail.

"Damn it," Willie whispered sidelong to his younger brother. "I knew we should've gone on over there in the first place. Now we've made ourselves look like a couple of rubes, him having to tell us where to go." He paused as they walked on, then said, "Makes it look like this is our first ambush or something. . . ."

To be on the safe side, the Ranger had left the trail a hundred yards below the top of the hill. There had been too many places where he knew he could be seen by anyone keeping watch above him. A hundred yards or less put him in a dangerous position. He didn't like moving forward with the threat of rifle sights beading down on him, even though climbing around the rocky hillside off the trail was no less dangerous.

The last hundred yards had taken him over a half hour, but upon easing up out of the rocks and brush behind the big boulder he realized the extra time had been worth it. As soon as he stepped up and slipped around the side of the boulder he looked down and saw the Cundiff brothers sitting huddled in a stretch of brush. Ready, waiting for him, he told himself.

A dry-gulch in the making . . .

Across the rocky trail from the Cundiffs he saw Cutthroat Teddy Bonsell and Jake Cleary. It was easy to see that these two had grown tired of watching the trail and stood leaning against a rock twenty-five yards away. Both of them were facing toward him, Cleary with his head bowed on his chest. Teddy stood smoking a thin black cigar. He fanned the smoke away after each puff.

So far so good, Sam decided. He stood still just long enough to check his Colt and rifle, taking stock of himself out of habit. Then he raised the Winchester to the pocket of his shoulder and steadied it alongside the boulder. This shot would be tricky, he reminded himself, but he wanted to take Cutthroat Teddy alive if possible.

Here goes. . . .

Taking tight aim on the Colt holstered on Teddy's hip, he let out a breath, feeling the rise and drop of the gun barrel with each steady beat of his heart. He relaxed his right cheek on the rifle stock as if settling in for a nap. Then he cut his breath short, saw the gun sights stop dead on their target; and he squeezed the trigger in that perfect moment of stillness, his breath, mind and heartbeat centered on the fine black point of his rifle sights.

"Jesus, God . . . !" he heard Teddy Bonsell shriek behind the roar of the rifle shot, throwing both hands up as if hit by a sudden attack of hornets. Sam levered a fresh round into the Winchester even as Bonsell's holster, Colt and all, fell to the ground at his feet. The startled outlaw's rifle flew from his hands as Sam's rifle sights swung to Jake Cleary and he fired again. Cleary jerked back against the rock behind him, then staggered forward bowed at the waist.

The Ranger quickly levered another round as he saw Bonsell sidestep and reach down for his rifle in the dirt. Aiming for the rifle stock, Sam fired again. But this time instead of hitting the rifle stock, his shot sliced two of Bonsell's fingertips off at the top knuckles and sent the bloody inch-long nubs flying up into the outlaw's face. Cutthroat Teddy let out another shriek, this one louder, longer.

"Don't shoot . . . !" Bonsell shouted, rolling down into a ball against the rock, gripping his left wrist, blood running from the mangled fingers. Both of his guns had fallen three feet away. He dared not reach for them. Jake Cleary lay rolling writhing in pain, still bowed at the waist, his feet scraping, walking him in a circle on the rocky dirt.

Sam swung the Winchester toward the Cundiffs as pistol shots resounded from their position. One of their bullets thumped the ground at his feet, another zipped past his shoulder. But before he could return fire, he saw the two brothers bounding in and out of sight, firing backward over their shoulders as they skittered down off the trail, breaking brush, hopping over rocks, stumbling back to their feet, continuing on without missing a beat.

That went well enough. . . .

The Ranger let out a tight breath. In the waft of gray rifle smoke he waited and watched the rocky hillside for a moment longer. Twenty-five yards away Cleary groaned in pain and Cutthroat Teddy hunkered and panted like a trapped mountain cat. Wild-eyed in disbelief, Bonsell stared toward the Ranger, gripping his bloody left hand.

"You've—you've shot the wrong men, Ranger," he cried out as Sam stepped away from the boulder and walked toward him, his Winchester hanging in one hand, and his Colt out and cocked, hanging down his right side.

"No, I haven't," Sam said confidently, walking closer. "You're Cutthroat Teddy Bonsell. That's Jake Cleary. Howdy, Jake."

Jake Cleary managed to stop groaning long enough to look up and give a stiff nod.

"Howdy, Ranger," he gasped.

Sam turned back to Bonsell.

"I've got both your names on a list here in my pocket, Cutthroat Teddy," he said. "Want to see it?"

"Hell no!" Bonsell said. "What if this wasn't us?" he said, holding his bloody hand up for the Ranger to see. "What if you was tracking the wrong men—*innocent* men?"

Sam didn't reply. He stooped and untied Bonsell's sweaty bandanna from around his neck and wrapped it around his bloody shortened fingertips.

"Hold it there," he said to Bonsell, placing the wounded outlaw's right hand around the bloody bandanna. Out of the corner of his eye he saw Jake Cleary struggle onto his knees and wobble there, clutching his lower belly.

"You okay there, Jake?" he asked over his shoulder.

"I'll do . . . ," Jake groaned, examining himself. Cupping his belly with one hand, he felt down his inner thigh past his knee. "Thank goodness," he said in relief. His voice strengthened. "I thought you put a bullet in my gut rack, but you didn't. It hit my CSA belt buckle, went down my leg and sliced down the side of my boot well." He paused, then said, "I'm obliged, Ranger. I mean it."

Sam stood and kicked Bonsell's Colt and rifle out of reach. He only nodded in reply.

Watching, Bonsell couldn't stand it.

"You're both making me sick!" he spat. "This lawdog ain't that good with a rifle—nobody is!" He spun a harsh look at Sam. "Are you, *lawdog*? Tell the truth."

Sam didn't answer. He only stared down at Bonsell. He had aimed at Bonsell's gun belt, but hitting Cleary's belt buckle was a fluke. He'd aimed at his belly. Yet, Sam knew that the less he told these men about his intentions, the better.

"Speaking of telling the truth, Cutthroat . . . ," he said, reaching down to help Bonsell to his feet. "You and I are going to talk some about Braxton Kane and his pals—"

"*Ha!* You won't have to go looking for Brax, Ranger," Bonsell sneered, cutting him off. "Soon as he hears you killed his brother Cordy, he'll come looking for you. Him, the Garlets, Buford Barnes and all the rest." He started to point his bloody wrapped index finger at Sam before he realized it was missing. "So there's no need in you talking to me—I'll tell you *nothing*!"

Sam just stared at him for a moment. *That's a good start,* Sam told himself. Cutthroat Teddy was already giving him names before he even asked. He'd heard of Buford Barnes, knew him to be one of Braxton Kane's regular gunmen. But the Garlets was a name he'd heard only a couple of times. Were they newcomers to the craft of robbing and killing? Maybe, he supposed, or they could be coming farther west having worn out their welcome somewhere else. Either way, he had their names. Now that he heard from Cutthroat Teddy that they were part of Kane's Golden Gang, he wanted them. He knew better than to get in too big of a hurry. He would get them all rounded up just like this, one, two and three at a time. The rest of the time he would be tracking them, watching, waiting and being there when the time was right.

"Have it your way, Cutthroat Teddy," he said quietly, and he nodded toward the horses. "Let's get on our way."

Chapter 2

Midland Settlement, Arizona Badlands

The Garlets—Foz, Tillman and John—rode into Midland Settlement in the heat of the blazing Arizona sun. John, the eldest, had a long-barreled shotgun standing propped up on his thigh. A long dusty beard hung to the middle of a faded bib-front shirt. The high crown of his hat had long fallen victim to the harsh desert heat and lay flattened down one side of his head. Tillman, the middle brother, also wore a faded blue bib-front shirt. Over his shirt he wore a ragged long riding duster. His headwear, a roomy frayed bowler held down by a strip of rawhide, rocked back and forth with each step on his big buckskin barb. A big Colt Dragon stood in a saddle holster above his right knee.

On Tillman's right, Foz Garlet, the youngest, sat atop a surly head-tossing blaze-faced roan that appeared on the verge of bolting out from under him. John tossed his younger brother and his horse a disdainful look.

"Settle that flea-bitten cayuse before I bend a pistol barrel between his eyes," he warned.

"I don't know what in the devil's hell has gotten into him," said Foz, not about to take such a warning without reply. "But I expect any pistol barrel that gets bent on my horse's head will come from my hand and no other." He gave a tough, broken-toothed grin and patted the ornery roan's withers. "Ain't that right, ole buzzard-bait?" he said to the horse. *"Yes sir, that's right,"* he said, speaking in a gravely mock tone that was meant to be the horse answering him.

John and Tillman looked at each other and shook their heads, riding on.

"You've never been worth a damn with horses, truth be told, little brother," said John, the three of them steering their horses over to a long, iron hitch rail outside a weathered plank-and-timber saloon.

"Is this going to be a day full of your opinions?" Foz asked flatly, stopping his horse between his brothers and swinging down from his saddle. His brothers slid down and the three men tied their reins. "If it is I need to get as drunk as I can as fast as I can and stay there until you run out of sour wind." He slid a rifle up from his boot, then seeing the look on both his brothers' faces, he caught himself, stopped and slid the rifle back down.

"A drink or two, fine, but this is not a day for getting slack-jawed drunk," John whispered. "Remember our plan. Like always we're going to play it real quiet and sly. Nobody's going to know why we're here, until we're done and gone."

"I know that," Foz whispered in reply. "Sly and quiet, just like always."

The brothers nodded in agreement and stood among their horses for a moment and gazed off along the dusty street toward the new Midland Bank building, still under construction. John gave the other two a coy smile and lowered his tone.

"There she is, boys," he whispered.

"Damned if she ain't," said Tillman. "I'll drink to banks and all that's in them."

John dusted his long beard with both hands and slipped his shotgun into his bedroll behind his saddle.

"You and me both," he said, stepping from between the horses, Tillman right behind him.

Foz looked back and forth along the street, and then he stepped out, following his brothers onto a short plank boardwalk. The three walked single file across the boardwalk to the open door of the saloon. They stepped through a waft of stale beer, whiskey and cigar smoke and walked to a long bar where a row of drinkers readjusted and made room for them.

"What'll it be, fellows?" asked a short, stoop-shouldered bartender wearing a sweat-soaked white shirt. A black ribbon-style necktie hung wet against his chest. He wiped the bar top in front of the three men as he spoke. "I've got Saint Louis whiskey, Pilgrim beer and an oversupply of loaded mescal made by a fellow right across the border. He is now deceased. Some say he was hacked to pieces by the very ones who harvested his agave for him. Others say he drank his mescal and kilt himself flat out."

The Garlets showed no interest in the mescal maker's tragic misfortune.

"*Oversupply* meaning it's cheap?" John inquired with a straightforward stare. "*Cheap* meaning nobody's buying it?"

"I prefer to say *adequately priced*," said the bartender, "since there'll be no more of it coming from this distiller's hands. As far as folks buying it, some do. But I caution them to only take a short sip, then let it alone for a while. Too much at once . . . *whew*! It's hard on a man."

"Either hacked to death or killed himself you say?" said John, only now taking an interest in the distiller's fate.

"Those are the two more reliable stories," the barkeep said with slight shrug. "There're others, but they get more sad and gruesome I'm afraid. One says he cut his own tongue out, but I find that a little far-fetched." His face beamed with a smile.

"You're a hell of salesman," said John with a mocking grin.

"Take serious note, please," the bartender said, his smile fading, "This is a *special*, powerful brew. Very, *very* powerful. I'd be an odious fool not to warn folks."

Standing near the three brothers, a grizzled prospector spat a stream on tobacco into a brass spittoon.

"*Special*, ha . . . Don't let Eland here josh you," he said with a sidelong glance at John. "Every Mex who can swing a machete makes mescal this time of year. The only difference is what they put in it."

The short bartender, Eland Fehrs, cocked his bald head toward the dusty old prospector.

"I'll advise you to keep your nose out of other

people's conversations, Old Time," he snapped. "I'm trying to tell these men about this loaded mescal. I will sell it to no man unawares."

The prospector grunted and looked away.

"Well, now that you've scared us all to death," John Garlet said with sarcasm, "pull some up, we'll see how strong it is. I can't resist anything that would get a man hacked to pieces or make him kill himself. If it won't stagger a bull ram, we don't want to waste our time with it." He dropped a gold coin on the bar top.

"Oh, it's strong," the bartender cautioned, "*very* strong, meant to be sipped slowly, like I said, over a long period of time." He pulled a clay jug from under the bar and jerked out a small rag and a short stick that held it corked. "I don't recommend it to just anybody who comes along. The deceased was known for his liberal use of red peppers, ground peyote buttons and cocaine to give it both body and a visual experience that—"

"Do you talk this much all the *damned* time?" asked Tillman, cutting the bartender short. "I'm starting to think you're *out* of mescal."

"My apologies," the bartender said meekly. He set three wooden cups on the bar, filled them from the jug and started to remove the jug. But John grabbed his wrist.

"Leave it," he said.

The bartender gave him a wary look. But upon seeing it would do no good to argue, he swiped up the gold coin and left the jug sitting.

"If you have any questions, feel free to summon me," he said, moving away down the bar.

"Lord!" said Tillman, "I thought he wouldn't shut up until we all three got saved." He raised the jug and took a long swig while the other two held their wooden cups out to be filled.

"What about us, Brother Till?" Foz said coolly.

Tillman let out a blast of hot breath and spoke in a strained voice as he set the jug down atop the bar.

"It ain't *weak* . . . I'll give it that," he said, his voice shutting down on him even as he spoke. He patted the clay jug; his face glowed a boiling bright red. A sliver of steam curled atop the open jug.

"Maybe we should have heard the bartender out," said Foz staring at the jug. "I've heard of this stuff but I've never drank any."

"How strong can it be?" said John, lifting the jug and filling the cups.

The prospector, Casey "Old Time" Stans, turned sidelong to them again, overhearing their words.

"It ain't so much how strong it is, as how blind-staggering wild-eyed loco it makes a man, real *pronto*-like," he said. He watched the three drink from their wooden cups and let out a rasping hiss. "It's fast, *awfully fast*," he added. "You almost need to hold on to something when you drink it. I believe that's what Eland would've said once he finally got around to it."

"You ask me, he's just too mouthy to work a bar," Tillman said, raising his cup for another sip. "We come from Kaintuck and Tennessee stock. We don't need telling how or what to drink." He tipped his cup toward his brothers. The three drank.

"There ain't nothing under cork that's too strong for a Garlet to muzzle up to," said John. His voice had already started to take on extra effort. He took another, deeper drink as if to prove his point. *"Whoooiee,"* he shouted. "Boys, if this makes me want to kill myself, hand me a rope I'm ready to die!"

"Again," said the prospector amid the laughter, "not wishing to belabor the matter. It's not the kind of *strong* a man gets from whiskey. It's different. If you've got business that needs doing you need to get it done first, is all I'm saying. You don't want to—"

"You going to start now?" Foz interrupted with a shiny stare. His cheeks were rosy red. "See . . . I'm starting to understand how a man would drink this and want to chop some fool to pieces." He glanced around as if searching for a machete.

"No sir, I'm not going to start in," said the prospector, "and I beg your pardon. But as one man to another, I have to give warning. The first, and *only*, time I ever drank it I lost the use of this eye for near a month." He tapped a finger to his left eye. "I could not stand the smell of live chickens, linen, cotton or spun wool going on six weeks." He gave a slight shrug. "There. That said, I wish the three of you nothing but the best."

"No offense, prospector, and I am not a doctor," Tillman said with a slight chuckle, "but it sounds like maybe your eye was a bit on the wane to begin with." He slid the jug to the prospector and nodded at it. "If you want to jump back in the saddle, have at it. If you go wild-eyed blind we'll lead you out of here and set you the right direction."

The old prospector thought about it.

"I'd better not," he said. "I was on the Sonora sand flats last time, thinking I was lost in the Rockies."

"It's up to you," said John Garlet. He looked around and laughed and said, "Where's my rope? I'm ready to hang."

"That's not funny, John," said Foz.

"Hanging never is," John replied, grinning. "But it *is* a fact of life."

The prospector reflected for a moment longer.

"Well, what's *one drink* I always say." He grinned and wrapped his hand around the jug handle.

John Garlet still held his grin.

"Have you got a name, prospec-*tor*, or do you just conjure in off the desert and let the dust settle around you?" He chuckled at his sudden cleverness.

"Casey Stans is my name," said the prospector, "But you can call me Old Time, like everybody else." He raised the jug to his lips and took a long swig. As he lowered it, he heard Foz Garlet let out a strange hooting sound. Other drinkers along the bar turned and watched as Foz high-stepped in place, his hands up under his arms, crowing like some demented rooster.

"Holy God, this stuff is *fast*," John Garlet said in amazement. "I don't have any toes on my right foot. My left is about gone too!"

"You ain't alone, brother," Tillman said after a nasty belch.

As the Garlets passed the big jug around among

themselves for the next half hour, the barkeeper stood marveling at their drinking prowess. When they weren't taking a swig they were staring waxy-faced at whatever grabbed their attention. Finally, after a long silence, Foz cleared his throat and spoke in a restrained voice.

"I can see what you mean about smelling stuff," he said to the prospector. Foz sniffed the air all around like a curious hunting dog. "I can smell"—he paused thinking about it; finally it came to him—"*stars!*" he blurted out with a strange laugh. "I smell *stars*, and it's still broad daylight out!" He laughed toward his brothers as if asking them to join in with him. Drinkers along the bar laughed along with them.

John and Tillman just stared at their brother. So did the prospector.

"I got to go," the prospector said in a strained voice. He started to turn away, but Tillman caught him by the shoulder of his fringed buckskin jacket.

"What's the hurry, Old Time?" he said, the black pupils in his eyes looking large, wet and shiny.

"Nothing," said Casey. He stopped and looked at each Garlet brother in turn. "Can't I leave if I've a mind to?" he asked meekly.

"You can . . . ," said Tillman. As he spoke he raised a Colt from his holster. He cocked the big gun, turned it around and stared down into the barrel as if checking whether it was loaded. Then he turned it toward Casey Stans. "Or, you can stand right there hospitable-like until the music stops." He grinned and slid the jug back to the prospector.

"What music?" Stans asked, looking all around. He was already feeling the slight effects of the powerful mescal.

"That's up to you," said Tillman. He nodded down at the jug again.

Chapter 3

Sheriff Dave Schaffer had already risen from the bunk in one of the empty cells and strapped on his gun belt as the first sounds of gunshots and horses' hooves thundered from down the dirt street. He walked along the short hallway connecting the cells to his office at a calm measured pace. By the time he stepped into his office, and grabbed a rifle from the gun rack and checked it, the front door flew open and Eland Fehrs ran in. Sweaty and out of breath, Fehrs skidded to a stop and motioned the sheriff toward the open door.

"Sheriff Dave, come running!" he shouted. "They are robbing our new bank right this minute!"

Dave Schaffer kept his same measured pace toward the door. He knew the danger of a lawman getting into too big a hurry before he had an idea what was going on.

"Who's robbing it?" he said moving along steadily, but not yet fast enough to please the excited bartender.

"Three men calling themselves Garlets," Fehrs panted. "They've drank a lot of loaded mescal and gone out of their minds. But they started bragging bold as brass that they'd come here to rob the bank, and by thunder that's what they're doing."

Sheriff Dave eyed Fehrs as he walked past him and out onto the front boardwalk. Down the street the gunfire continued. A woman screamed; men shouted back and forth. Two armed riders rode away in opposite directions and disappeared around the two far corners of the street. Gunfire marked their locations as they circled the block into a long back alley.

"Loaded mescal, huh?" the sheriff said, levering a round up into the rifle chamber. "I thought I told you to stop selling that poison, Eland, before you got somebody killed."

"What you said was, '*take it easy* selling it,' " said the sweaty, short bartender. "And I have, that's the gospel truth. I warn everybody—anybody who'll listen, that is. But these three would not hear of any warning. No sir, they knew they could handle that damnable stuff." He struggled to catch his breath. "So I shut up and sold it to them."

The sheriff looked along the street and saw a remaining rider spinning in the street on a blaze-faced roan, firing a long revolver in every direction. Gray smoke loomed.

"And you're sure it's these Garlets doing the robbing?" he asked, hesitant to advance into the gunfire.

"Hell yes, I'm sure," said the bartender. "They got wild-eyed and admitted that was why they were here. Said they come to be the first men to rob our brand-new bank."

"Well then . . . ," said the sheriff letting out an exasperated breath. "I expect that's all I need to know." He started walking purposefully toward the single circling shooting rider as people watched from behind whatever cover they could find. "How bad a shape are they in?" he asked.

"Bad enough," said Eland, hurrying along to keep up with the long-legged sheriff. "Merlyn the bank manager said they charged in shooting, scared everybody, made him unlock the teller's door, then ran behind the counter and never stole a single dollar! Took off without taking any of the money!"

The sheriff gave him a doubting look as they moved along toward the circling rider.

"Never took a dollar? Are you sure?" he questioned the panting bartender.

"As crazy as it sounds, I'm not making it up," the bartender replied. "Merlyn Oates said one of them opened his fly, shook himself at a woman customer. Then he grabbed a desk chair up in his arms and carried it out the door! They got outside and took to shooting at everything in sight—his exposed crotch still flapping and bobbing."

"This sounds bad," said the sheriff. "Get somewhere safe and take cover, Eland. I don't want to have to worry about shooting you if this thing gets hot and heavy."

"I'm gone," said the bartender, ducking and running away as the circling rider brought the scrappy roan into a run and started shooting wildly at the sheriff. In the long alley behind the street the shooting had ended suddenly, a cloud of thick dust billowed above the roofline.

What the . . . ?

The sheriff looked at the rise of dust where the guns had fallen silent, but he had no time to contemplate. The blaze-faced roan charged straight at him, its rider letting out a yell, still firing mindlessly. With no place near him to take cover, Sheriff Schaffer took a standing position, his feet shoulder-width apart, his Colt raised, leveled and cocked. He forced himself to take his time—make the first shot count. The rider charged, seventy feet, fifty feet. Schaffer held his ground and squeezed sure and steady on the Colt's trigger.

But just before his Colt fired, the rider on the blaze-faced roan cut the horse sharply away. The whinnying animal skidded and slid in a tight abrupt turn, redirected its charge and ran straight toward the hotel. The sheriff stood staring, his Colt still up and ready, but as yet unfired.

"Holy gods in heaven . . . !" he said aloud, seeing the roan lunge up and across the boardwalk, its rider reared back on the reins to no avail as the two of them crashed headlong through the closed front doors. "He's gone into the hotel . . . ?" Schaffer said, stunned, glancing back and forth as if searching for someone to confirm what he was seeing.

On the street, the sheriff stared transfixed through the broken-down double doors, seeing the horse's rump ascend quickly and disappear up the hotel stairs. The sound of breaking boards and shattered banister resounded as the roan plowed its way up to the second-floor landing, turned a sharp left and ran along the hallway leaving broken floorboards flying up in its wake. The sheriff

and a few venturing townsfolk gawked and followed
the sound of breaking wood and smashing hooves along
the inside of the large hotel. Another crash resounded,
a woman screamed as the roan blasted through a door,
across an occupied room above the street. The stunned
onlookers watched the roan launch itself and its cling-
ing rider through a closed window in a spray of glass,
shredded curtain and broken sash. The animal landed
skidding and backpedaling on the tin-clad overhang
five feet below the window.

"He's come out!" someone shouted, seeing the rider
bowed and gripping the horse's neck for dear life, his
boots out of his stirrups flapping against the roan's
sides. Sheriff and townsfolk watched, stunned, as the
horse's hooves slid out and down the tin overhang.
Beneath the overhang the support posts broke away and
collapsed just as horse and rider sprang out off it onto
the street.

Hitting the street, the rider flew from the horse's back.
The horse stumbled and rolled away; the rider flew off in
a high arc and fell with a splash, flat on his back in a
horse trough full of water. The impact of the falling outlaw caused the water trough to burst at its corner seams
and send a wave of water rolling onto the street.

With no more than cuts and scratches from broken
glass and splinters, the horse rolled to its hooves and
stood shaking itself off in a cloud of dust. Shredded curtains fell from its rump. Its twisted saddle hung on its
side. In the flattened horse trough fifteen feet away, the
rider, Foz Garlet, soaking wet, stunned and wild-eyed,

struggled to his feet and sloshed wobbly away as if nothing had happened. His crotch had somehow fallen partially back behind his open fly.

"This is all a *first* for me . . . ," Sheriff Schaffer murmured to himself almost in disbelief. He uncocked his Colt and left his thumb over the hammer.

"There he goes, crazy as a goose!" shouted Eland Fehrs, who had eased back into the street, seeing the spectacle unfold.

Foz Garlet, dripping wet, looked around at the sound of the bartender's voice with a lost and vacant expression. His eyes appeared to swirl with madness.

"Where's my damn horse?" he asked no one in particular. His voice was thick and distant sounding.

The sheriff stepped forward quickly, noting the empty holster on the wet man's hip.

"You won't need him," he said. Expertly, he grabbed Foz's shoulder with his free hand and kicked his feet out from under him. The would-be robber fell to the mud offering no resistance.

As the sheriff bent forward and reached for the handcuffs he carried behind his gun belt, a townsman ran toward him from the alley behind the main street.

"Sheriff, quick!" the man shouted, seeing the man on the ground, the broken glass, the horse, the curtains at its hooves, "there're two more down back in the alley. They rode headlong smack into each other!"

The sheriff straightened from cuffing the downed outlaw and looked at the townsman Arthur Polks in disbelief.

"I mean it, Sheriff!" said Polks, a middle-aged lawyer. "It's the damnedest thing I ever saw!"

"Ha!" said Fehrs, "you didn't see nothing—you should have been here." He gestured toward the fallen overhang, then upward at the open hole where the window used to be.

"Eland," the sheriff cut in firmly, "stand here and keep a foot on this one."

"Me . . . ?" the barkeeper protested.

"Yes, *you,*" said the sheriff. "It was your loaded mescal that caused all this."

"But what if he tries something?" said Fehrs.

"Look at him," said Sheriff Schaffer, nodding down at the hapless Foz Garlet. The cuffed outlaw babbled mindlessly up at the sky. His tongue wagged in his gaping mouth. "He don't know where he's at or how he got here."

As the sheriff stepped away and let the barkeeper plant his boot on the downed man's chest, Merlyn Oates, the bank manager, hurried forward.

"Thank God you caught these blackguards, Sheriff!" he called out proudly. "Caught them right in the act." He offered a firm smile, glaring down at the mindless Foz Garlet.

"I understand they didn't take any money?" The sheriff asked.

"That's correct, Sheriff," said Oates. "I have never seen such a fouled-up piece of work. It was hardly a robbery at all." He looked toward the broken desk chair lying in the dirt a few yards away. "I suppose I can take my chair back to the bank, see about repairing it?"

The sheriff considered his request for a second.

"Not right now," he said finally. "Better let me hold on to it for a while."

"For heaven's sake, Sheriff, why?" the banker asked.

Before the sheriff could answer, Arthur Polks stifled a laugh and said, "It may well be *evidence*, Mr. Oates." He looked the banker squarely in the eyes.

"That's nonsense!" said the banker. He turned a glare to Schaffer.

"Attorney Polks is right," the sheriff said. "If it's the only thing stolen, it's *evidence*. Unless you want to see these men go free."

"Go free?" said Oates. "They robbed the bank!"

"Did they *demand* any money?" Polks cut in.

"No, they did not, but they demanded I unlock the door to the teller counter," Oates offered. "They held guns on me!"

"Did they *take* any money?" Polks proceeded dryly.

"No, but—" The banker stopped abruptly, seeing where the lawyer was leading. He pointed a finger at Polks. "Listen to me, Polks, you slick-talking son of a—"

"Easy now, Merlyn," Polks warned. "You don't want to start saying things about me that could cost you money should I take offense and pursue it—"

"Shut up, the both of you," Schaffer said, fed up with them. He turned back to Eland Fehrs. "Keep this one pinned down. I'll be right back." He looked at Oates. "Go back to the bank, for now." He looked at Arthur Polks. "Come with me, Polks, and do me a favor. I'm going to need a qualified legal opinion from an officer of the court here."

"Any way I can help, Sheriff," Polks said, giving Oates the banker a sly smug grin. "Any way *at all . . .*"

It was late evening when the Ranger rode into the Midland Settlement with Jake Cleary and Cutthroat Teddy Bonsell, both of them handcuffed, riding along in front of him. Sam held on to a lead rope that ran from one wounded outlaw to the next, a loop drawn around each of their waists. Bonsell held his hands up against his chest, his right thumb hooked in his shirt, supporting his injured left fingers. The bandanna around his fingers had turned almost black, covered with thick congealed blood. Cleary sat stiffly upright to help lessen the pain in his bruised lower belly.

Along the boardwalk townsfolk had begun to gather as soon as the three riders came into sight. They stood armed and ready, holding rifles, shotguns, pistols, pick handles. Fear and hatred shadowed their faces. Yet upon seeing the two men handcuffed and the Arizona Ranger badge on Sam's chest, they eased back, lowered their weapons, and watched as he followed his prisoners toward the hitch rail in front of the sheriff's office.

"Not a real friendly bunch here, are they?" Jake Cleary said, eyeing the townsfolk. The three looked at the collapsed overhang in front of the hotel and the broken support posts.

"Something bad's gone on here," Sam replied quietly. "They look a little edgy."

He looked at the broken window glass and ragged curtains in the street, the ripped-out window frame on the hotel's second floor. Two men carried the busted double doors away from the hotel. Two others stood in the broken glass with brooms and shovels.

"*Edgy* is putting it mildly, Ranger," Bonsell said in a lowered voice. "I see hanging ropes in their eyes."

"You two keep your eyes down and your mouths shut," Sam replied. "Let's see what the sheriff's got to say." Ahead of them, he saw the sheriff step out of his office and stand looking toward them from the boardwalk.

As the Ranger and his prisoners rode closer, the sheriff eyed his badge and let his hand fall away from the butt of his holstered Colt. He watched the Ranger touch his hat brim as the three stopped in the street a few yards away.

"We've never met, Ranger Burrack," Schaffer said, touching his hat brim in return. "I'm Sheriff Dave Schaffer."

Sam gave him a questioning look.

Shaffer explained, "I recognized your sombrero," he said with a thin smile. "I heard you were riding a black-point dun these days. Sometimes a man's horse and hat gear is easier recognized than the man himself."

Sam only nodded and returned the thin smile.

"Pleased to meet you, Sheriff," he said. Gesturing a nod toward the street behind him he said, "I can see you've had your hands full here."

"Yep," said the sheriff. "Three brothers calling themselves the Garlets rode in and tried to rob our new bank." He aimed a narrowed glance toward the Midland Settlement Bank. "Left us with a mess, but didn't get away with any money."

"I've been hearing their names of late," Sam said. "I

just put them on a list I keep. Good job catching them. It saves me the trouble."

"Obliged, Ranger Burrack," said Schaffer. "I'd like to take credit for catching them, but I can't. The truth is they got so broken-down on mescal and cocaine beforehand, two of them rode smack into each other, the third idiot rode his horse up the hotel stairs and out the window, glass and all. . . ." He paused and nodded at the mess of broken glass, wood and curtains in the street. "You see how well that worked for him." He shook his head. "I've got all three of them locked up. Can't make sense out of anything they say."

Cutthroat Teddy snickered under his breath.

"That would be ole Foz doing the fancy riding," he said. "That's one fool that shouldn't be allowed on a horse's back."

"Shut up, Cutthroat," Sam said.

The Sheriff looked at Bonsell, then at Sam.

"This one would be Cutthroat Teddy Bonsell, I take it?" he queried.

Cutthroat Teddy looked proud of being recognized for his growing notoriety.

"What gave me away, Sheriff?" he said, his chest a little puffed.

"It's known that you never keep your mouth shut," the sheriff replied sharply.

Sam said to Schaffer, "Yep, that's him all right. And this one is Jake Cleary. I expect you've heard of him, too."

Jake Cleary only looked down at his boots.

"You bet I have," Sheriff Schaffer said. He touched

his hat brim toward the older gunman almost in a gesture of respect.

Not liking the way the two lawmen were paying more attention to the older gunman than to him, Cutthroat Teddy spoke loud enough for gathering bystanders to hear him.

"If you two lawdogs think you're cleaning up this badlands you've got another think coming—"

"Shut up, Teddy," Cleary said, cutting him off. "Can't you see folks are on a sharp edge here?" He gave a wary look around the street at the stark, angry faces gathering in closer.

"Shutting up is wise advice; you'd best take it," Schaffer quietly warned Bonsell. Bonsell looked all around at the faces of the townsfolk, then lowered his head. Sam looked at Schaffer.

Schaffer nodded over his shoulder toward his office door and spoke to the Ranger.

"This is a good time to get in out of the sun," he said. "Bring your prisoners on in, Ranger Burrack. This is one robbery you'll likely want to hear about sitting down."

Chapter 4

With the two prisoners in a cell next to the Garlets, the Ranger and the sheriff walked back down the short hall to the sheriff's office. Schaffer closed a thick wooden door separating the jail from the office area and sat down behind his desk. The Ranger leaned against a support post in front of the big oak desk while Sheriff Dave Schaffer related the whole botched robbery attempt to him.

He took off his sombrero and glanced questioningly at the big wooden door and hesitated before speaking.

"Don't worry, Ranger," said Schaffer, "they can't hear nothing we say back there. It's been tested."

"It crossed my mind listening to you," Sam said. "At some time or other, every man back there rides with Braxton Kane's Golden Gang, out of Colorado Territory— the gang I'm trying to round up and put out of business. I'd like to get them all back to Nogales at once if I can."

"Oh . . . ?" said Schaffer. "Why's that, if you don't mind my asking."

"I killed Braxton's brother, Cordell, just the other day," Sam replied.

"Whoa, I see," said Schaffer. "So, Braxton's going to be sending his whole gang after you, soon as he hears about Cordy. The more of them you get out of the way now, the better?"

"Something like that, Sheriff," Sam said. "Once I get Braxton Kane in my sights I can cut the head off the snake, so to speak. But for now, I have to keep moving forward, taking them down one and two at a time when I can catch them."

"I realize how it is with these big robbing gangs," the sheriff sighed. "Gunmen drift in and out, job after job. You never know who all's riding with them and who ain't."

"There it is, Sheriff," Sam said. "If it's all the same with you, I'd like to take these Garlets off your hands tomorrow morning, get them out of here before Kane hears about his brother."

"You're welcome to them, Ranger," Schaffer said. "The truth is, I've been wondering how to keep the town from swinging a rope over a timber post." He gave a short grin. "You'd be doing us all a favor taking them to Nogales come morning. In fact I'll ride with you, if that's suitable."

"I welcome your company," the Ranger said. As he finished speaking, a knock resounded on the front door and the attorney, Arthur Polks, walked in without waiting for an invitation.

Before acknowledging Polks, Sheriff Schaffer turned his eyes back to Sam long enough to say, "It's all settled then, first thing in the morning, Nogales?"

"First thing," Sam said.

"I hope you're not planning on moving these Garlet brothers, Sheriff," Polks cut in, as if having been there for the whole conversation.

Sam and the sheriff both looked at the rosy-faced lawyer. Polks grinned confidently, took off his stovepipe crowned hat and jerked a pencil and a thick book pad from inside it.

"Because if you'll permit me to say so . . . ," Polks said thumbing through notes he'd begun writing down shortly after the Garlets' melee in the dirt street. "These men must not be charged with bank robbery, no indeed." He thumbed through more pages of notes. "Even bank manager Merlyn Oates has stated that these men asked for no money, nor did they abscond with any," he continued in an officious tone, "although there was *in fact* money there in the open safe for the taking had they chosen to do so."

"What kind of shenanigan are you trying to pull, Polks?" Schaffer said.

"No shenanigan, Sheriff Schaffer," Polks beamed. "You asked for my legal opinion as an officer of the court earlier, did you not?"

"I did . . . ," said Schaffer hesitantly. "But I didn't expect you to go boring away at it full tilt."

"I could give the matter no less than my full and earnest attention," Polks said smugly. "If you expected otherwise from me, you were mistaken, sir. The law is not frivolous in such matters and as an officer of the court of this fine territory I am called not to treat it so."

Here we go . . . , Sam said to himself, noting how much the attorney seemed to enjoy the sound of his own voice.

"Of course I wanted a sound opinion from you, Polks," Schaffer said. "But I need to hold them, charge them with something. Look at the mess they've made here. They shot up the town, tore up the hotel, broke up a desk chair."

Polks stepped closer, consulted his pad again and flapped it shut.

"Yes, they undisputedly did all that," he said. "And I'm certain they might well stand trial for everything from public drunkenness to indecent exposure." He raised a finger for emphasis. "But not for bank robbery." He paused and grinned again. "Any lawyer with half a mind can beat this case for them. God knows I would."

"What about *attempted* bank robbery?" Schaffer asked, sounding disgusted. "We all know that's what they had in mind before they got lit up on mescal."

"Knowing it and proving it is two different things, Sheriff," said Polks. "Bank money was lying there, they didn't *attempt* to take it. So, there goes a bank robbery charge out the window. I'm advising you, trying to convict them will be a waste of time and money."

"My goodness," Schaffer said, shaking his head. "The more civilized the law gets, the less sense it makes. No wonder townsfolk like to drop a rope and watch these fools wiggle their bootheels." He looked at the Ranger. "Have you got them wanted for bank robbery anywhere else in the territory?" he asked.

Without taking his eyes off the grinning lawyer, Sam only shook his head without commenting.

"Then I'm afraid your best bet is to charge them a fine for all the mess they made here, Sheriff," Polks put in. "And at that, I caution you not to fine them so high that they can't afford to pay, or you'll be stuck with them in your jail, feeding them on the taxpayer's money. How much do you think the townsfolk will like that?"

Schaffer looked at the Ranger.

"See what I mean about the law making less sense?" he said.

Sam only stood watching, listening.

"Here's something else you're not going to like much, Sheriff Dave," said Polks. "Being the only qualified attorney in town, it is my duty to offer my services to the Garlets should you decide to try them here on any charge more than a simple—"

"Jesus, Polks!" said Schaffer, cutting him off. "Do you just sit around dreaming up this crazy, mindless—?"

"I beg your pardon, Sheriff, this is the law," Polks cut in indignantly. "You *did* ask me for an opinion. I would be remiss if I gave this matter anything less than my best effort."

The sheriff cooled and let out a breath. "Pay me no mind, Arthur," he said to Polks. "I know you're quoting law, chapter and verse. But sometimes *the law* piles up on itself like rat turds in a barn loft."

Polks said, "Fine them and get them out of town, Sheriff. That's my best advice."

Schaffer looked back and forth between the attorney and the Ranger.

"Hunh-uh," he said. "I'm not turning them loose today. Not in the shape they're in. Look at them. They're all three off somewhere goosing butterflies. For their

sake and the town's, I'll hold them until they sober up enough to lift themselves into a saddle."

"Oh, and then . . . ?" said Polks.

"Then I'll chase them out of here, like you said," Schaffer replied grudgingly. He turned to Sam and said, "Unless you still want to take them to Nogales, Ranger Burrack. If you do they're all yours."

"*Ranger Burrack*, did you say?" Polks queried, a look of surprise coming to his face. He quickly looked the Ranger up and down. "The Ranger Burrack I've heard so much talk about of late?"

"Most likely," Sam said flatly, knowing he was the only Ranger named Burrack riding for the Arizona Territory Rangers.

"Sheriff, where are your manners?" Polks said to Schaffer. Then he said to the Ranger, "Please allow me to introduce myself, Ranger Burrack. I'm Arthur B. Polks, attorney-at-law." He smiled. "No hard feelings over what I've said here, I hope."

"No hard feelings at all," Sam said.

"Watch him, Ranger. He's gotten as slippery as an outhouse ditch today," the sheriff cautioned Sam with a half-joking smile.

"Shame on you, Sheriff Dave," Polks said with an affable chuckle. "You know that I always have the matters of this town at heart." He turned to the Ranger with a smile and tipped his hat back atop his head.

"To answer your question, Sheriff," Sam said, getting back to the Garlets. "If you can't make a case against these three, there's no reason for me to take them to Nogales. Turn them loose. I'll just have to wait until there is a charge that'll stick." He gave a slight shrug. "I shouldn't have to wait long."

"I wish I could be more help, Ranger," said Schaffer.

"Obliged all the same," said Sam. "This is how it goes busting up a big gang like this. I'll take Cleary and Bonsell back to the Ranger outpost. By the time I get back out here, maybe Braxton Kane will hear about his brother, and him and his pals will come calling."

"I apologize if what I've said causes you any problems doing your job, Ranger," Arthur Polks said.

"Don't apologize for the law," said the Ranger. "I'm used to situations taking sudden turns and peculiarities. That's why I carry extra bullets."

In the darkening shadows of evening, behind Eland Fehrs' First Street Saloon, Prew Garlet and a half-breed Mayan-Mexican Indian called the Bluebird stepped down from their horses and looked all around the dusty alley. Earlier, the two had heard the shooting from a distance of two miles out of town. A full hour after the shooting had stopped and no sign of his brothers had appeared along the trail, Prew and the Bluebird had led their horses down from among a rise of rocky cliffs and followed the trail toward the Midland Settlement with caution.

Now, they reined their horses to one of the hitch posts standing alongside a row of dilapidated public outhouses. The horses twitched their ears and grumbled under their breath at the terrible stench of human urine and excrement.

"Are you sure that stuff is safe here?" Prew asked the

Bluebird, nodding toward the bulge of homemade dynamite in the Bluebird's saddlebags. "If we blow up these horses, we're going to be in a tight spot here."

The Bluebird only stared at Prew blankly as he spoke. When he saw that Prew's lips had stopped moving, he only nodded his head, his long, shiny black hair hanging from under his hat brim.

"All right, I'll take your word for it," Prew said, not realizing that the Bluebird couldn't hear anything quieter than a clap of thunder. "Stay back here close to them. Nobody's going to let you into the saloon anyway."

The Bluebird grunted, but continued walking alongside Prew toward a small, narrow alleyway leading alongside the First Street Saloon.

Seeing the Bluebird still beside him, Prew stopped and held a hand toward him.

"No, damn it," he said firmly, shaking his head. "Stay here with the horses until I check things out." He pointed down at the ground as he spoke. When he finished, the Bluebird looked all around, then nodded his head.

"Jesus," said Prew. "You need to brush up on your *Ingles*, if you expect to make it in this business."

The Bluebird only nodded again and watched him turn and walk away toward the rear door of the saloon. When he saw Prew step aside for two men walking out to use the outhouses, he backed away into the shadow of a building and sank onto his haunches and watched, seeing a smile crease Prew's otherwise hard and leathery face.

"Evening, gents," Prew said as he allowed the two

men to walk past him, one of them weaving a little on his feet. The two men nodded and walked on purposefully. Prew caught the back door before it swung shut and walked inside, making a show of rebuttoning his fly as he walked across the plank floor of the crowded saloon.

At the bar, he sidled in between two drinkers who had left a sliver of space between them and summoned the bartender with raised fingers.

"Another beer and rye here," he called out as if he'd been drinking there all evening.

"Another beer and rye coming up," said a tall, powerfully built bartender with a pockmarked face and a tangle of thick black hair. He hooked a clean beer mug from the bar top and drew back on a tap handle in one sleek quick motion.

Watching the mug fill, Prew pulled out a gold coin and spun it on the bar top. The bartender stood the foamy beer mug in front of him and filled a shot glass with rye from a bottle, almost before the coin stopped spinning and flattened onto the bar.

"I have never knowingly participated in that practice," the big bartender said, nodding at the coin. His wide hand scooped it up and closed around it like a thick clam.

"Could have fooled me, fast as you are," said Prew. He gestured down at the rye bottle in the bartender's other hand. "Leave it," he said. And before the bartender could turn and make change from a tin box under the bar, Prew asked, "What was you saying a while ago about some shooting that went on here today?"

"What part?" said the bartender, spreading his big

hands along the bar edge, his eyes checking along the line of drinkers.

Prew gave an offhanded shrug.

"Well, all of it, I reckon," he said.

"It was the damnedest thing I ever saw," the bartender said, "a horse flying out a window that way, the second floor? You ever see something like that?"

Good God . . . !

Prew stood staring, taken aback for a second.

"No, I can't say I have," he finally replied. "There was three of them, I heard?"

"Yep, three," said the bartender. "Each one as wild-eyed crazy as the other. Got blind-flying drunk and decided to rob our new bank."

Wild-eyed crazy . . . ? Prew had to think about that one for a second. Finally he shrugged again.

"I expect they're all headed for Boot Hill now?" he queried.

"No," said the bartender, "they all lived through it, don't ask me how. They say it's hard to kill a lunatic." He pointed a big finger off along the street out front. "They're all in our jail. But it's likely they'll swing by morning. There're some townsmen mulling it over right now. Add some whiskey into the mix, I'd say they'll be reaching for ropes most anytime." His hand went below the bar and came up with change for Prew's gold coin. "They liquored up right here on loaded mescal before they did their deed," he added matter-of-factly. He dropped the change onto the bar top.

Prew, sweeping up the change, said, "Man, that must be some powerful mescal."

"I'll say so," said the bartender. "The owner had me take it off our offerings till mescal season next year. Said this was just too strong a mix for these desert pilgrims." He gave a tight, thin smile. "But I myself will have to slip in a drink or two before I go casting judgment. It's out in the woodshed—what's left of it."

"That's the only way to know for sure." Prew nodded, raised his shot glass, drained it, filled it up, and drained it again. "Hearing all this makes me curious about it myself." He paused thinking how powerful the mescal must be to have sidetracked his brothers so quickly. Then he said, "Say they're about to hang those three?"

"Oh yes," said the bartender. "They'll swing for certain."

"Well. . . ." Prew sighed, swept the bottle of rye up, corked it, and touched his hat brim toward the bartender. "I suppose if a man's got to swing, drunk is the best way to do it." He turned and walked out the rear door. He saw the Bluebird stand up from the shadows as he closed the door behind him.

"Well, Bird," he said, walking up to the waiting half-breed. "I found out what happened, and where my brothers are."

The Bluebird only nodded, seeing Prew's lips move.

"They're in jail," Prew said, the two of them walking purposefully to their horses, "and we're going to get them out, right now. Get your stuff." He motioned the Bluebird toward his saddlebags.

As the Bluebird took out a homemade bundle of four

dynamite sticks from his bags he turned to Prew and saw him hold up three fingers.

"I want all three of my brothers out of there alive—do you understand me?"

The Bluebird looked at Prew's three fingers and only nodded; he turned back to the saddlebags.

"All right, get it ready to blow," Prew said. "I'll get their horses out of the barn. He turned and unhitched his horse's reins. Before leading his horse away, he looked at the woodshed where the bartender had placed the jugs of mescal. "One more thing I've got to do," he said. He patted the Bluebird on his back as the Indian pulled out two more bundles of dynamite sticks and tucked them under his arm. Bluebird only nodded without looking around.

Chapter 5

At the wall of iron bars separating the three Garlets' cell from the cell housing the Ranger's two prisoners, John Garlet, Cutthroat Teddy and Jake Cleary huddled and whispered back and forth in the slice of moonlight slanting through a rear window. Behind John Garlet, Foz and Tillman lay sleeping beneath a steady rise and fall of snoring and mindless babble. Behind Bonsell and Cleary, Casey Stans, the prospector, lay on the plank floor, using his wadded-up hat for a pillow. The sheriff had placed him in the cell to keep him from sleeping on the street.

Jake Cleary gave the sleeping prospector a guarded look, then turned back to John Garlet.

"Don't worry about that old desert rat," John Garlet said in a lowered voice, still sounding woozy and somewhat disoriented. "He's with us, leastwise until we say he can leave."

Bonsell and Cleary gave each other a dubious look.

"All right, here's the way I see it," said Cleary, knowing he could spend all night waiting for John Garlet's head to clear. "You hombres *did not* rob the bank, so get that part out of your mind right now."

"We meant to," said John, a little confused.

"*Shhh,* just hush saying that," said Cleary. "Don't even let it in your mind. You rode in here, the barkeeper sold you some mescal liquor that would stagger a bull ram. You had no idea in hell what you were doing when you went into that bank."

"That part's true," John said, scratching his throbbing head. "One minute we were drinking big swigs, the next, Tillman and me were on our backs in the dirt where we run each other down in an alley."

"That must be some powerfully good stuff," Cutthroat Teddy put in. He sat lowered on his haunches, his bandaged left hand hanging between his knees, his two shortened fingers throbbing like the beat of a drum.

Cleary eyed Bonsell and said in a gruff whisper, "Pay attention, Teddy. Stick to the matter at hand." Then he looked back at the striped shadowy moonlight crisscrossing John Garlet's face. "One question, is your brother Prew coming for you?" he asked.

"Hell yes, you can count on it," John said, knowing that much for certain. "I'm surprised he's not here already."

Cleary let out breath in relief and relaxed a little.

"Then that's that," he said. "It doesn't matter if the law says you're guilty or not. You'll be out of here soon as Prew hears about it. He don't want to leave you here and risk a lynching while the law scratches its butt deciding what to charge you with."

"Yep, that's kind of how I see it," John said, sort of understanding the conversation in spite of his mind still floating on a sea of mescal.

"My question is," said Cleary, "can I count on you and your brothers letting me and Cutthroat out, too?"

"We all ride for the Golden Gang," said John. "How can you even ask me something like that?"

"Sorry, John," said Cleary. "The shape you're in I wouldn't want to get forgotten about here."

"You won't be forgotten . . . uh," said John, leaving his words hanging under a confused stare.

"Damn it, *John*, it's us—me and Jake Cleary. Look at me," said Cutthroat Teddy, seeing the outlaw struggle to remember who he was talking to.

"Okay, *okay*," said John, raising his eyes to Bonsell's shadowy face through the bars, "I forgot for a second. I know it's you. I'm not a damned idiot." He paused and cupped his unsteady hands to the sides on his head. "I'm getting sober here." He paused again, then said, "But I swear I can hear a bug crawling down the wall."

Cleary looked around the dark cells, seeing no sign of any crawling things.

"Get yourself sober," he coaxed John.

"I'm trying," John said. "I'm just coming and going. One minute I'm here, the next I'm somewhere else."

Cleary and Bonsell looked at each other again. Bonsell stifled a laugh and grinned.

"That has got to be some awfully good stuff," he repeated.

Cleary gave him a sour stare.

"What . . . ?" said Bonsell. "You hear about something that makes a man act like this and you ain't even curious?"

"No," Cleary said, tight-lipped. "I've been as drunk as I wanted to be my whole damned life. I don't need no Mexican *whoopiee* potion making me walk upside down." He shook his head and looked around again as if searching for bugs crawling on the walls. "You young outlaws are killing us, dragging the whole profession down."

John Garlet sat staring blankly at the floor, his head in his hands.

"John," said Cleary. He waited, got no response. *"John,"* he said again. "John," he said a third time. When John looked up from his hands and back through the bars at him, Cleary said, "Can you get up, walk around some?"

"Where we going . . . ?" John asked as if in a dream-like state.

Jesus . . .

Cutthroat Teddy even took it seriously, seeing that the outlaw had gained little ground toward reclaiming his senses.

"John, get up and walk around the cell some," he said. Then he turned to Cleary as John struggled to his feet. "He was all right a minute ago," he said in amazement.

"This ain't *a minute ago*," said Cleary. "This is *now*."

"I'm over here," John whispered for no reason at all, having staggered his way toward the rear window.

"We know that, John," Cleary whispered. "Keep quiet." He spoke with slow calm words, like a man hoping to steer a lunatic away from a high ledge. "See if you can wake your brothers, easy like—"

Cleary stopped short at the sight of a black silhouette blocking the moonlight at the rear window.

"Get back," said a stiff voice from the darkness outside, "I blow these bars out."

"Get back where?" John said dreamily. He looked baffled.

"No! No!" said Cleary, trying to shout in a whisper. "Not yet! Let us get ready!"

"Get down . . . ," said the voice as if ignoring Cleary's desperate pleading. "Here goes."

"Wait! For God's sake, *wait*! What's *wrong with you*?" shouted Cleary, hearing the sudden sizzling sound of a wick burning outside the window. Seeing nothing would stop the sizzling wick, he shouted at John, throwing silence to the wind. "Get your brothers under the bunk! Get down yourself; take cover!" even as he spoke, he and Cutthroat Teddy flung themselves to the floor and belly-crawled under their bunks.

Cleary grabbed a thin straw mattress, pulled it under the bunk with him and hugged it to himself quickly. He drew a deep breath like a man going underwater and held it as the whole jail building seemed to jump a foot off the ground and hang there. Before squeezing his eyes shut he saw the world turn into a spinning, churning fireball. He heard a sound like cannon fire, and in the roar of it he felt a second blast, this one louder, harder.

In the midst of the two blasts he saw John Garlet fly away, spread-eagle on a section of bars that had ripped loose from between the two cells. He thought he caught a glimpse of the devil's red-blue hand reach sidelong out of some netherworld and slap him out from under his bunk like a matron's broom sweeping away a mouse. Behind the blast, the world slammed back into place with the breath of hell's fire and brimstone.

In his hotel room a block away, the Ranger awakened fast and felt himself suspended in air for a split second. Then he felt himself and his bed jar back down onto the plank floor.

Dynamite . . . Jailbreak . . . Was that one blast or two? he asked himself as he batted sleep from his eyes.

Almost before the hotel had stopped trembling he rolled from the bedside to his feet. Grabbing his Colt, holster and all from the bedpost, he slung the gun belt over his shoulder and grabbed his trousers from a chair back. He stepped into his boots as he buttoned his fly. He stamped his boots into place and grabbed his Winchester rifle from against the wall on his way to the door. From the direction of the blasts came a relentless round of bullets exploding randomly.

On his way down the newly replaced steps to the hotel lobby, Sam saw men and women alike running along the hallway from their rooms in housecoats and slippers. The boards of the hallway floor were likewise new, still unpainted, having replaced the tread and risers left cracked and broken behind the hooves of Foz Garlet's galloping horse.

Sam made it to the stairs ahead of the other awakened guests. He descended the stairs and was out the front door in the dirt street as the townsmen hurried here and there staring in disbelief at the black fire-streaked smoke boiling and billowing along the rooftops.

While men gathered to form a bucket brigade at the town's water troughs, Sam ran up the street under a low looming cloud of smoke. From inside the smoke, bullets continued to explode. He crouched beside the town doctor who knelt over Sheriff Schaffer lying prone in the dirt. Schaffer's face was black; smoke curled from his scorched shirt.

"I'm all right, Ranger," the sheriff said, gasping for breath.

"I've got him," the doctor said, looking up at Sam. "Get the horses out of the barn!"

Sam looked around at the chaos growing along the street. Men and women ran back and forth. Bullets still exploded from within the black smoke; debris and bits of burning wood lay strewn everywhere. Following the doctor's orders, Sam moved on through the smoke, seeing one of the outlaws, John Garlet, still lying spread-eagle, pinned to the ground by the section of ripped-out bars.

But he didn't stop to check on the downed outlaw. Hearing the sound of whinnying and neighing coming from the direction of the livery barn, he hurried on through the smoke. But he didn't have to turn the frightened animals loose. At an alleyway leading back to the barn, he heard the thunder of hooves running toward him and jumped aside just in time to see horses emerge from the roiling smoke. Like apparitions fleeing a nightmare, the animals raced past him, smoke gusting from their nostrils.

When he spotted his black-point dun running out of the smoke, he took a chance, leaped out, grabbed its mane with his left hand and swung up onto its back as the horse cut away from the others and turned onto the street. Feeling the weight, the sudden clutch of a human hand, the big copper dun tried slinging him off sideways. But Sam held fast, allowing the horse to buck and fight for a second. Then he settled it with a firm familiar hand, made it realize it was him, his feel, his touch, his weight and scent atop it.

"Easy, Copper, easy, boy . . . ," he said, realizing from the graveled strain in his voice how badly the black smoke was getting to him. Beneath him the dun settled, grudgingly at first, careful not to be tricked. Sam, reaching farther up the dun's neck, took another handful of mane and leveled the horse's gait into a slower, waning pace, then down to a trot, the Ranger's grip holding firm control.

As soon as the dun settled under him, Sam tapped his knees to its bare sides and set it at a run to the end of the street and back around to the livery barn. In front of the barn the smoke from the explosion had drifted away enough for him to look into the long empty barn and out the rear door into the purple night. He heard no whinnying, no neighing from within the smoke-streaked barn, and he knew the stalls were empty, or any horses still inside were dead.

Bullets continued exploding; a big explosion rose straight up inside the fiery smoke with a whistling sound that ended in an orange-red ball of fire high up the darkness. With another tap of his knees, Sam spun the dun and headed back to the gathering chaos on the dirt street. Smaller fires had already sprung up everywhere. Flames danced on bits of strewn debris along the street and alleyways. Townsmen called out to one another as they ran back and forth, some with buckets of water, others with shovels.

"This one's alive, Dr. Croft!" Sam heard a man call out. The man stood holding the section of iron bars off John Garlet's chest. The outlaw's clothes emitted curls of smoke.

"Get the bars off him," the doctor shouted, standing crouched, dragging the sheriff away by his shoulder.

Sam slid from his dun's back beside an overturned buggy in the street. He took one of the loose buggy reins, hitched the dun and hurried over to help the doctor. The townsman standing over the outlaw struggled and managed to raise the section of iron bars and turn them over. He dropped the bars into the dirt.

The doctor and Sam kneeled over the smoldering, half-conscious sheriff. Pressing the end of a stethoscope to Schaffer's chest, the doctor listened intently. He turned his eyes up at the Ranger in relief.

"I think he's going to be all right," he commented. As some townsmen ran up to them, he said, "Our sheriff's alive. Get him to my office. I'll be right along."

As the townsmen carried Schaffer away, the doctor hurried over and stooped down beside John Garlet. He raised Garlet's hand and moved it back and forth slowly as if inspecting it. "Why was this man walking the street at this time of night?" he asked no one in particular.

"He was in the jail, Doctor," Sam said. "There were five prisoners and a prospector in the cells." As Sam spoke he looked over at the thick flame-streaked black smoke and where the new jail had stood. Bullets still exploded from the burning remnants of the mercantile store next door.

"I expect they're all dead men now," the doctor said. He laid Garlet's limp hand down on his chest. "This one looks like he's broken every bone in his body." John Garlet lay flat in the dirt with the imprint of the bars stamped on him, head to toes.

As the doctor shook his head and stood up, his medical bag in hand, his stethoscope hanging around his neck, a voice up the street called out to him from in front of a burning building.

"Doc Croft, we need you here, quick!" the voice said.

The doctor clamped his black bag to his side with an elbow and gave one last look down at Garlet.

"Somebody get this one to my office, too," he called out. He gave Sam a level gaze.

"I expect you'll be the law here until our sheriff's back on his feet?" he asked pointedly.

Sam looked off into the black smoke and fire still shrouding most on the long block of burning buildings, at bucket brigades hastily formed, made up of men and women alike who passed buckets of water from the water troughs along a row of waiting hands. In the street a half block away a fire wagon stood with its hose rolled into the smoke and flames. A townsman held the team of frightened fire wagon horses in place while two men worked frantically, turning the pump handle that fed water from the wagon's supply tank.

"I'm here for as long as I'm needed, Doctor," the Ranger said, the raging firelight glittering in his eyes. Even if the ones who'd blown up the jail were still alive and had made their getaway, he couldn't leave here now. Rounding up the Golden Gang would have to wait, he told himself, seeing what destruction the pursuit of his prey had wrought upon this unsuspecting town.

Seven miles out of Midland, lying in the dirt beside a narrow creek, the six blackened and smoked outlaws dropped from their saddles and fell to the ground at the water's edge. Jake Cleary coughed and hacked and spat up black-gray saliva. His hair had been singed from the front and both sides of his head. His eyebrows were missing. His beard was frayed and ragged. While his horse drank its fill, Jake stuck his blackened face down into the water and swished it around and raised it. He stared at the Bluebird three men down from him as the Indian cupped water to his face with both hands and washed black sweat from his cheeks.

"I want to kill this son of a bitch . . . worse than I've ever wanted to kill anybody in my life," he wheezed in a broken voice. He stared hard at the Bluebird. "He's come damn near . . . blowing us all to hell." As he spoke he rubbed his bare hip where his gun would ordinarily be holstered. Unable to hear Cleary's threats, the Bluebird didn't even look around.

"Take it easy, Jake," Prew Garlet said to the scorched

and blackened gunman. "Nobody wants to kill him more than I do. I've got a brother missing back there."

"I hate to tell you, Prew, but your brother John is dead," Cleary said, his voice still raspy from smoke. "If he's not, he's wishing he was. Last thing I saw was him riding a piece of jail bars out through the front wall." His words ended in a hard cough.

Foz and Tillman both raised their faces from the water at Cleary's news. They looked at their brother Prew, then at the Bluebird. The Indian continued washing black sweat and grit from himself, not realizing he was the topic of bitter conversation.

"Don't kill him," Prew warned. "Brax wants him. Says the Bluebird here is the man to have with us if we need something blown up."

"I can sure as hell believe that," said Cleary with dark sarcasm.

"This Mex-Injun worked setting up explosives for mining companies blowing down whole mountains— learned to make his own dynamite from the South American Suala Soto. I expect you've heard of him."

"I've heard of him," said Cutthroat Teddy, also in a raspy voice. "I've heard he's dead—blew himself up somewhere."

"Brax wants the Bluebird," Prew said, "so we're taking him to him." He shook his head and added, "Anyway, what happened back there is the jail wall blew into the mercantile and the mercantile must have had lots of gunpowder on hand."

"Maybe so," Bonsell replied, "but the jail wall

wouldn't have blown into the mercantile if this fool hadn't used so damn much explosive."

"I don't know how that happened," said Prew, unable to deny it. "I think he doesn't *habla Ingles* so good." He looked over at the Bluebird and said, "Ain't that right, Bird? You don't understand English?"

The Bluebird didn't even look around.

"Jesus . . . ," said Cleary. "Now I think he's just ignoring you."

Foz wiped water from his blackened face and looked around at his brothers, Tillman and Prew.

"I don't know if it's the blast or that damned mescal, but I'm still not right in the head," he said.

"There're some would say you never have been, Foz," Prew said, rising to his feet. "I heard all about that mescal. I even brought some along in case I want to see for myself how strong it is."

"Don't drink it, Prew," Foz warned, also pushing himself to his feet. "It's ruined me."

"I won't," said Prew. "Not now anyway."

Foz stared at Prew grimly and said, "I ain't joking. There's something wrong with that stuff."

Prew gave his brother a dismissive chuff under his breath.

Cleary and Bonsell stood up, water running from their scorched faces.

"If that damned Ranger ain't dead, he's going to be after us," said Bonsell.

"He won't be for long," said Prew. "There're plenty of Golden Riders between here and Kane's hideout. One of us will kill him before he gets too close. If not,

Brax will stop his clock when he hears about him killing Cordy." He turned to his horse and picked up its
reins. The horse's tail was frazzled and burnt on the
ends. "Either way, Burrack is now just a killing waiting
to happen." He swung up into his saddle. The men
swung up as well, except for the Bluebird who sat staring out across the night sky.

"Let's go, Bluebird," said Bonsell. Then he repeated
himself in Spanish. Still, the Indian just sat staring. As
Bonsell stepped his horse closer, the Bluebird saw the
dark shadow of the animal stretch out on the water.
Looking around he saw the men atop their horses, and
stood up himself.

Bonsell looked at Prew and said, "Just one more
hardheaded Injun is what I think."

"Might be," said Prew turning his horse away from
the water toward the trail. "Let's go get ourselves some
guns and take the Bluebird to Kane's hideout." He nodded at the Bluebird's bulging saddlebags. "I don't like
traveling with dynamite behind me."

PART 2

Chapter 6

For three full weeks the Ranger kept the law in Midland Settlement while Sheriff Schaffer recuperated from his injuries—the burns, broken ribs and numerous cuts and contusions the explosion had inflicted on him. During that time, marshaling town law had not been difficult. The people of the settlement were too busy rebuilding their town to participate in the drunkenness and brawling that might ordinarily take up much of a sheriff's time. It helped that for the first week and a half the saloon itself had been closed for repairs, due to the domino effect the explosion had created racing along the main street.

"I don't mind telling you, Ranger," he said, "I'll never sleep at my desk again—if I ever have another desk, that is."

"You'll have a desk, Sheriff," Sam said. "I ordered you one up from Texas. Should be here in a month."

"Obliged, Ranger," said Schaffer. He sighed. "By my estimation, we lost a full third of our businesses right there," he said, gesturing a bandaged forearm toward the new buildings under construction across the street from where they stood out front of the doctor's office. "Not to mention my jail and office building," he added. "When the jail blew, the explosion ripped through the mercantile stockroom. Smitty, the owner, said he had four and a half kegs of black powder stored there. That did it. We're lucky we didn't all land in Mexico."

Sam only nodded, gazing along the row of unpainted flat-plank-and-adobe buildings. Almost miraculously, a band of Mexican adobe craftsmen had shown up from across the border and began constructing the structures with blocks made from mud mixed on-site in the charred, blackened earth.

"We only found one body sifting around the jail site," Sam said, staring in that direction. "We'll never know who it was—it could've been the prospector."

"Could've been that they all blew into pieces and burned in the street," Schaffer said, looking at the countless black charred spots on the wide dirt thoroughfare.

"Could be . . . ," Sam replied deftly.

"But you don't believe it?" said Schaffer.

"I can't allow myself to," Sam said, his thumb hooked in his gun belt. "Not just yet anyway. Besides, even if the Garlets and my prisoners are all dead, there's still Braxton Kane. Still enough Golden Riders to keep me busy for a while."

Sheriff Schaffer stood with his weight steadied on a walking cane, his left arm in a sling, salve covering his red, raw forehead and the back of both hands. His eyebrows and lashes were gone; his head was covered with fresh white gauze. One bootless foot had a thick bandage covering it almost up to his calf, his trouser leg ripped open up the seam to accommodate it.

"To tell the truth, Ranger, you're ready to get on the trail, aren't you?" he said to Sam as if it was confidential between the two of them.

Sam stared straight ahead, seeing a Mexican lead a reluctant mule loaded with fresh adobe brick on its back.

"To tell the truth, *yes*, I'm ready to get on the trail," he said. "But not until the doctor says you're in shape to get back to work."

"Fact is, I'm as right as a spring peach, Ranger," the sheriff said, his mustache and goatee gone. He pointed his cane at a large ragged saloon tent standing in a vacant lot. "The saloon's back in business, but there's no piano, no billiard table anymore. That's where most trouble always comes from. Men can't hear music and not fight. Can't seem to hold a stick for long without swinging it at one another—it's born in them," he confirmed.

"Obliged, Sheriff," Sam said. "But make sure you're up to it, before I cut out of here."

"Like I said," Schaffer reiterated, "I'm right as a spring peach." He pounded himself lightly on the chest with his bandaged forearm in the sling. "Did you ever get anything out of that Garlet idiot?" He gestured a nod toward the doctor's clapboard building behind them.

"No," Sam said. "Nothing yet. I'll talk to him again before I leave."

"And if he won't give up their hideout?" said Schaffer.

"I rode out into the hills and looked around some

while you were unconscious," Sam said. "I found some tracks that were riding wide off the trail, headed south."

"So, that's why you're suspecting some of these men might still be alive?" Schaffer asked.

"Bonsell's horse was wearing store-bought shoes, has a nick in one the size of my thumbnail. I saw that nick while I was looking around."

"Could be the horse was running away from the fire," said Schaffer.

"Could be. But whether they're alive or not, it's as good a place as any to start looking," Sam said. "They were headed south when I took up the hunt. They did a change around when I started getting close. I figured they did it to lead me away. From what I hear, Braxton Kane is not a man who'd stand for his riders bringing the law down on him."

Schaffer looked him up and down and nodded.

"That he ain't," he said. "Nor is he the kind of man who'll shy away when somebody's killed his kin. I can't say that enough, Ranger," he added.

"Obliged, but you needn't warn me, Sheriff," Sam said. "I don't want him shying away. I want him coming at me full bark-on. Killing Cordy might be the only way I can flush Braxton out and take him down."

Schaffer shook his head warily at the Ranger's methods.

"That's playing too fast and loose for my blood anymore," he said. "I expect I've lost my stomach for that kind of hard killing." He turned as he spoke and gestured his walking cane toward the side door to the doctor's building. "Come on, I'll question John Garlet with you," he said. "I'll wear this stick out on him—make him cooperate, if you want me to."

"Let's see how it goes," Sam said, walking in front of the sheriff and opening the door for him. "What is Dr. Croft saying about this one?"

"Says he's lost his mind," Schaffer said. "Says the blast didn't help any, but he thinks he was poisoned from the mescal and it's boiled his brain. Aside from the peyote, cocaine and God knows what else is in it, Doc says it might be full of metal from up around the mines where it was made. Metal poison alone can eat a man's brain plumb out of his skull."

Sam just stared at him, listening.

"Anyway," said Schaffer, "I'm glad we've seen the last of that stuff around here. No telling how many it's sent into raving madness. Still they like to drink it, seeing how strong it is. The more they hear about it, the more they have to try it."

As the two stepped inside and saw John Garlet stretched out in a corner, his arms out spread-eagle, thickly bandaged and strapped down on splint boards to keep his broken bones in place. His legs were also strapped to boards and bandaged. His feet rested in slings that hung from thin cables on pulleys attached to a metal frame that stood over the bed. A wooden frame mantled his shoulders and held his head in place on a round board, held there by rigid wires screwed in place. His head was covered with thick bandage, his face partially concealed by gauze.

"Did you . . . think to bring me . . . a gun?" he asked from within a dazed laudanum stupor.

"No gun, Garlet, you can't hold one anyway," the sheriff said. "It's me, Sheriff Schaffer, and the Ranger, Sam Burrack. The Ranger wants to ask you some questions."

"I don't know . . . anything about it," Garlet said groggily.

"About what?" the sheriff asked.

"About . . . nothing," said Garlet. His mouth hung gapping in a crazy half smile.

"See?" Schaffer said to the Ranger. "Still doesn't have the sense God gave a goose." He shook his head and said to Garlet, "All the same, talk to him, Garlet. It might make you feel better."

"Can I . . . have a gun . . . one bullet?" John Garlet asked, adrift on the laudanum. His dark eyes swirled in madness. Saliva ran from his mouth down his chin.

Sam stopped short before walking any closer.

"It's useless talking to him," he said. "Dr. Croft is right. He's lost his mind." He stepped back to the door. "I'm leaving come morning."

"I'm holding him here and putting him on the jail wagon from Yuma when it gets here," said Sheriff. "He's a danger to himself. They'll stick him in a lunatic cell."

Sam looked at John Garlet again and shook his head. Then he and the sheriff stepped out the door and closed it behind them.

After the first two weeks of riding northwest through a succession of frontier mining settlements and hill towns, the three Garlets, Bluebird, Cutthroat Teddy Bonsell and

Jake Cleary stopped at every opportunity to search for arms and ammunition. One of the first had been Poco Fuego. In the wispy first light of dawn they had ridden scorched, singed and blistered into the high border town and spilled into a small cantina owned by a one-legged Confederate war veteran named Virgil Piney.

There they spent a week lying in the cool water of a shallow creek and eating anything Piney and his old Mexican man-servant Jeto would kill, chop and roast for them.

Being the only one fully armed and carrying money, Prew bought two of Virgil Piney's spare guns, a long-barreled muzzle-loader shotgun and a battered—but still vicious—nine-shot LeMat revolver. The big French-made horse pistol hosted a twenty-gauge shotgun barrel beneath its long .42 caliber pistol barrel. The shotgun he gave to his brother Tillman, the LeMat to Jake Cleary who had carried one like it when he'd ridden with a band of Alabama guerillas in the great civil conflict.

When the men had finished their week's stay and prepared their horses for the trail, Foz saw Cleary check the big LeMat and shove it down into its worn saddle rig hanging beside his knee.

"What about me, Prew? Hadn't I ought to get a gun?" Foz asked his brother.

Prew studied his brother's eyes for a moment, scrutinizing him closely.

"How you feeling now?" he asked.

"What do you mean *how do I feel*?" said Foz, a little taken aback.

"I mean have you gotten your senses back yet?" Prew said bluntly.

"Hell yes, I've got them back," said Foz, sitting upright in his saddle. "What are you saying, that you don't trust me holding a gun?"

"Last night you said you were seeing things, things that had you shaking and carrying on," said Prew. "How's that going now?"

Foz jerked angrily on his roan's reins as the animal began getting restless beneath him.

"Last night I *was* seeing things," he said. "Today I'm *not* seeing them. Do I look shaky to you?"

Prew just stared at his brother's hairless, browless smudged face.

"Next guns we come upon, you get first pick," he said, placating Foz. "Does that suit you?"

"That'll suit me," Foz said. He looked all around at the other faces as he spoke. "I'm warning everybody here and now, if I keep hearing you whispering and laughing about me behind my back, somebody's going to die, gun or no gun."

The men, except for Tillman, sat staring blackly at him. Tillman sat looking off into the distance with a dreamy wistful look on his face.

"Take it easy, Foz," Prew said quietly, seeing his brother getting agitated.

But Foz would have none of it.

"Don't deny it," he said, ignoring Prew. "You've all been doing it, haven't you?" His eyes stopped on the Bluebird who upon seeing Foz's lips move, nodded his head, agreeing with the delusional outlaw although he hadn't heard a word he'd said.

"Jesus . . . ," Prew said under his breath. He turned his horse to the trail. "Come on, Foz, you and Tillman ride beside me a while. I want to hear more about what to expect from this jug of mescal I've got here." He gestured toward his saddlebags. "Tell me what you all were seeing last night." He took Tillman's inattentive horse by its bridle and pulled it alongside him until Tillman seemed to snap out of a trancelike state and collect himself.

Bonsell and Jake Cleary gave each other a guarded look and slowed their horses to fall behind the three Garlets.

"This is worrisome, the way they're acting," Cleary said under his breath.

"I hear you, Jake," said Bonsell. He nudged his horse forward, following the Garlets. He stared forward at the jug bulging in Prew's saddlebags. "This keeps on I'm going to start getting curious about that stuff myself."

The Bluebird rode beside the two, staring ahead at the endless Mexican hill country. And they rode on.

By that afternoon they had made a camp on a hillside in the shelter of tall pines and rock. The next day, in the early afternoon, they arrived at an ancient nameless Mexican trade settlement overlooking a wide stretch of Sonora desert valley. There they gathered more guns, gun leather and ammunition from a Mexican gunrunner named Sibio Alverez, who was known to show partiality to the Kane brothers and anybody associated with the Golden Gang.

The settlement had become a stopping point for any of the Golden Riders to lie low and lie the trail grow cold behind them. At Alverez's cantina, two such men, Lester Stevens and Mason Gorn, had been drinking and carousing with four loose women who made their living off passing gunmen along the border badlands trails. Looking out through a window they recognized the six riders moving their horses along the dusty street.

"All right," said Stevens, grinning, staring through the wavy window glass. "It's about time we had some company show up." He threw back his shot of rye and set his glass down hard and snatched the bottle by its neck. He and Gorn walked out front and met the men as they rode up to the hitch rail and stepped down from their saddles. The four women ventured out behind them and stood hanging and leaning on to the two and staring at the newcomers. In the doorway, Sibio Alverez stood chewing on a short black cigar. He grinned across gold teeth and raised a hand in welcome.

"Look real pretty, senoritas," he said in border English, "these hombres can do for you what your daddies never could."

As the riders climbed down from their saddles, both Stevens and Gorn stepped forward, Stevens holding out the bottle of rye as a welcoming gesture. But upon seeing the men's condition, the two stopped. Stevens let the bottle hang down his side.

"Jesus, Prew, what the hell has happened to you fellows?" Stevens said, staring at their singed hairless faces, their scorched clothes. They looked at Cutthroat Teddy Bonsell's bandanna-wrapped hand.

"Too much to talk about out here," said Prew, reaching out and motioning for the bottle, which Stevens handed to him. Prew turned up a long swig of whiskey and passed the bottle to Jake Cleary standing nearest to him.

"Then do come inside," said Sibio Alverez with a sweeping gesture of his hand. "Let these lovely senoritas show you some sympathy."

The Bluebird, knowing his place, stayed at the hitch rail with the horses as the bedraggled men filed into the cantina and took up position along a long, ornately carved bar. The four women sidled into their midst, ignoring the men's condition, the smell of burnt hair, of charcoal and gunpowder. Slipping around behind the bar, Alverez set up shot glasses and a row of three new bottles for the arriving gunmen. He filled the shot glasses and began filling beer mugs from a tap as the men threw back their first shots and refilled them as if in reflex.

Prew glanced at one of the women who suggestively rubbed up against him and eased her hand inside his sweaty shirt. She looked up and gave him a smile.

Prew turned his attention from her to Lester Stevens.

"We had a robbery go bad on us," he said grimly.

"My God, they set you on fire?" said Stevens, looking along the line of charred gunmen.

"No," said Prew. "The Mex-Injun out front is the Bluebird, he blows stuff up. You ever hear of him?"

"Yes, I have," said Stevens. "He did all this?"

"Him and I did this, getting my brothers out of jail. The explosion went bad too. My brothers turned into idiots on bad mescal." He nodded toward Tillman and Foz who stood staring at their empty shot glasses as if in deep contemplation. "It's been one mess after another this whole trip." He shook his head in despair.

"Jesus . . . ," said Stevens. He looked at Gorn on his other side, then back at Prew. "Brax sent us here to watch for any of our bunch and guard their back trail if they need it. I expect you fellows *need it*?"

"Oh, yes, we need it," he said. "We've been riding for over two weeks, getting away from the Midland Settlement and heading to the hideout to tell Brax his brother is dead."

"Cordy, dead?" said Gorn, looking around Stevens at Prew.

"Yep. Killed by Ranger Sam *by-God* Burrack, according to Bonsell and Cleary there," he said bitterly. He threw back his shot of rye and set his glass down hard. "We'll be leaving here come morning. If Burrack comes through behind us, kill him."

"We'd love to, Prew," said Stevens, him and Gorn both nodding in agreement. "And so you know, if he slips around us we've got gunmen in every little town between here and the hideout. Nobody's getting through this stretch of hills." He raised a shot glass as if in toast. "Here's to killing Rangers," he said, "be it for *good reason*, or just *good sport*."

"Damn right," Prew agreed. He raised his refilled shot glass and drank it down. "That aside . . . ," he said, looking back at the woman's hand inside his shirt.

"Little darling, how would you like to give me an all-over bath and send my clothes out to get boiled and beaten clean?"

She gave him a red-painted smile.

"For two dollars, I'd be both thrilled and delighted," she said. "What about your friends?"

Prew looked along at the bar at the miserable, stinking gunmen, realizing that he was the only one with any money. He thought about it, then said, "Yeah, why not? You gals get them all cleaned up and smelling better. Me first though"—he drew her against him—"in case you run out of water too soon."

Chapter 7

In the morning, Prew stepped from the front door of a dusty plank and adobe hotel onto the even dustier street. The men following him stopped and watched as Prew looked down at the Bluebird sitting wrapped in a ragged blanket, leaning against the front wall. The flat brim of the Indian's hat hid his face.

"Wake up, Bluebird," Prew said. He reached his boot sideways and jingled his spur near the Bluebird's ear. The Bluebird didn't move. *"Hey . . . ,"* said Prew, a little louder. He tapped his boot against the Bluebird's leg. The Indian stood up—too quickly to have been sleeping—Prew thought, and turned and looked at him from beneath his hat brim. "Let's eat and get out of here," said Prew.

The Bluebird nodded his head, unwrapped himself and held the ragged blanket over his shoulder.

"Look at this, Prew," said Cutthroat Teddy. He nodded at the horses lined along the hitch rail, saddled and ready for the trail. A few loose grains of feed lay in the dirt at their hooves. The night before, the men had unsaddled the animals and lined their saddles along the edge of the short boardwalk.

"My, my," said Prew, "but I do like a Mex-Injun who's willing to pitch in and help out a little." He looked at the Bluebird as he spoke. The Bluebird nodded and walked to his horse. The men walked to their respective horses and looked them over good, pleased to see that the animals had been well attended to the night before.

"I believe we ought to let the Bluebird take care of the horses from now on," Bonsell chuckled. He looked at the Bluebird who saw his thin smile, saw his lips moving as he looked at him. "What do you say to that, Senor Bluebird?"

The Bluebird only nodded again. "Yes, even so . . . ," he said tightly. Again, he nodded.

"*Whoa*, did you hear that?" said Bonsell as if taken aback at the sound of the Bluebird's voice. "This Mex-Injun can talk after all!"

"Don't act like an ass, Bonsell," Prew said. "We all knew he could talk."

"I swear I didn't," said Bonsell with a shrug. "I knew he had a hinge on his neck, kept his head bobbing up and down. But I haven't heard him talk till now."

"Don't make a big thing of it," Prew said. "Maybe he don't feel like jawboning all the time."

"Yeah," Cleary cut in, giving Bonsell a look. "There's some of us here who could take a lesson from it."

"Go to hell, Jake," Bonsell said. He turned and looked at the Bluebird and said, "I didn't know if he couldn't talk or was just being half-cross with us." He grinned at the Bluebird. "No offense intended though." He shook his head a little.

The Bluebird shook his head along with him.

"See? He's as good-natured as the next fellow," said Cleary, also gathering his horse's reins.

Bonsell chuckled, looking the Bluebird up and down.

"Did you mean it, Bluebird, offering to take care of our horses for us?" he asked.

Looking at Bonsell, the Bluebird nodded and backed his horse onto the street with Tillman and Foz.

"Yes, even so . . . ," he said in a short tone. Prew and Cleary backed their horses and turned them beside Foz and Tillman.

"See?" said Bonsell. "Now that he's started talking you can't shut him up." He chuckled under his breath and looked at the others and shook his head. Backing his horse, he turned it in the street and rode up alongside the Bluebird. "You even rubbed this cayuse down for me!" he said, running a hand along his horse's clean withers as if amazed. He looked at the Bluebird.

The Bluebird nodded.

"Yes, even so," he said.

Bonsell laughed aloud and slapped his thigh.

"I like you, Bluebird," he said. "We're going to be pals, you and me."

Hearing Bonsell, Cleary looked down and shook his head.

"Listen up, everybody," said Prew, booting his horse to the front of the riders.

"I did," Foz said for no reason, sitting slumped in his saddle, Tillman beside him, riding in the same manner.

Bonsell and Cleary looked at Foz and Tillman. So did Prew with a concerned expression. Then, ignoring his brother's remark, he turned from his brothers and looked around at the other two gunmen.

"We're riding all day and night till we get where we're going. We're making sure we've got some gunmen waiting in each place we stop. The way we always do when we gather up for a big job."

Bonsell and Cleary both nodded, acknowledging him. The Bluebird, Foz and Tillman rode looking straight ahead.

"It just ain't getting no better out here," Prew said to himself under his breath. He batted his boots to his horse's sides and they rode on. Behind them, Stevens and Gorn looked at each other.

"I'm not going to stay here and face that Ranger, are you?" Gorn asked.

"Ha, I ain't that stupid," said Stevens. "Soon as the dust settles, I'm headed up out of here. We can tell Braxton Kane whatever suits us. The shape that bunch is in, they'll be lucky if they even get there."

"That's what I say," said Gorn. He grinned and spat and stared after the riders until they fell out of sight in their own wake of dust.

The Ranger left the Midland Settlement atop his black-point copper dun, leading two spare horses alongside him on a lead rope. One of the horses, a big brown-and-white paint, carried two canvas bags across its back, one carrying grain for the horses; the other carried enough provisions and extra ammunition to get him across the badlands hill country and deep into Mexico if the trail led him that far. He switched the supply sack from the paint horse to a big, easygoing buckskin every few hours to keep both horses fresh when he'd ridden his black point out and needed to switch his saddle to one of the spares.

When he'd first ridden out to where he'd found the fresh tracks the day after the jail break, he looked down at those tracks only in passing, noting how much three weeks of dry, hot breezes had caused them to fade into the rocky earth. Yet, luckily, there had been no rain up here, he reminded himself, or else he would have found no tracks at all.

So far, so good . . .

It never hurts having luck on your side, he told himself, looking out and down across the sloping sand rises where the presence of both jagged rock and smooth rounded boulder appeared to compete for the desert floor. Beside him the copper dun pushed its muzzle against his arm and chuffed.

"All right, I'm coming," he said. "You don't mind if I look around some . . . ?" He rubbed the dun's muzzle with a gloved hand. The two spare horses gathered closer, their muzzles pushed out toward him. He'd rubbed them in turn. Then he'd stepped into the saddle, collected his reins and the lead rope and rode until late afternoon.

At dark, Sam stopped at a water hole to let the horses cool and drink their fill and he grained them with feed from the canvas. He rested himself and the animals until a three-quarter moon revealed the desert hills in broken shadows and purple moonlight. Then, with his saddle on the paint and the supplies atop the buckskin, he set out without benefit of track or sign to follow along the rocky hill trail. But at this point it made no difference. He'd seen the faded hoofprints enough to know that these were not runaway horses fleeing a fire.

The tracks, however obscure, were not meandering. There were riders on these horses' backs, keeping them regimented, he was growing more certain of it. Ahead of him, he knew the only logical direction for men would be through a few small mining camps dotting the trail. They would stop and rest at the old Mexican trade settlement, then on to Poco Fuego—*Little Fire*—then on to Alta Cresta—*High Ridge*—he decided. He knew he could save time by riding up and bypassing the Mexican trade settlement. So he did.

Switching and resting his horses in turn, he kept moving fast and steady. When he reached Poco Fuego it was midmorning and he was met in the dusty street by Virgil Piney and a French-Canadian gunman named Henri Stampos. A burly gunman, Stampos rode with the Golden Gang now and then when he was beckoned in by Braxton Kane. He had shown up a day after the Garlets and the others had left. With Stampos rode a Texas killer known as Shotgun Lloyd. Kane had sent the Texan to bring Henri Stampos to him. Shotgun Lloyd stood at a corner of an alley, his ten-gauge shotgun hanging down his side.

When the Ranger saw the two men standing in the street, he was riding the buckskin. He brought the buckskin to a halt, his Winchester rifle across his lap.

As the other two horses bunched up beside him, he looked ahead along the rooflines of shacks, of crumbled adobe ruins and hovels standing on either side of the trail.

"I'm surprised you made it this far, lawman. But you won't be riding through here tracking my pals," Piney called out in a harsh voice. "Not alive anyway." He stood holding another big nine-shot LeMat with both hands, the saddle mate to the big LeMat he'd sold Prew Garlet.

The Ranger saw the third man standing at the alleyway. He turned his three horses in the narrow street, rode the buckskin over to a hitch rail and stepped down from his saddle. He walked back to the middle of the street, his rifle half raised in his left hand.

"You three need to stand down, Virgil Piney," he called out boldly. "You're interfering with an Arizona Ranger in the pursuit of his job."

"Job, ha!" said Piney. "You mean in pursuit of killing men who are good friends of mine—" He stopped short and gave the Ranger a curious look. "How do you know my name, Ranger Sam *son-of-a-bitch* Burrack?"

The man had just set aside any doubts he may have still had about the Garlets and his two prisoners being alive and riding this way. Piney had just admitted they did. He kept his Winchester half raised in his left hand.

"There's no need in that kind of name-calling, Piney," Sam admonished him. "It's a weakness of mind and spirit. And yes, I've heard of you, Piney," he finally replied. "I know you're a bird dog for the Golden Gang."

"Now who's name-calling?" Pine said venomously.

"*Bird dog* is not so bad," Sam said quietly. As he spoke he starting drawing his Colt up from its holster slow, easy, as if with no ill intent. "I've heard much worse—"

"*Whoa! Whoa!* Hold it right there!" Piney shouted, taking his left hand off the LeMat and pointing his finger at the Ranger. "You ain't pulling that trick on us!"

"What trick is that?" Sam asked calmly, still raising the Colt smoothly, clear of his holster. He cocked the big gun and let it hang down his side, his finger over the trigger.

"That trick *right there*, damn it to hell!" Piney shouted, enraged, realizing the Ranger had pulled the gun trick even as the angry outlaw warned him not to. Piney let his finger drop as if exasperated. He gave Stampos a sidelong look. Stampos just shook his head, as if he could not believe he'd let the Ranger get the drop on them. He stood stone still, his hand poised at his holstered gun.

"Tell your shotgun pal in the alley to come out here in the street with the rest of us, Piney," the Ranger said, both his rifle and Colt cocked and ready.

"And if I don't?" said Piney defiantly.

"Then I'm going to put a bullet in you the next words out of your mouth," Sam said calmly. He called out to the alley, "You over there. Either show yourself or get out of here."

Shotgun Lloyd took a step forward onto the street.

"Stay there, Lloyd!" Piney barked. "This man ain't giving orders—"

Piney's words stopped short as the Ranger's big Colt

swung up and a shot exploded along the street. The bullet hit Virgil Piney in the dead center of his chest and sliced though him, sending him flying backward. A bloody mist hung in the air for a second as did his left boot as it flew from his foot. The big LeMat hit the ground and sent a twenty-gauge blast of buckshot pellets into Stampos' right leg. His leg flew straight back out from under him with such force that it caused him to slap the rocky ground face-first like a man who'd slipped and fallen on ice.

Sam fired at Shotgun Lloyd as Stampos struggled and yelled, rolling back and forth on his big round belly, unable to stand. Shotgun Lloyd grunted and fell to his knees as the Ranger's shot hit him high in his shoulder. He fired the ten-gauge straight at the Ranger, but the out-of-range buckshot only scooped dirt along the street fifteen feet short of its target.

"Drop the shotgun. Stay down," Sam warned, taking aim with his smoking Colt cocked and ready.

"Like hell!" Shotgun Lloyd shouted. He dropped the shotgun on his way up to his feet, his left hand clutching his bleeding shoulder. He tried reaching for his six-shooter at his waist, but the Ranger fired his Colt again. This time the shot hit Lloyd in his chest; he did a backflip and settled, relaxed, dead in the dirt.

Sam stepped forward, the Colt out in front of him smoking in his hand.

"Stay down, mister. You're not going anywhere," he warned Henri Stampos. But when he got to the large gunman, Stampos had managed to push himself to his feet with much effort. Yet, as Sam stepped closer, he kicked

Stampos' good leg out from under him and watched the large man fall with a grunt. "Now stay down there, or we'll keep doing this all day," Sam said. He reached down and took a Remington from its holster and stuck it down behind his gun belt.

"For your information, you did not shoot me, Ranger," Stampos said stubbornly. "He did." He gestured toward Piney lying dead in the dirt. "Had he not shot me in my leg, you would be dead this very minute. I am not a man to take lightly. You should have killed me while you had the chance."

Sam just stared at him for a moment. Then he leveled the cocked and smoking Colt at the big man.

"It's not too late right now," he said.

The French-Canadian gunman gave a toss of his hand.

"You will not kill me now," he said. "It is too late. You lawmen are all alike. You must defend your precious law at all costs, even when it is not in your best interest."

"Keep it up," the Ranger said quietly. "I bet you can talk me into it."

"All right, I will stop. Maybe I am wrong about you," said Stampos, now wary that the Ranger might just pull the trigger. "But if you try to get me to betray my friends, you will not succeed. I will tell you nothing."

"I understand," Sam said. "Your pal here already told me the men I'm looking for were through here the other day. I don't need to ask you anything. We both know there're going to be gunmen waiting for me everywhere between here and Braxton Kane's hideout."

Henri Stampos gave the Ranger a short crafty smile and eased up onto his knees and stopped there. His thick right hand fell down his side and laid easily, close to his boot well. Sam took note, but said nothing.

"Yeah, you know there will be gunmen waiting along the trail for you," he said. "But you don't know how many, do you?"

"No," Sam said quietly, "you've got me there." He took his eyes off Stampos for a second. "I'll just have to wait until they come out and make their moves on me."

"Aw, and by then it will be too late, Ranger," Stampos said with the same crafty smile. His right hand moved quickly. It went into his boot well. Sam heard the metal on metal cock of a gun down there. He saw a Colt .36 caliber pocket gun come out of the boot and swing up at him. But the gun never came up enough to take an aim; Sam's big Colt bucked in his hand, still smoking. The bullet hit the large French-Canadian in his wide chest and sent him sinking backward onto his calves. He bobbed there, swaying, trying to catch himself as blood spewed through the bullet hole in his shirt and ran down his broad belly.

"Why . . . ?" he lamented. "You saw what I was . . . doing. You could have . . . told me to stop."

"Yes, I could have," Sam said, and he fell silent.

He sat staring at Stampos for a moment, seeing the question swirl deep in his dark eyes. He let the Colt slump at his side.

"It was better this way," Sam said finally, fresh smoke rising from his gun barrel, caressing the back of his hand like a silver-gray serpent's tongue. "I don't have time to take you in."

He watched as the big man rocked again on his under-turned calves, then toppled onto his side and seemed to melt onto the rocky ground.

Yep, this is how it is going to be, he told himself. There would be gunmen positioned along the trail all the way to wherever he would find Braxton Kane. *So be it. . . .* Maybe Kane would run out of gunmen before he got there. He stepped over and picked up the big LeMat. Nine .42 caliber rounds and a twenty-gauge shotgun blast to boot. He hefted the big, heavy gun in his hand and shook his head. He turned and walked away, back to his three waiting horses.

Chapter 8

Toby Delmar and his twin sister, Lindsey, finished burying their father deep in the sandy soil. They spent the next half hour rolling rocks over from the sloping hillside and covering the grave to keep out desert scavengers. While they worked, the mule, Dan, stood hitched to the small covered wagon that contained everything they and their father had owned in the world. The mule watched them and chewed hungrily on a clump of wild grass that grew sparsely strewn along the base of the rocky hills.

"Go easy on that water, Sis," Toby cautioned the slim, auburn-haired girl. "We don't want to run out before we find more of it around here."

"I'm just touching it to my lips," the girl replied. She watched as Toby sat down on the rocky ground and untied rawhide strips from around his worn-out shoes. As he untied the strips, the thin soles of the shoes gapped like the mouth of some strange land animal. He pulled the shoes off and cast them aside. He yanked up his dirty ragged socks, tucked the holes of the sock toes under his feet, and then stuck his feet into his father's heavy miner's boots.

Lindsey looked away across the desert floor as Toby stood and stamped his feet in the big boots.

"It—It don't seem right you wearing Pa's boots. Not this soon anyway."

"Sis, I'm going on sixteen years old," Toby said quietly, being as patient with her as he could under the circumstances. "I need footwear that I don't have to keep looking back to see if I've walked out of." He stepped over closer to her. "If Pa could say something right now, he'd tell me to take these boots and wear them. You know he would."

Lindsey didn't reply. Instead she looked back out across the desert floor to the stretch of hills lining the far side.

"What are we going to do now?" she asked pointedly. "Pa's dead. His claim and map are no good. We've got no provisions. Dan is thirsty and falling off with hunger. He'll likely die of starvation, if the wolves don't eat him first."

"Whoa, now, Sis," said Toby. "Don't try prettying things up on my account." He gave her a look. "Sounds like you think we're in bad straits here."

The girl shook her head and gave a thin, sad smile in spite of herself.

"You sound just like Pa, Toby," she said. "Always hoping for a gold mine while your belly growls out loud that there's none to be found."

Toby, having heard the same thing recited so many

times he managed to join in and finish her words along with her.

She stopped talking and looked at him.

"Now guess who you sound just like, Sis," he said.

"I know," she said, "but Ma was right. Pa *did* put too much into searching for *what's not there*."

Again her brother finished her words right along with her, and gave her a look.

"It's not funny, Toby," she said.

"It's not funny," Toby mimicked.

"I mean it. Stop it," she said. "It's not funny at all."

"I'm not laughing," Toby said, turning more serious. He reached out, took the canteen from her, capped it and walked it to the small covered wagon. He pointed toward a tall stand of rock farther along the hill line beside them. Afternoon shadows had begun to stretch long across the desert floor. "There's the water hole we come to on the way out here," he said. "Pa called it Dutchman's Tanks. We need to get there before dark."

"Are you sure that's it?" Lindsey questioned. She held a hand above her eyes as a visor against the afternoon sun glare.

Toby took a deep patient breath.

"That's where we left it, Sis," he said. "These water holes hardly ever move around."

Lindsey looked at their trail behind her, then back toward the stand of rock.

"Every critter in the desert will be there tonight," she said warily.

"Good," said Toby. "I'll shoot one and we'll eat it."

"One what," Lindsey said, "a *wolf*, a *coyote*?"

"I was thinking more of a jackrabbit, or a fowl of some sort," said Toby. "But if it's a coyote you want to cook, I'll see what I can do."

"It's not funny, Toby," said Lindsey.

"I'm not laughing," Toby replied again. "Come on; let's see if we can get Dan on the move again."

Lindsey turned with him and stepped over to the mule. She stood by the lank animal and rubbed a hand against its tall, upright ears.

"Look at him. The poor thing is starving to death before our eyes," she said.

"He could use a good graining or two, that's for certain," Toby said. "But he's a long ways from starving. So are we. We've just got to keep our heads and keep moving. Long as we keep moving we'll come upon something."

"I hope you're right," Lindsey said. She reached down and plucked a twist of wild grass, as if the mule could not reach down and do it for himself. The mule stared at her, already chewing a mouthful of grass.

Toby reached into the driver's side of the small wagon and picked up a battered, long-barreled shotgun and lay it up over his shoulder. To conserve the mule, they had not ridden in the wagon for the past week. But they had hauled their father's body in it when he'd died yesterday evening on the way down from their hillside claim.

"I am right, Sis," Toby said, his tone turning more serious. "I will get you through this. You're my look-alike twin. Anything happens to you, it happens to me too. I won't let nothing happen to you, not ever."

"You'd better not," she said in a mock threat. She managed to give him a trace of a smile. Standing beside the mule she took Dan's wagon reins with one hand and one of his long ears with the other. The mule balked a little, but then stepped forward reluctantly, as if having to first pull his hooves free from the ground. "Come on, Dan," she said. "You heard Toby, we're in *good hands.* Let's get you watered. . . ."

"I'm not joking, Sis," Toby said, hearing her. "I mean it."

"I know you do, Toby," said Lindsey as the mule stepped forward grudgingly.

Four gunmen from the Golden Riders had met with the Garlets, Cleary and Bonsell two days earlier and agreed to come out and set a trap for the Ranger or any other lawmen on their trail. The four had crossed the border, rode all night the night before and arrived at the Dutchman's Tanks in the early afternoon. They brought a long telescope with them. They set up against a large boulder behind a lower stand of rocks overlooking the desert trail, knowing that any rider coming from the same direction as the Garlets would have to come this way—come this way or die of thirst somewhere on the water-barren trails ahead.

"I wish you'd look who's coming here," said a gunman named Arnold Pulty, staring out through the telescope. "We've got pilgrims coming, one of them looking as sweet as candy."

"We see them," said a Kansas gunman named Roy

Mangett. "Hell, we can see them *without* a telescope. You must be near blind, Arnold."

"The hell I am," Pulty retorted.

A young blond-haired Texas gunman named Joey Rose shifted slightly and looked out and down across the top of the rock at the small covered wagon as it came into sight on the desert floor.

"What do you think they're doing out here?" He checked all around the small wagon, seeing no one else in sight, just the two figures trudging through the sand, one on either side of the gaunt mule.

Sitting back from the others, a disgruntled gunman named Chris Weidel coughed hard, spat and wiped a wadded bandanna across his parched lips.

"They're damned fools, whatever they're doing," he said without looking toward the desert floor. "So are we, you want to know the truth. I've swallowed enough dust I'll soon be leaving bricks behind me."

"Nobody made you come out here, Chris," said Roy Mangett, the self-appointed leader of the group. He stepped over as he spoke, took the telescope from Pulty and looked out.

"Nobody told me not to either," said Weidel, his words ending in another cough. "I hope to hell the Garlets appreciate us doing all this, without even paying us."

"It ain't just the Garlets we're doing it for," Mangett said over his shoulder, watching the mule, the wagon, the young man and woman. "We ride out and watch each other's back trail every time Brax gathers us in."

"Yeah, Chris," Pulty said to Weidel, "and every time we do it, you carry on like it's griping your ass plumb up to your elbows."

"Only this time, we're not just watching a back trail," said Weidel. "We're fixing to kill us a lawman." He spat again and blotted his lips.

"So . . . ?" said Mangett. "You saying that's a bad thing? Is this your first lawman?" He lowered the telescope and handed it sidelong to Joey Rose.

"No, I'm not saying it," Weidel snapped, "and it won't be my first. . . ." Standing up from the rock where he sat, he moved over among the others in a crouch, staying out of sight from the desert valley below. "But I never killed any lawman in my life that made me a dime better off."

"Arnold," Mangett said to Pulty, "have you got a dime?"

"Might have," Pulty said, staring out with his naked eyes onto the desert floor.

"Give it to Chris so he'll stop bellyaching," said Mangett.

"Sonsabitches," Weidel growled to himself. He sat down in the dirt, his rifle across his lap.

"What about these two," said Joey Rose, the telescope to his eye. "Looks like they're coming here."

"Hell, of course they're coming here," Weidel groused. "You see any other water nearby?" He waved his hand holding the wadded bandanna all around.

"I'm just saying, is all," Joey Rose said in a stiff tone. He turned back to Mangett with an expectant look.

Mangett breathed deep and stared out across the desert floor as if in contemplation.

"Let them get watered and get on out of here," he said. "We've got a lawman coming most any time. We want things looking smooth and ordinary here." He turned his eyes to Arnold Pulty, singling him out. "I see you looking at the woman with your hands in the wrong place, I'll chop them off," he warned.

Pulty's face turned red-blue. "I don't do that no more," he said.

"You're damned right you don't," said Mangett. He looked all around at the men bunched together against the side of the boulder.

"Jesus . . . ," he said, "*Damn it!* All of you spread out and get out of sight somewhere. You want them thinking they've come to a birthday party?"

Toby and Lindsey Delmar led the mule up a short rock slope half circling the water hole and with their last ounce of strength, they collapsed onto their knees at the water's edge. Toby pitched three empty canteens in the water in front of him to fill them up. Turning to his sister, he wobbled in place and gave a weary grin.

"See, Sis?" he said. "I told you we'd be all right." Then he dropped forward onto his chest and stuck his face down into the tepid, yet soothing water. Lindsey did the same, letting the mule's reins fall from her hand. Dan stepped forward into the water up to his knees and stuck his muzzle down into the water. Silence fell around the water hole for a long moment as the three drank and slaked their thirst.

Lindsey, coming up first, gasped in a breath of air and propped herself on her elbows, her long auburn hair hanging in wet strands, water running down it. She looked around, seeing the mule still drinking, her brother's torso lying limp and bobbing, his face still under the water.

"Toby?" she said. She stared at him. When he didn't make a move, she said, "Toby . . . ? Are you all right?"

She looked at him warily. The water around him took a red sheen.

"Toby!" Frightened, she started to reach over and grab him. But just before she could, he came up suddenly, noisily, and slung his wet hair back and forth.

"Whoo-ieee!" he said loudly, propping up on his palms. Water ran from his chest, his face, his hair. "I had to *come up soon* or drown," he said. He gave his sister a half-silly smile. But seeing the look on her face, his grin vanished. "What is it, Sis? What's wrong?" he asked. Rising up, he awkwardly knee-walked the short four-foot distance to her.

"Nothing . . . ," Lindsey said, a relieved tone to her voice. She glanced back at the red sheen on the ripples in the water, noting now that it was only sun glare. "I'm just tired. I'm not thinking straight."

"Well . . ." Toby raised the filled canteens, held them out and let water run off them. "While you rest *some*, why don't I go scout around and see if I can rustle us something to eat." He held the canteens closer and began capping them.

"Remember, Pa never liked firing the goose gun unless we had to," Lindsey reminded him.

"I know that," Toby replied patiently, "and I *won't*, unless I have to. But we've got to eat, Sis."

Toby walked the dripping canteens to the small wagon, reached over and lay them inside the bed. He picked up the long-barreled shotgun and propped it up over his shoulder.

"Wish me luck," he said, turning and walking along a game path around the water hole.

Lindsey watched until her brother stepped out of sight into a stand of brush.

"Good luck . . . ," she whispered to herself. Her stomach tightened just thinking about food. But she put her hunger aside as her father had taught her and her brother to do. She made herself think of something else, anything but food.

She reached around and unbuttoned her dress and stooped back down at the water's edge. She cupped a handful of water and raised it as she lowered the front of the wet dirty dress. She sighed to herself, washing herself with her hand, feeling relief as water cleansed the crusted perspiration from her breasts.

She let the front of the dress fall and washed her sides, her neck, under her arms. She stood up and thought for a moment, then decided to push the dress down, to step out of it.

But a sound caught her attention and she looked around quickly. On a thin, steep path leading up between two large rocks she saw dirt and fine, small gravel trickling down. *A coyote . . . ? An animal of some sort? No!* She didn't think so. She heard a muffled grunt like someone who'd fallen and was trying to keep it quiet.

Grasping her dress, she yanked it up and held it against her.

"Who's there?" she said in shaky voice. More dirt and gravel spilled down. "Who's up there?" she demanded, in a louder tone of voice.

"Don't be scared, little lady," a thick voice called out from up the path, more dirt and small rock spilling down. "I'm not going to hurt you any."

Lindsey saw a large bare head appear around the side of the rock beside the path of spilling dirt. A bare arm reached out and waved at her. A broad grin appeared through a thick ragged beard. "I'm just looking at you, is all."

"Who are you? What do you want?" She called out, backing away as she spoke, hoping her brother would hear her and come running with the goose gun.

She stared in terror as the man stepped out naked onto the thin path and stood with his hairy arms spread wide. His organ stood out short and stiff, bobbing as if on a spring.

"Don't worry none. I'm just plain ole *Arnold* here," the man called down to her, stepping forward into full sight. "Nekked as the day I's born!"

Lindsey let out a scream.

Thirty feet away, two more men stood up from behind a cover of rock.

Lindsey screamed again. She watched the two men stare at the naked man as if in disgust and disbelief.

"Arnold, you *son of a bitch*! *I warned you!*" she heard one of the men call out. She saw him raise a pistol toward the naked man. He cocked the gun and took aim. But before he fired, the second man grabbed his wrist and pulled the gun down.

"Don't shoot him, Roy!" she heard the second man call out. "We don't want gunshots!"

Chapter 9

Toby Delmar, hearing his sister's shrill screams had
turned from his unsuccessful hunt and ran loping down
the hillside like a deer, bounding over brush and rock to
get to her. Falling, he slid down a path on his rump the
last twenty feet, then rose into sight at the water's edge.
He saw his sister run to the side of the wagon and climb
inside quickly, still screaming. He saw her through the
open front of the canvas cover as she rummaged wildly
among the wagon's meager contents.

The naked man advanced across thirty feet of rock
ground toward her.

Without hesitation, Toby threw the goose gun to his
shoulder and fired. The sound of the blast rolled and
echoed out across the desert floor. As soon as he fired
the big single-shot shotgun, he pulled a fresh load from
his pocket and fumbled with it, trying to hurry and
reload.

Among the rocks on the hillside, Roy Mangett
slumped, his cocked Colt still in hand and watched the
large naked gunman take the shotgun blast in his chest
and fall backward onto the ground, blood flying.

"Damn it to hell," Mangett said to Chris Weidel standing beside him. "There goes keeping things quiet." The two looked down the hillside at Toby reloading the shotgun. Shaking his head, Mangett raised his Colt as Arnold Pulty struggled up onto his feet, bleeding all over from the load of buckshot.

"Yep," said Weidel, "it don't matter now." He raised a big Remington he'd drawn and held down his side.

"Adios, Arnold, you crazy bastard," Mangett said under his breath. He pulled the trigger on his Colt just as Toby finished loading the shotgun and raised it to his shoulder. Before Toby could pull the shotgun's trigger, he heard three shots in close succession and watched the naked man bounce backward a step as each bullet nailed him hard in his bloody chest.

"Damn, Roy, that was good shooting!" remarked Joey Rose, standing up from among the cover of rock on the hillside.

"Yeah . . . ," said Roy, "you keep that in mind, before you ever go acting a-fool like that." He nodded down at Arnold's body in the dirt.

"Jesus, Roy," said Joey Rose, an offended look on his face. "I'd never do nothing like that—"

"You up there," Toby called out, the shotgun still raised and pointed up the hillside. "Drop your gun . . . keep your hands where I can see them. Walk down here, *real slow.*"

Mangett and Weidel looked at each. They gave guarded grins and looked downhill at Rose, then at the young man holding the shotgun pointed up at them.

"I know we've made what you might call a real bad

first impression," Mangett called down to Toby. He gestured a nod at Arnold's bloody, naked body in reference. "I'm wishing we can start all over and forget that fool ever skint out of his pants." As he replied, he started walking slowly down the hill path. Weidel followed a step to his side. Mangett slipped his cocked Colt down into the holster on his hip.

"Hunh-uh, mister, stop right there," Toby demanded, advancing forward, closer to his sister as he spoke. "I didn't say *holster* it, I said *drop* it!" His eyes and gun barrel moved back and forth quickly among the three, seeing the older gunman step farther away as the two descended the last few feet of the hillside.

Feeling a little safer now that she saw the big naked man was lying dead in the dirt, Lindsey stepped down from the covered wagon bed, a long butcher knife in her shaking hand.

Instead of stopping, instead of raising their guns from their holsters and dropping them, the three men remained spread out, and walked slowly closer to the wagon. Toby hurried. He got to the wagon first and stood close to his sister's side, the shotgun held firmly in his hands.

"I got this side covered, Roy," said Joey Rose.

Mangett only nodded.

"I'm warning the three of you!" he said loudly. "Not one more step." He placed his face on the gun stock as if to take aim.

"Now you see, young fellow," Mangett said calmly, without slowing a step, "we're not going to drop our guns. That would be foolish." He raised a finger as if for emphasis. The three stopped fifteen feet away. They kept spread out a few feet between them. "We saw what that idiot did," he said, "and you saw how we dealt with it." He gave a slight shrug. "That's all you get." He looked from Toby to Lindsey, then back. "You might have guessed, that ain't the first gun that's ever pointed at us." He nodded at the barrel of the goose gun.

"Don't try nothing," Toby warned, unrelenting, but looking a little shaky about his situation.

Mangett shrugged again.

"We won't," he said. "Like I told you, I wish we could start all over. All we want to do here is water our tired cayuses, and ourselves. Then we're gone." He nodded, looking back and forth between the two closely, curiously. "Say, you two look just alike, except that—"

"We're twins, mister," said Toby, cutting him off. "This is my sister." He still held the shotgun up, but he let the barrel slump, easing his grip a little. Mangett took note of it and stepped in closer.

"Twins, you say?" he gave a thin smile, eyeing them each up and down. "Well, I'll be damn—" he caught himself. "*Darned*, that is," he corrected quickly, touching his hat brim toward Lindsey. He noted the big butcher knife in her hands. She gripped it tightly.

"All right, then," Mangett said, "in the spirit of starting anew, ny name is Dave Johnson. This here is Jack and—"

"He called you Roy," said Toby, cutting him off again, stiffening his grip on the big goose gun.

Roy winced at his mistake.

"Yes, you're right. He did," he said. He half turned to

Joey Rose as he said, "But this one—?" He shook his head. "Hell, it don't matter," he said, dismissing it. He turned back quickly, grabbing the shotgun barrel quickly, jerking it so hard Toby had to let it go, or fall.

Catching himself, Toby started to grab and retrieve the gun, but the gun reversed itself in Mangett's hands. The metal-trimmed butt came forward with a hard snap and struck him squarely in his forehead. Lindsey shrieked as she saw Toby fall backward and lie limp on the ground. She lunged at him with the butcher knife as she screamed. But Chris Weidel caught her by her wrist and slung her around.

"Where you going with that pigsticker, little gal?" he said gruffly. Before she could catch her balance, he dealt her a hard backhand slap across the face and wrenched the knife from her hand as she fell backward herself.

Joey Rose's gun came out of his holster. But he stood only watching now that everything was over. Stepping in over Toby, he stared down at him, at the vicious rising gash on the young man's forehead. Toby eyes were half open, turned severely upward. His boots twitched in the dirt, his shoulders jerked spasmodically.

"I believe you've killed this one, Roy," he said.

"Did I, sure enough?" said Mangett. He stepped over and stared down at Toby with a bemused look on his face. "Damn, I expect I don't know my own strength sometimes." He looked at the metal cover on the goose gun's butt plate and wiped a streak of blood from it with his thumb. "If he stops wiggling and carrying on, tie him to the wagon wheel. See if you can keep him alive."

"We going to leave them here?" Rose asked.

"Was going to," Mangett said. He looked back and forth at the twins, trying to guess their ages. "Now, I'm not so sure. I know traders south of the border would thump down a chunk of money for a real live pair of twins."

Joey Rose, stepped in closer and looked down at the two. Lindsey had begun to recover; she sat up in the dirt, hand to the side of her burning face.

"I hear what you're saying, Roy," said Rose. "They might pay for this girl." He nodded at Lindsey.

"They'll pay for both, Joey," said Roy. "Use your head. What good is one twin without the other?"

"I am using my head," Joey replied. "I know what they'll do with a young woman. But what are they going to do with a boy?"

Roy Mangett just stared at him; Chris Weidel gave a chuff under his breath. He grinned flatly.

"You've got a lot to learn, Joey Rose," he said knowingly.

It was dark when Toby awakened, propped back against the wagon, his hands behind his back, tied around the wheel. The front of his head throbbed with pain. His vision took a few seconds to clear, so did his memory. But as the plight of his sister and himself came back to him, he sat still, and looked around guardedly.

He saw Lindsey lying in the dirt only inches away, her hands also tied, only hers were tied in front of her. A long rope circled her waist, knotted at the center of her back. The rope ran from her back to the wagon wheel, long enough to allow her to move around in a ten-foot radius.

Keeping his head lowered, Toby gazed sidelong through the pain in his forehead and saw the three men seated around a small fire. He watched and listened as Joey Rose stood in a crouch and refilled Mangett's tin cup with hot coffee from a blackened coffeepot.

When Joey finished filling Mangett's cup he stepped over to Weidel and offered to pour.

But the older gunman pulled his cup away.

"No, thanks," he said. "If that little gal is as bad at everything else as she is boiling coffee, you'd better sell her quick then run like hell."

Mangett and Rose gave a short laugh.

"She'll have to learn as she goes," Mangett said, "just like everything else."

Up the side of the hill came the sound of thrashing in the dried brush along the rock paths. Amid the thrashing, a sharp yelp, followed by a deep growl.

"How far off did you drag that son of a bitch?" Mangett asked Rose. Glancing at the horses tied a few yards away, Mangett saw them grow restless and mill back and forth at the sound of wolves.

While Toby listened, he felt around behind him and ran a thumb along the sharp metal edge covering the face of the wagon wheel. The hot desert sand had honed the metal as surely as a grinding wheel over the past weeks.

"I don't know," Rose replied to Mangett with a shrug. "Far enough I reckon."

One of the horses nickered. At the wagon, the mule stood stone still as if frozen in place.

"I hope you did," Mangett said. "I'm not going to spend the night tossing while every wolf in the badlands is chewing and lapping at Arnold's innards."

Weidel gave a short dark chuckle.

Toby wasted no time. He began rubbing the rope on his tied hands against the steel edge of the wheel behind him. He kept watch on the men around the fire as he worked, making sure they didn't hear him, and look around. He knew the metal edge was doing its job, he could feel it cutting into the rope. Knowing it, he rubbed faster.

Toby stopped rubbing suddenly as Mangett stood up and slung coffee from his tin cup and dropped the cup to the ground.

"That is some terrible coffee, sure enough," he said. He looked over at Lindsey lying a few feet away. "I might better check and see what she *is and ain't* any good at." He stepped over to her.

Toby saw his sister spring up and try to scoot away in the dirt.

"Stay away from me," Lindsey cried out. "Don't touch me!"

But Mangett grabbed the rope and yanked her to a halt. He laughed, looking down at her. He loosened his gun belt and laid it aside.

"Settle down. You ain't going nowhere," he said.

Toby rubbed harder, faster on the rope, his head bursting with pain. The two gunmen turned and watched over their shoulders.

Holding Lindsey by the rope, Mangett stooped down, held her face in his hand and studied it closely.

"How old are you, little darling?" he asked, tightening his grip on her face to keep her from pulling away.

Lindsey didn't answer; at the wagon fifteen feet away Toby rubbed harder, feeling the rope widening as the metal bit deeper into it.

Mangett shook Lindsey's face in his hand.

"I asked you a question," he demanded.

"Check her teeth," Weidel called out with a dark laugh.

"I will," said Mangett. "Open your mouth," he ordered the frightened girl.

"Hunh-uh!" Lindsey shook her head.

Mangett squeezed her cheeks until she was forced to open her mouth. He put his thumb against the edge of her teeth and ran it back and forth.

"Ouch," he said with a dark laugh. "She's a young one, Chris."

"Stop it, Roy," said Joey Rose, sounding nervous at such rough play.

Mangett ignored Rose. At the wagon wheel Toby continued sawing back and forth madly, knowing where this was headed.

Mangett let go of Lindsey's face. He reached down and unbuttoned his fly.

"How old are you, young lady?" he asked.

Lindsey lied quickly, hoping, praying. . . .

"Thirteen," she said in a shaky voice.

Mangett slapped her, not hard, a warning slap.

"Damn it, Roy, don't do this!" said Rose. His hand

went to the gun on his hip. But he stopped as Weidel gave him a warning stare.

"I know you're not twenty, girl," Mangett said. "I know you're not eighteen." He grabbed the top on her dress, twisted it in his fist, ready to tear it away. "But I know *damn well* you're not thirteen."

"Please, *please*," she sobbed, struggling against his grip.

"If you're going to lie, I ain't going to listen," Mangett said. He tightened his grip.

Toby sawed madly at the rope.

But just as Mangett started to rip the dress away, a terrible yelping, growling, snarling sound came from the hillside so intensely that it pulled Rose and Weidel to their feet.

"Jesus!" said Weidel. "A wolf fight."

"Damn it to hell!" said Mangett, springing up, buttoning his fly quickly. "I ain't having this." He stepped over, grabbed his gun belt up from the dirt and slung it around his waist. "How damn far did you say, Joey?"

Weidel reached for his rifle.

"Not damn far enough," he said, before the younger gunman could answer.

"How far, damn it?" Mangett asked again.

"At the top of the path there," Rose replied.

"Right on the path?" Mangett asked.

"Well . . . yeah," said Rose. "I figured nobody's going to be coming along—"

"Right," Mangett said in disgust, steeping over to the fire where he grabbed his rifle from his saddle lying in the dirt by his bedroll. "Come on, Chris," he said.

"Bring your horse. Let's drag his dead ass away from here." He looked around at Rose. "You stay here with the girl. I come back and see your prints on her, I'll feed you to the wolves too."

At the wagon wheel, Toby felt the rope give way. He stopped rubbing the metal edge. He kept his head lowered as Mangett and Weidel both looked over at him.

"Had I better check him before we go?" Weidel asked.

Toby felt fear clutch tight in his chest. But he managed to keep himself from making a move. He could leap up and run, but he wasn't about to go anywhere without his sister.

"Naw," said Mangett, dismissing the matter. "Leave him be. He ain't waking up for a while . . . if he ever does at all."

Chapter 10

No sooner had Weidel and Mangett stepped away out of the firelight and disappeared up the path onto the rocky hillside, Joey Rose walked over to where Lindsey lay sobbing on the ground. Stopping, he placed a cup of steaming coffee in front of her and watched her brush a strand of hair from her face with her tied hands. Then he reached out and brushed a strand from her other cheek and tried to give her a thin smile.

"Careful, that cup is hot," he cautioned her.

She just stared at him. Atop the trail sixty yards up the wolves still snarled and growled and fought one another in the brush.

"I—I just want you to know I was having no part in what was going on here," he said.

"You weren't stopping it either," she snapped back at him. She scooted away from him.

"I would have though," Joey said. "I was fixing to when the wolves started."

Lindsey only stared at him skeptically. She eyed the butcher knife lying on a rock by the fire.

"I mean it," Joey said. "I'm not that kind of man. I

believe women ought to be treated—" His words stopped short as a fist-sized rock in Toby's hand slammed down atop his head. The attack came silent and sudden. Lindsey was even caught off guard by her brother's fast, decisive move. She gasped as Joey Rose crumbled on the ground in front of her. She started to say something, but Toby clasped his hand over her mouth and pulled her to her feet.

"*Shhh*, don't talk, Sis," Toby said. "I've got to get you out of here before they get back. He untied the rope around her wrists, turned her around quickly and untied the rope from around her waist. She stepped over quickly to the fire and picked up the butcher knife and clutched it to her. With Toby's arm around her, the two started to run toward a stretch of rock and brush on the far edge of the water hole.

Stopping suddenly, Lindsey looked back at their wagon, at the dark silhouette of the mule still hitched to it.

"Wait. What about Dan?" she asked in a whisper.

The sudden stop had almost thrown Toby off his feet. When he didn't answer her, Lindsey grabbed him and looked at him closely. In the purple starlight she could see his forehead and left eye was covered with dried blood. Yet, even worse, she could see that the white of his eye was not white at all. It was filled with blood.

"Toby! Buck up!" she whispered, shaking him, feeling his unsteadiness.

"I'm all right, Sis," he replied, seeming to shake off a dizziness. "Just weak, is all." Looking back he pulled her on toward the rocks. "No time . . . to get Dan," he said brokenly.

"I know," Lindsey said, realizing her brother was barely able to stand. "Keep going. . . ." Arms around each other, the two hurried on in the darkness. Lindsey wielded the big butcher knife in her hand.

As they reached the stretch of rocks and started up into them, they heard Joey Rose's slurred voice in the darkness behind them.

"Stop, damn you!" he shouted. His voice was followed by a series of six wild pistol shots in their direction. The two ducked into the rocks as bullets ricocheted and spun all around them. "I'll kill you!" Rose screamed. "I was going to be good to you!"

Beside her, Lindsey heard her brother grunt, felt his arm stiffen around her for second. But as she stumbled, he shoved her up the rock path into the black shadowed darkness.

"Keep going, keep going," Toby said.

Behind them they heard the voices of the other two gunmen as a rifle shot replaced Joey Rose's pistol shots.

"You damn fool," they heard Roy Mangett say to Rose, "you let them get away?"

"I didn't let them, Roy, damn it," they heard Rose shout in reply. "The boy got loose . . . hit me from behind."

"They're headed up into the rocks," shouted Weidel. Another rifle shot resounded from Rose's rifle in the darkness.

"Stop shooting, Joey," Mangett demanded.

"Don't stop, Sis," Toby said, shoving his sister up the rocky path deeper into the rocks.

"Toby, are you all right?" she asked over her shoulder, noting he had slowed and appeared to be struggling along behind her. She stopped, looked around and saw him backed against a tall rock, his hand clutching his lower belly.

"No, Sis . . . ," he said. "A bullet nicked me. I'm bleeding."

"God, no!" she grabbed him by his shoulders. "What are we going to do, Toby?"

Gripping his belly tightly, Toby shoved her away with his free hand.

"You're going on, Sis," he said.

"No, I'm not," Lindsey said.

"Don't argue with me," Toby said harshly. "I'll slow you down. You've got to go on. Get over these rocks and down to the trail. Stay out of sight come morning until you know they've given up and gone on."

"What about you?" she asked, realizing the shape he was in. "I can't just leave you here to die."

Toby heard her trembling, tearful voice.

"Who said anything about dying?" he said, trying to keep his voice strong for her sake. "I'm just not . . . able to run right now. I'll get over into these rocks. They'll never find me."

"But, Toby—" The sound of a wild rifle shot cut her short.

"Don't argue with me, Lindsey," Toby snapped, giving her a shove. "Don't worry about me. I'll be close behind." Another wild rifle resounded. "Get going," he demanded, "before you get us both killed!" He shoved her again with his free hand. This time at his coaxing she turned and ran as fast as she could as another rifle shot rang out behind her.

"Stop shooting, damn it, Joey," She heard Roy Mangett shout as she disappeared farther into the rocks.

At the campfire, Mangett grabbed Rose's rifle from his hands.

Chris Weidel shoved Rose backward.

"Why don't you just start calling out for that damned Ranger by name, you idiot."

"My head's been busted, Chris!" shouted Rose. "Look at me." He tipped his bare head enough to show the large bump on top. His revolver lay smoking in his holster where he'd stuck it after empting it at the fleeing twins. He stepped forward to give them a look.

But instead of looking, Mangett shoved him away angrily.

"You're lucky I don't kill you!" he shouted. "Chris, get up in the rocks after them. "We'll bring the horses around and meet you down at the main trail. There's no point in staying here any longer, this fool has given us away."

"You've got it, Roy," said Weidel. He handed Mangett his rifle, turned quickly without another word on the matter and headed for the path into the rocks.

"Roy, I swear, there's nothing I could do—" Rose managed to say before Mangett cut him off.

"Shut up, Joey!" Mangett shouted. "Get the horses. You'd better hope to hell we catch those two. I'm wondering if you let them go on purpose."

"On *purpose*? Roy, look at my head!" Rose pleaded. "He busted me with a rock, knocked me cold!"

Mangett glared at him.

"Have you got those horses yet?" he said harshly.

Fortunately, the Ranger had not a made a camp for the night. In order to make better time, he had rested, grained and watered his three horses and had lain stretched out on the ground for little over an hour. When he'd heard the sound of gunfire from the direction of the Dutchman's Tanks, he arose quickly, dusted himself off, and wasted no time getting under way. With a three-quarter moon in the starlit sky, he'd ridden at a brisk pace throughout the purple night. At first light he'd spotted the outline of the low hills surrounding the water hole and after looking all around, he'd left his horses among the rocks and slipped down quietly and looked all around.

At the water hole the gaunt mule stood alone in front of the wagon, staring straight ahead, his ears twitching a little as the Ranger eased up to him and placed a hand on his muzzle. In the rocks above the water hole the snarling and growling of wolves had settled a bit, but was still going on. Sam could tell the animal was frightened, but managing to hold his ground pretty well.

"Easy, boy, I'm not a wolf," he whispered. "See?" He rubbed the animal's muzzle all over, giving him his scent. "Looks like somebody left you in a tight spot here," he whispered.

Looking all around again, seeing shoe prints and boot prints in the rocky ground and the signs of an abandoned campsite, he leaned his Winchester against the wagon and freed the mule from its hitching. He dropped its bridle on the ground.

"I've never seen anybody forget their mule," he said quietly, sensing the calming effect his voice was having on the nervous animal. "A wagon either for that matter." He still searched all around. In the distant east, a glow of silver morning spread upward across the purple sky. Up the path where the wolves fed, the snarling seemed to fall away with the coming light.

"All right, get on out of here," he said to the mule. "Sounds like that bunch has gotten their bellies full." He shoved the mule around with a firm hand and slapped its rump. The mule sprang forward at a gangly trot. But at more than fifteen feet the animal stiffened to a stop and stood with its hooves spread as if determined to not go an inch farther.

"Suit yourself," Sam said, "I know better than to argue with a mule." He turned, picked up his Winchester and walked all around the campsite. He saw spent rifle shells in the dirt. Six pistol shells lay where they had been dropped in a tight pattern nearby. *Here's where the gunshots had come from,* he told himself, stopping, picking up one of the rifle shells, inspecting it. When he tossed it aside, he saw the short length of rope lying on the ground where the boy had untied his sister. Sam studied it. The twist of the rope told him it had been used to bind something, *or someone,* he reminded himself. But he wasn't sure what.

He stood and started to walk forward to the blackened campfire. Behind him he felt something shove him hard in the middle of his back. He swung the rifle around quickly, tensed, only to look into the mule's face as it blew out a breath and twitched its ears.

"You might want to warn a fellow before doing that," he whispered. He stepped away and looked back over his shoulder. The mule stepped forward with him.

"All right," he said quietly. "I can't blame you. Just stay back some, don't get yourself shot."

He walked forward and all around the campsite. When he'd circled wide around the campsite, the mule right behind him, he spotted the place where the horses had been tied. He spotted a set of boot prints and shoe prints running off away in the opposite direction. Stopping where he'd dropped the mule's bridle, he stooped and picked it up. The mule stood perfectly still and let him slip the bridle back onto its muzzle.

"Come on then," Sam said, "let's see who's running away."

He followed the prints in the grainy morning light, seeing them lead to the game path at the far end of the water hole, opposite the path where the wolves had fed in the night. Fifty yards up the meandering path he saw the first smear of blood dried on a waist-high rock. He touched the smear, making sure it was dry, then moved on, looking for more, the gaunt mule picking its way steadily along the rocky path.

Here we go, he told himself, seeing the next streak of blood fifteen yards farther up. The blood was dry, but now there were several drops in the dirt at his feet— *somebody bleeding bad,* he told himself, walking forward with caution.

He stopped a few feet farther along and made the mule stop behind him. Listening close he heard the sound of labored breathing coming from among a stand of brush off the side of the trail. Looking down he saw more dried blood in the dirt.

"Hello, the brush," he said calmly. Not knowing who was lying in there bleeding, he kept his rifle half raised, cocked and ready for anything. "This is Arizona Ranger Sam Burrack. I can see you're wounded. Step out with your hands where I can see them."

After a tense silence, a weak, broken voice rose from the brush.

"I can't . . . I'm shot too bad . . . ," the voice replied.

Sam didn't bother saying any more. Instead he took three steps forward and walked quietly into the brush from a different angle. The mule lagged back and stood with its muzzle tipped forward toward the Ranger.

Deeper into the brush, Sam saw the young man on his back, leaning against a rock, his belly covered with thick, pasty blood.

"I've got . . . no gun," Toby said, looking relieved at the sight of the badge on the Ranger's chest. He raised his bloody hands a little but hadn't the strength to keep them up.

"Lie still then," Sam said. He looked at the belly wound as he stepped in and stooped beside the young man. "I heard shooting in the night," he said, seeing the questioning look on Toby's face.

Toby looked him up and down. He coughed and swallowed and clenched his teeth against the pain in his lower belly.

"I've never had . . . nothing hurt like this," he said in a pained voice. "This is . . . gut-shot?"

"Yep, I'm afraid so," said Sam. He reached in and tore open the bloody shirt at the bullet hole for a better look. Black, pasty blood had partly firmed up around a half-moon-shaped ricochet wound, but still there was bleeding that had to be stopped.

"Am I . . . dying?" Toby asked, his voice carrying a shiver.

"I hope not," Sam said flatly. "Looks like you caught a ricochet." He reached up and untied his dusty bandanna from around his neck and shook it out. "Who shot you?" He wadded the bandanna as he spoke, and waited for the young man's answer, knowing it would be too painful for him to speak when he pressed the bandanna down on his belly.

"Three men . . ." Toby said. "They had my sister. I . . . got her away, but they shot me. . . ." He eyed the Ranger, seeing the raised wadded bandanna. "I heard them . . . talking. They were . . . waiting to ambush somebody."

"That would be me most likely," Sam said. "This is going to hurt." He lowered the wadded bandanna and pressed it against the wound.

Toby winced and clenched his teeth but keep himself from yelling out loud.

"God . . . it does," he rasped.

Sam took the young man's bloody right hand and laid it on the bandanna.

"Keep it pressed here," he said, "the hurting will

ease some. We've got to stop this bleeding." He patted Toby's shoulder. "Now, what about your sister?"

Toby managed to keep talking as the pain in his belly lessened beneath the wadded bandanna. Sam turned him slightly onto his side and looked at the bleeding exit wound. The ricochet had flattened even more on its way through the flesh and sliced out wide, like a knife wound. Fortunately, the flat exit wound was drying over better than the bullet hole in front.

"My sister . . . Lindsey, got away . . . but I've got to get to her," Toby said, his voice sounding stronger as he thought of his sister out there alone, three gunmen stalking her. He tried to raise himself. He was too weak, not to mention the searing pain in his belly.

"This ricochet is going to cost you a shirtsleeve," Sam said. He reached up from his boot with his boot knife and cut Toby's shirtsleeve at the upper seam. He ripped the seam all around and pulled the sleeve down off of his arm. Toby watched him split the sleeve down its middle into two strips and tied their ends together into one long strip. As he started to reach the strip under Toby's back, the mule stepped forward into the brush noisily. Sam almost swung around toward it.

"That's your mule from the wagon, I take it?" he asked, having been once again surprised by the animal's sudden appearance.

"Yes . . . that's Dan," Toby said. The mule stopped three feet away and stood peering at the two of them.

"Is he always so curious?" Sam asked.

"He's part prospector's mule . . . and part pet." Toby's

voice grew stronger, finding renewed hope for him and his sister now the Ranger was here.

Sam finished reaching the strip of cloth under him and tied it around his waist, holding the bandanna in place and putting some pressure on the exit wound.

"Can you ride that mule?" he asked. "If you can't I've got three horses near here. I'll bring you one."

"Is it quicker . . . me riding a horse?" Toby said.

"It doesn't matter," said Sam. "You can't keep up with me with this wound. I want you to keep slow and follow my tracks. I can't wait up for you, not if we're going to find your sister."

"I can ride Dan," said Toby. "The main thing is we get to Lindsey."

"That's what I figured you'd say." Sam reached down and helped Toby rise to his feet. The young man gasped in pain but overcame it and kept himself standing.

"It's turning daylight. Let's get down to water and take it from there," said Sam. He raised the young man's arm across his shoulders and led him out of the brush, the mule right behind them.

Chapter 11

———

Lindsey Delmar had spent the night running blindly in the maze of boulder, rock, capstone and brush. When she'd begun to realize how disoriented she was, she'd stopped searching for a way out. Like a frightened rabbit she'd simply taken cover and conserved her energy until the next sound behind her sent her darting from one spot to the next, and taking cover again. With the butcher knife in hand, she'd made up her mind that she would fight for her life if it came to that. But for now— *keep moving*, she commanded herself.

At each new hiding place she lay in the dirt listening closely, wondering if her brother was coming; wondering how she would know it was him if she did hear anything. She had seen a shadowy silhouette in the moonlight at one point; but just as she'd started to call out, she saw that it wasn't Toby. It was the gunman, the one the other two called Chris.

As dawn had begun to rise in the east, she'd taken cover on a cliff and waited for daylight to reveal a path down to the sand flats. Lying there she heard the sound of hooves clicking softly on the rocky trail below. She had started to rise up and look down toward the trail when she was startled by a voice near her calling out in the darkness.

"Roy, up here," she heard the voice say. "I'm coming down."

In the grainy light she saw Chris Weidel step into sight less than twenty feet away and look all around. His face appeared to stop and look straight at her for a moment. Then he turned away and walked down the path toward the main trail. She went weak in her chest for a moment and lowered her face to the dirt. But she collected herself quickly and forced herself to rise enough to gaze down over the edge of a rock and watch Mangett and Rose ride forward at a walk, Rose leading Weidel's horse by its reins.

"They're lying down somewhere, the both of them," she heard Weidel say, the three of them talking only a few yards below her. "One of them's hit, I saw some blood. But I've beat this blasted hillside to death." He stopped and coughed and hacked for a moment. "They ain't coming up," he added in a choking voice. He held a wadded bandanna to his mouth.

"Damn it," said Mangett as Weidel took his horse's reins from Rose. "I want those two. I want them *bad*." He stared at Weidel.

"I'm done with it, Roy," Weidel said, half speaking into the bandanna. "Far as I know they might have circled back to their wagon. They ain't got very far if they did."

"Damn it," Mangett said again. "We can't keep running back and forth. This whole ambush idea has turned into a damned mess. We're going on to Kane's hideout." He paused for a moment, then said, "Still . . . I hate giving up twins, knowing what they're worth, knowing they're up there somewhere. We can give it one more try."

"I'll hang back and get them," Rose volunteered. He'd already decided, even if he found the twins, he wasn't bringing them to Mangett. He would send them on their way, maybe even apologize. Things had gotten out of hand, but he could make them right. This whole thing had happened because of that fool Arnold Pulty— *the son of a bitch.*

Mangett chuffed at him and looked all around in the gloom. "I mean it, Roy," Rose said. "I'll duck into the rock up there and watch for them come morning light. They can't make it long without heading down to the water."

"Yeah? What if they're already gone like Chris says," Mangett replied.

"Then I'll find out, and I'll catch back up to you along the trail," said Rose.

"You couldn't find horseshit with both hands up a mustang's ass," Weidel said.

In the brush and rocks above them, the young woman lay listening as silent as death.

Rose let Weidel's insult go unchallenged; Mangett gave a short scornful laugh and sat considering it for a moment.

"If you could find them as easily as you let them get away, we'd do well leaving you to look," he said.

"I'll find them, Roy," said Rose. "Find them, or see

where they went back in the night and slipped away from here."

"Find them, goddamn it," said Mangett, jerking his horse around onto the trail. "Since you came up with the idea, either find them or don't come back."

Weidel chuckled and turned his horse beside Mangett.

"How's that for a bargain?" he said to Rose. "Roy and me win either way."

"Now wait a minute, Roy," said Rose, hedging a little. "I'm trying to help out here. But now I either have to find them or I'm cast out?"

"Like Adam out of Eden," Weidel laughed over his shoulder as the two booted their horses up into a gallop.

"Damn it, Roy," Rose called out as they rode away. "Oh, I'll find her—find them both, that is," he corrected himself. "Just you wait and see." There it was, he'd said plenty. When he caught up with Mangett later, who could say he hadn't done his best.

Listening, Lindsey watched the young gunman turn his horse and nudge it over onto the steep, narrow path. She ducked again and lay stonelike until she heard the horse's hooves pawing, scraping, struggling up the path only a few feet away. She wasn't sure where Toby was back there, but she wasn't about to let the gunman ride back and find him. She took a deep breath to clear her head and crawled over to the edge of a low cliff and waited while the rider drew closer. She gripped the butcher knife in her hand.

As Joey Rose rode by unsuspecting, she lunged out from the cliff, four feet down and landed atop him, slashing, stabbing and screaming. Rose's terrified horse reared and bolted from under him, sending him and Lindsey crashing to the rocky ground. Rose felt the burn of the knife blade across his face, his side; he felt the sharp stab of steel into his shoulder, his ribs. The two rolled and fought, Lindsey putting all her entire strength and effort into killing the gunman, for her sake, for her brother's. She knew she was fighting for their lives. She knew Toby would be doing the same thing were the tables turned.

But instead of dying right away as the young woman somehow felt he would, Rose fought back hard, realizing that he too was fighting for his life. As soon as she had lunged down on him, he'd realized it was her. As they fought, he tried at first to grab her wrist, grapple with her and get the knife out of her hand. Yet, feeling the blade cut him time after time, he instinctively abandoned any notion of grabbing the knife. Instead he shoved himself away from her, struggled to his feet, drawing and cocking his gun.

Seeing the gun aimed at her, Lindsey jumped aside. Rose, his face and eyes covered with blood, tried to focus on her and get off a shot. But before he could, Lindsey leaped off the path into the maze of rocks and ran down and away toward the flatlands below.

"You've killed me; damn you, girl!" Rose shouted and sobbed. "I never done nothing to you!" Holding his sliced face together with a bloody hand, his Colt hanging down his side, he staggered back and forth in the path, still stunned by the attack. The girl had swept down, caught him off guard, cut and stabbed him viciously, and disappeared, screaming as she went. Now the path was silent, except for the sound of him panting, catching his breath.

And now he stood staggering in the silence, bleeding all over, looking along the path through a veil of blood at his horse standing twenty yards away. The animal had settled quickly. It looked back at him curiously, as if wondering what strange circumstance had brought on the young woman's sudden outburst of wild behavior.

"Damn it, girl . . ." Rose said in a broken voice, stooping, picking up the butcher knife, seeing drops of his blood splatter into the dirt at his feet. "I was only trying to help. . . ."

Lindsey ran hard and fast down the winding game path, through tangles of brush. She leaped over rock, ducked around stands of spiky barrel cactus and never slowed until she collapsed at the edge of the desert floor. Then she lay gasping for breath for only a moment. Looking back over her shoulder, she shoved herself to her feet and staggered to a rock and leaned back against it, keeping watch on the path behind her. She knew she had stabbed and sliced the young gunman many times. But she didn't trust the outcome, not after finding out firsthand how hard it was to kill a man.

She'd thought at the outset that a butcher knife would make short work of him. But she'd been wrong. Her hope now was that he would bleed to death up there along the path. Or, at least be badly enough wounded that he wouldn't bother coming after her, or going on after her brother.

Her brother . . .

She gazed upward along the hill line behind her in the direction of Dutchman's Tanks, as if hoping Toby would appear up there, wave at her, and soon come bounding down to her, fit as ever. The whole thing had been nothing but a nightmare—a bad dream that had vanished with the passing night. Now that daylight shined bright and clear . . .

Stop it, she said to herself.

Last night had been real and terrible, but nothing had gotten any better with the coming of daylight. She was alive, that meant something. But Toby was still back there somewhere, hurt, maybe dead for all she knew. Thinking of him, she pushed herself up from against the rock. She had to follow this main trail along the bottom edge of the hill line and get back to where the path ran up to the water hole. She looked all around. She had to do all this and at the same time stay out of sight. For all she knew the gunmen could come back looking for her. She'd heard them say they were riding on, but she couldn't trust it. She couldn't trust anything, she reminded herself.

She walked down the last few sloping steps of the sandy hillside to the main trail. She stayed along the inner edge of the desert trail and walked back to where she knew they had turned up on the path to the water hole. She kept the rocky hills near her side should she suddenly need their shelter.

She had walked steadily, nonstop for an hour when she came upon the sound of thrashing in the dried brush a few yards up on the sloping hillside. Stopping and freezing in place, she stared in terror, expecting to see the wounded gunman who had somehow circled above her and lay in wait. Yet, as she stood watching, she saw a large, bloody wolf—one of the losing combatants in last night's contest over Arnold Pulty's corpse—step out of the brush and stand staring down at her, its fangs showing.

Oh God . . . !

She backed away a slow step. Wolves never came out in the daylight, she told herself. *Did they?* She backed another step, the wolf stalked forward slowly. She saw a deep, bloody tear in its fur. *No, they don't,* she answered herself, not unless something was wrong. She backed another step, telling herself not to run. If this monster saw her running, it would strike out after her. But she only moved slowly, quietly, showing no threat—

Oh no . . . !

The wounded wolf leaped forward, charging down at her in a full run—limping in its hindquarters, but running all the same.

Lindsey ran with all her strength along the sandy lower edge of the hill line, veering out every step farther onto the desert floor. She had no idea where she was running to, she only knew to run, put distance between herself and the wolf. For how long or far she didn't consider, to what inevitable end she dare not imagine.

The harder she ran out onto the barren desert floor, the more the deepening sand slowed her down. She looked back, seeing the big limping wolf gaining on her. Beneath her, she felt her feet moving as if she were running in a bad dream, running hard, getting nowhere.

She screamed. It made no difference to the wolf.

"Get away!" she shrieked, but the wolf ran on,

getting closer, too close. She heard the panting rattle of its breath, heard its paws striking the sand. When she looked back again, she knew it was over. The big animal made a long final leap, as was its instinctive move when it knew it had its prey.

Lindsey stumbled to her knees, rolled in the loose, hot sand, trying to cover herself with her arms. The wolf had her; she knew it. But then she heard the animal let out a terrible yelp. As she looked through her protecting arms, she saw it fly sideways, its direction changed in midair, a ribbon of fresh blood streaking from its side. Then the blast of a rifle shot caught up with itself from among the rocks along the lower hillside. In the sand, the mortally wounded wolf dragged itself forward, its fangs snapping at her foot. Lindsey scooted quickly forward away from it, the wolf's paw digging at her, striking against her shoe. She struggled to her feet on the run, looking back wide-eyed. She'd gone three steps when the wolf's body bucked hard in the sand and seemed to melt there. The report of a second rifle shot came down from the rocks and echoed out across the desert floor.

Lindsey felt a sudden rush of relief, but also the dizzying press of heat, of thirst and exhaustion. Even as she tried to focus on the figure standing atop the line of rock in a drift of smoke where the shots had come from, she felt the world spin around her, and she fell backward, limp onto the burning sand.

The Ranger looked out across the desert floor from up in the rocks atop a narrow cliff. He saw the wolf dead in the sand; he watched the young woman fall to the ground. With his Winchester in hand he climbed down among a stand of boulders, walked around to where he'd left the horses, and led them along a slim path to a downhill trail. At the bottom of the sloping hill line he stepped up into his saddle and shoved the Winchester into its boot.

Riding the easygoing buckskin, leading the black-point copper dun and the big paint alongside him, he raced out through the sand to where the young woman lay collapsed beneath the hot morning sun. She struggled up onto her elbows as the sound of the horses drew closer. Seeing the rise of dust from the three horses, not realizing it was a lawman riding toward her, she struggled the rest of the way to her feet and started running all over again.

Sam kept the horses pounding straight at her across the sand. As he drew closer, he let go of the lead rope to the two horses and leaned off low to the side. On his way past her, he swept her up across his lap and held her there. She kicked and screamed and lashed out at him with her fists, managing only to hit him on his leg.

"Easy, *Miss Lindsey*, easy," Sam called out. "I'm Arizona Ranger Sam Burrack. Your brother Toby sent me. I'm here to help."

Hearing her name, hearing her brother's name, she settled a little and looked up at the Ranger. Seeing the badge on his chest she settled the rest of the way. Tears filled her eyes.

"Toby sent you?" she said.

"Yes, ma'am, he did," the Ranger said. He lifted her

and sat her more securely onto his lap as he brought the buckskin to a halt.

"He's—he's all right then?" she asked, her eyes already full of tears.

"He's on the trail behind me," Sam said. As he spoke he raised a canteen from his saddle horn. He uncapped it and held it to her lips. She drank thirstily. "Now that I've got you, we can ride back and join him." He pulled the canteen away and capped it.

Lindsey cried against his chest as Sam turned the buckskin and rode over and gathered the lead rope to the other two horses.

"You just rest a spell," he said quietly. "Everything's all right."

When he'd gathered the horses and she'd collected herself and stopped crying, Sam nodded at the dried blood on her hands, the front of her dress.

"Are you all right?" he asked.

"Yes, I am . . . now," she said, sniffling. "This is not my blood. Are you the lawman they were waiting to ambush at the water hole?"

"That would be my guess," Sam said. "Whose blood is it?"

"A gunman they call Joey Rose," she said. "He was going back to look for my brother, but I stopped him."

"Did you kill him?" Sam asked gravely, again noting all the dried blood.

"No," she said. "I meant to, but he drew his gun. I barely got away alive." She paused and took on a troubled look just thinking about the morning's events.

"We'll talk about it later," Sam said. He looked her up and down. "You've had a rough morning. Are you able to ride?"

"Yes, I can ride," she said.

"Good," said Sam, before she'd hardly gotten the words out of her mouth. "Here's a horse for you." He scooted back off his saddle and slipped expertly over from the back of the buckskin onto the paint.

"There," he said, "you even get a saddle." He looped a length of the lead rope into a makeshift hackamore and leaned forward and slipped it onto the paint's head and muzzle.

Lindsey adjusted herself in the saddle, her ragged dress gathered above her skinned knees.

"All set, Ranger Burrack," she said.

"Then let's go find Toby," he said, sitting bareback on the big paint beside her. "He'll be glad to see you."

Chapter 12

Toby Delmar spotted his sister and the Ranger when the two had ridden their horses as far as the winding hill paths would allow. They had stepped down from the horses' backs and led the three animals around a large boulder when Toby saw them and stood up in the cover of a downed juniper.

"Sis, over here," he called out to Lindsey, limping forward, his hand to the bandanna covering his belly wound.

Sam reached a hand out in time and took the buck-skin's reins as Lindsey pitched them to him and ran to her brother. The two met with a hug in spite of their wounded, battered conditions. Sam stood watching, glad he'd been able to help. Yet, now that these two were together, both of them alive, reasonably well after the situation they'd been through, he realized their welfare would have to come first. He had to attend to getting them safely off the desert floor and find them help and shelter before turning his attention back to Braxton Kane and his Golden Riders.

So be it. . . .

That was the job, he reminded himself. Besides, in a strange roundabout way, these two had kept him from facing an ambush. He nodded to himself, watching the reunited twins. When they turned and walked back to him he was stricken by how much they looked alike regardless of their difference in gender.

"Ranger Burrack," Toby said gratefully, "you did it. You found my sister and brought her back, unharmed." He smiled and hugged his sister on his good side.

"And you found Toby," Lindsey put in, gesturing toward her brother's bloodstained side. "You saved his life." She smiled, tearfully, and swung an arm toward the mule, who stood to the side chewing on dry wild grass. "You even saved Dan."

"We can never thank you enough," Toby said.

Sam touched his hat brim, a little embarrassed, not accustomed to hearing thanks from anyone, save for perhaps some town sheriff when he'd saved the town the cost of a hanging, by shooting an outlaw dead in the street.

"You're both very welcome," he said. "Now we need to get over this hill—get back to the water hole and get your wagon."

The two nodded in agreement.

"Are you going to be able to ride?" Lindsey asked her brother, noting his wounded lower belly.

"Sis, I've been riding," Toby replied. "The Ranger says this ricochet sliced through me clean, never hit anything."

Lindsey looked at Sam as if for affirmation.

"It appears so," Sam said. "Had it hit anything vital

we'd have known before now. He's been riding the mule on these hill paths all day."

Lindsey looked relieved.

"All the same," Sam added, "we need to get him to Alto Cresta and have a doctor look him over."

"Yes," Lindsey said nodding.

"These men you're after, Ranger," said Toby. "Will they get away now, while you ride with us to Alto Cresta?"

"No, they won't," Sam said, "not for long anyway. I'll catch up to them. I've been tracking them for a while. I have an idea where they're headed."

"I don't want us holding you back," Toby said.

"You're not," Sam said. "I've got a notion Alto Cresta is in the direction they're headed."

"So, you might catch up to them there?" Toby said.

"That's possible," Sam said. He saw something at work in the young man's mind.

"And you'll take them prisoner, right there in the street?" he asked.

"Prisoner . . . ?" said Sam. "That's not likely. I'll give them a chance to turn themselves in. But the kind of men I hunt usually don't choose to go to prison." He paused, then said, "Likely as not these men would rather die."

"Or else kill you?" Toby offered.

"Toby Edward Delmar!" Lindsey said, aghast by her brother's words. "Don't say such a thing as that." She gave Sam an apologetic look.

"That's all right," said Sam, "it's true. It's not some fact I'm unaware of."

"Then—then, *you* will kill *them*. . . ." Toby said,

seeing they had eliminated any other option. "That is what lawmen do, if need be?"

"That is the calling," Sam said. He gave the appearance of wanting to dismiss the matter.

Lindsey started to say something more, but Toby cut her off.

"Come, sit down, Sis," he said. "Rest a few minutes before we go get the wagon." He looked at Sam and asked, "Is that all right, just for a minute or two?"

"Yes," Sam said, "rest a few minutes." He led the horses away from the twins and stopped and looked out across the desert floor. He saw the body of the wolf stretched out in the sand. The big ferocious animal was now only a black speck in the wavering heat from where he stood. *Or else kill you,* he recounted the twin saying only a moment ago.

"That is the calling . . . ," he repeated quietly, this time to himself. He turned his eyes from the body of the wolf and looked off along the distant hill line in the direction of Alto Cresta.

It was close to midnight when Chris Weidel sprang up on his blanket. Colt in hand he looked all around the darkened campsite, a bed of orange glowing coals smoldering inside a wide circle of stones. No sooner than he'd sprung up, the sound of the Colt cocking caused Roy Mangett to do the same on the other side of the glowing coals.

"What the hell, Chris?" Mangett said in a harsh whisper. He jerked his Colt from its holster lying beside him. He fanned it back and forth, cocked, staring into the dark shadows of boulder and rock that blocked out the purple moonlight.

"I heard something," Weidel whispered in the same tone. "Heard it plain as day. A horse I believe. . . ."

The two sat listening on their blankets. After a moment Mangett stood up, flipping his blanket aside.

"I'm going to check around," he whispered.

Weidel also stood up, picking up his rifle that lay along his side.

"I've got you covered," he said quietly, a gun in either hand.

As Mangett started across the campsite into the darkness, a breaking of brush resounded out among the rocks. Turning toward the sound with their guns drawn, they saw Joey Rose's horse step into the campsite and stand looking at them. Joey Rose lay slumped on the horse's back, his bloody face lying forward on its neck, covered with blood.

"Holy Jim and Gilbert," said Weidel, "it's Rose! Look at his face." Blood had streaked down the horse's withers and dried there, thick and black all the way to its knee.

"Please . . . ," Rose said in a pained voice. "I'm dried here."

"Damn," said Weidel, seeing strands of the horse's mane matted to Rose's face. "He's ruint!"

"Help me get him down," said Mangett, lowering his Colt, shoving it down in the waist of his trousers.

"This poor son of a bitch. We've got to put him out

of his misery," said Weidel. He stepped around and helped Mangett pull strands of mane from the deep slash wounds on Rose's face.

Rose tightened at the sound of Weidel's suggestion.

"Shut up, Chris," said Mangett. "Help me get him unstuck." To Rose he said, "Take it easy, Joey. Nobody's putting you out of your misery."

"I'm cut . . . all to hell, Roy," Rose groaned.

"Yes, I'd say you are," Mangett said.

"Which one did this to you, pal?" Weidel said with very little sympathy. "Don't tell us that skinny gal, or you'll never hear the end of it." He gave a dark chuckle.

Rose didn't reply.

The two gunmen lowered him from the horse and carried him over beside the glowing coals. Loose, blood-matted mane hair hung from his face like some strange and scraggly beard.

"I—I checked my belly," Rose said in a strained distorted voice. "I'm . . . not hanging out nowhere."

"Lucky you," Weidel quipped darkly.

"Am I . . . ?" Rose asked, uncertain.

Laying the wounded Rose on the ground, Mangett pulled the front of his shredded shirt open and peeled it loose from the dried blood covering his chest, his belly. As he looked Rose over good, he spoke to Weidel over his shoulder.

"Stoke up the fire, get his bedroll down here," he said. "Get your canteen from your saddle."

"Why *my canteen*, Roy?"

Mangett gave him a scathing look.

"Because I'll kill you if you touch mine," he said flatly. When Weidel turned to Rose's horse without another word on the matter, Mangett called out to him, "There's a Captain Marcy emergency kit in my saddle-bags somewhere. Get it."

"Needle . . . ?" Rose managed to say.

"Yes, a needle, Joey," said Mangett. "You need some tucking in and closing up here and there."

"I'm not . . . hanging out nowhere am I?" Rose asked again, this time running a blood-crusted hand over his belly, feeling the slick, fresh blood atop older dried layers.

"No, Joey, all your guts are where they should be," Mangett said. Looking more closely at the young outlaw's carved-up face in the dim light of the glowing coals, he added, "But your chin's hanging half over on your jaw."

Joey sobbed and groaned at the news.

"You'd best hope he can sew it on, Joey boy," Weidel said in a taunting voice, getting the items from Mangett's saddlebags. "If he can't he'll have to cut it off." He gave his dark chuckle. "Think how that's going to look."

Rose groaned again.

"Don't listen to him, Joey," said Mangett. He looked around at Weidel. "Chris, enough's enough. Get the fire stoked and let's put this poor bastard's face stitched back together—leastwise till we can take him to town."

"Whatever you say, Roy," said Weidel, pitching Rose's bedroll onto the ground beside him. "I'll get the fire stoked up good and bright. I want to see every bit of this." He pitched the emergency tin and the canteen down next to the bedroll.

Mangett gave him a harsh look.

"What?" said Weidel. "You never know, I might have to do the same thing someday."

"Spread his bedroll out. Let's get him on it," Mangett said looking away from him. "Find a strong piece of wood for him to bite down on."

"Hear that, Joey boy," said Weidel. "I'm going to get you a piece of wood to bite on." He grinned cruelly. "Meaning, this is going to hurt like a sumbitch."

At a corner table in Chavez's Cantina, Tillman and Foz Garlet sat sipping rye whiskey while their brother, Prew, Cutthroat Teddy Bonsell and Jake Cleary stood at the bar talking with a Golden Rider named Ed Dorsey. The four looked over at Foz and Tillman, whose faces had taken on a greenish pallor ever since they'd left Poco Fuega. Their eyes were still bloodshot, brown and watery. Their eyebrows and all other facial hair were gone owing to the blast set off by the Bluebird in Midland Settlement. The Bluebird stood out on the boardwalk staring onto the dusty street, his arms folded across his chest. Behind the bar, Bruno Chavez stood watching, listening, pouring rye, keeping their shot glasses filled.

"Looks like you Garlet boys have rode a hard trail getting here," said Dorsey, having heard about their jail break, the loaded mescal, and the Ranger being on their trail. He raised his shot glass to his lips. "Nothing

I can do about those two being mescal-poisoned, but as far as the Ranger, if Roy Mangett and his three gunnies don't stop him back there"—he jerked his head toward the desert hills—"we'll stop his clock right here if he shows his face." He set his empty shot glass down hard on the bar top. Chavez filled it.

"Mangett and his pals are good," Prew said with shrug. "So, I've got a feeling the Ranger is already dead in the sand. My brothers and I are riding on to Kane's hideout." He looked at Cutthroat Teddy and Jake Cleary. "What about you two, Bonsell?" he asked.

"I've got to go shake the snake," Bonsell said. He turned toward the rear door, but answered on his way, "Oh, we're going to stick here a while longer, just in case Mangett and his pals don't take care of the Ranger."

"Come to think of it I've got to shake the snake myself," said Dorsey. He shoved his shot glass forward; Chavez filled it as he followed Bonsell out back to the jakes.

Cleary started to follow the other two, but he stopped and stayed at the bar when Prew directed the conversation to him.

"That's what you think Brax would want you and Bonsell to do, wait here?" he asked Cleary.

Cleary shrugged.

"Once he hears about his brother being dead he might come riding this way himself, just to make sure the Ranger's dead. I would if it was my brother," Cleary said. "We'll stick here in case he does."

Prew nodded and tossed back his shot of rye. Chavez refilled his glass.

Bonsell and Dorsey walked back through the rear door and reclaimed their places at the bar. Bonsell took another shot of rye and considered things for a moment. The others looked at him as he let out a breath and drummed his fingers on the bar.

"This is a bad time to be having all this trouble," he said. "Brax losing his brother, your brothers poisoning themselves on loaded mescal. All of it while we're getting ready to pull off a big job."

"How big a job, you suppose?" Ed Dorsey asked. He raised his glass and he asked.

"*Awfully* big, I figure," Prew Garlet put in. He nodded toward the boardwalk out front. "That's why Brax has me bringing the Bluebird to him."

"That's the Bluebird . . . ?" Ed Dorsey looked around toward the front door, then back to Prew.

"Yep," said Prew.

"I've heard of him," said Dorsey. "He's said to be the best there is at blowing things up."

"So they say," said Prew. "I don't mind saying I'll be glad to get rid of him, let Brax deal with him."

"Peculiar, huh?" said Dorsey.

"*Damned* peculiar," Prew emphasized. "All I can get out of him is a nod now and then, if that. He's supposed to be a Mexican-Indian half-breed. I don't think he understands a lick of English, Spanish or anything else."

"From what I hear the Bluebird could blow the doors off hell if the devil locked himself out," said Bonsell. He grinned; his eyes shined in the cantina's dim lantern light.

"Locked out of hell. . . ." Ed Dorsey raised his shot glass with a wide half-drunken grin. "I'll drink to that. The Bluebird too, and all the money he's going to make for us."

"Hear, hear," the other three gunmen said in unison, raising their glasses.

Chapter 13

As the four men stood drinking, Prew getting ready to take his brothers and the Bluebird on to meet up with Braxton Kane, they all looked around when the Bluebird stepped inside out of the evening light and stood off to the side. Behind him came Roy Mangett with Joey Rose hanging limp at his side, Rose's bloody arm looped over Mangett's shoulder. The men watched in silence as Mangett walked over to a wooden chair where Tillman and Foz sat nursing their rye. He dropped Rose into the chair and stepped back and looked down at him.

"Take a good look," Mangett said. "This is what a slip of a woman can do with a butcher knife if she takes a mind to."

"A woman . . . ?" said Ed Dorsey.

"That's right, Ed, a woman," said Mangett. "Not a very big woman at that."

"You men went out to set up an ambush for the Ranger," said Dorsey.

"Maybe you didn't hear me, Ed," said Mangett, his hand falling near his holstered Colt. "I said, this is what a woman can do with a butcher knife. I didn't mention any Ranger, now did I?" He gave Dorsey a scorching stare. "We never even saw the Ranger." He looked over at Prew Garlet at the bar, at the two Garlet brothers sitting at the table. "We're getting Joey here patched up. We'll take care of the Ranger when he gets here . . . if he even comes here at all."

Outside the door they heard boots walking across the boardwalk. As they turned and looked, Chris Weidel shoved the white-haired town doctor, Davies Milton, inside the cantina and followed him across the floor. The doctor, red-eyed, his hair disheveled, saw Joey Rose's bloody, sliced and stitched-up face and stopped ten feet away.

"Yep, that's your patient, Doc," said Weidel with a cruel little smile.

The doctor stepped right over to Rose.

"My, my," he said, "let's see what we have." He lay his black medical bag on the table and flipped it open as he studied Rose's face. Noting many of the slashes on Rose's face had been stitched shut, yet many were still open and bleeding even though crusted heavily with blood, the doctor asked the two gunmen, "Who did the sewing, and why did you stop?"

"I sewed him," said Mangett. "I stopped when I ran out of thread."

"If it needs doing over, Doc," said Weidel, staring at Rose as he spoke, "we can always pull these stitches out and let you go at it anew."

Rose groaned and tried to shake his head.

The doctor ignored Weidel as he took off his shiny, black suit coat and pitched it over a chair. He rolled up his shirtsleeves.

"I'll need some hot water, some soap and some fresh clean bar towels—plenty of them," he said to Chavez who stood watching from the edge of the bar. Chavez turned to do the old doctor's bidding. The doctor leaned in and began peeling a wadded blood-soaked bandanna from one of the unstitched wounds on Rose's chest.

"That's where I ran out," Mangett said, watching the doctor work.

The doctor only nodded. As he reached over and dropped the bandanna onto the tabletop, he glanced at Foz and Tillman Garlet, who sat staring blankly, their glasses of rye in their hands.

"What's wrong with these two?" he asked.

Hearing the doctor, Foz straightened in his chair.

"Not a *damn thing*, sawbones," he said, appearing to bristle at the doctor's question.

Prew stepped over from the bar and held a hand out toward Foz as if prepared to shove him back down into his chair.

"They got ahold of some loaded mescal, Doc," he said. "They're about over it now."

"They don't look *about over it*," the doctor said, seeing the greenish pallor to the Garlet brothers' skin, the empty leer in their bloodshot, watery eyes.

Foz started to rise again; again Prew held his hand out at him, keeping him seated. Tillman only sat staring.

"Doctor, maybe when you get Rose sewn up you can look these two over good?" Prew asked.

"I can do it now while I'm waiting for water to boil," said the doctor. He stood at a spot where he could place a palm out on each of the Garlet brothers' foreheads. Foz started to object, but Prew grabbed him by his shoulder and gave him a warning stare.

"Neither of them's running a fever," Dr. Milton said. "Always a good sign." He stooped a little and looked at the brothers' eyes more closely, in turn.

"What do you think, Doc?" Prew asked.

"No signs of severe vomiting or dysentery?" the doctor asked.

"No," said Prew, "none of that. What does that mean?"

"It means most of the poison has worked its way out of their bellies," said the doctor.

Prew looked relieved.

"But it's still in their blood," the doctor said. He paused, then said, "Once it's completely out of their blood we'll be able to determine whether or not their mental condition is going to improve."

"You mean . . . they could both be idiots for the rest of their lives?" Prew asked.

The doctor looked at him with a flat expression.

"That's putting it bluntly, but yes," he said, "that is a possibility. There have been folks who've poisoned themselves on mescal and never been the same afterward."

"Hey, don't call me a damned idiot, me sitting right here listening to every word," Foz said, staring coldly at the old doctor.

"He didn't, Foz," said Prew. "I did."

Foz looked sidelong at Tillman, who sat staring blankly, then off at the far wall.

"All we need is our horses under us," Foz grumbled.

"What can we do to help them over it?" Prew asked the doctor.

"At this point, nothing," the doctor said, "except let them ride it out. Drinking lots of water helps. Back east they've been giving folks tincture of mercury for similar poisoning." He shook his disheveled head. "I'm of a belief that mercury might do as much harm as it does good. But you can't tell the experts nothing."

Chavez carried a pan of water and set it down on the table. Beside it he took clean towels from over his forearm and laid them beside the pan.

"Mescal improperly prepared is bad enough, sir," the old doctor said to Prew. "But mescal loaded with cocaine, peyote and God knows what else, poisons both the body and the brain. People die from it all the time." He shook his head. "Still, they drink it. I'll never understand."

Prew looked at his brothers, then the men standing at the bar, then at the Bluebird who stood off to the side with his arms folded.

"Get up, Foz, Tillman," he said. "Mescal poison or not, we're headed out of here. We're delivering the Bluebird to Braxton Kane. I'm telling him what happened to his brother."

Cutthroat stood at the bar, watching, his eyebrows gone, hair missing from the backs of his hands.

"Make damn sure you tell him me and Jake here are the ones who told you about Cordy," he said.

Prew didn't answer. He watched his brothers struggle to their feet and walk mindlessly toward the front door.

It was after dark when the Ranger and the twins stepped down from their saddles in an alley behind the doctor's house on the main street of Alto Cresta. The Ranger and the young woman quietly hitched the horses and the covered wagon to a hitch rail. The two helped Toby down from the wagon on which he'd ridden the last ten miles of their journey. Owing to the pain in his wounded belly, the Ranger looped the young man's arm over his shoulders and helped him walk to the rear porch, Lindsey close beside them.

Opening the rear door, Sam called out in a guarded tone before stepping inside the darkened house. Hearing no reply, the three walked farther inside, down a shadowy hallway to a room where soft lamplight spilled out onto the wooden floor.

Before Sam could call out again, a Mexican woman stepped into the hallway rubbing sleep from her eyes.

"Que est la . . . Qué est . . . ?" she said in her native tongue.

"Arizona Ranger Sam Burrack, ma'am," the Ranger said. "We've got a man here who needs the doctor to treat a belly wound."

"Dr. Milton is not here," said the woman. "He goes to the cantina earlier to treat an injured man."

Even as she spoke the woman led the three into the room and gestured for them to lay Toby down on a surgery table. Looking at Toby's face, then at Lindsey's, she gave a short smile.

"Gemelos, sí?" she said.

"Yes, we're twins," Lindsey replied, fluffing a pillow and adjusting it under her brother's head. "How long do you think the doctor will be?"

"I do not know," the woman said. She had moved in close and began taking the big boots from Toby's feet. "But I will get the wound washed, so when the doctor arrives he can immediately see your brother's condition."

"Gracias," Sam said before Lindsey could answer. To Lindsey he said, "I'll go to the cantina and look inside, see how long he might be."

Lindsey looked concerned.

"But, you said there could be Golden Riders here," she said.

"Yes, I know," Sam said. "Don't worry. I'm not going in. I'll find a window or a back door—I'm good at watching without being seen." He gave her a reassuring smile and turned and walked toward the door while the Mexican woman peeled Toby's shirt from his bloody belly.

Outside, Sam had started down the street toward the cantina, staying in the darker shadows close to the storefronts. The street lay empty except for an occasional pedestrian arriving at a hitch rail for their horse or buggy. As Sam walked the last fifteen yards to the cantina he saw the stooped, elderly doctor walk out onto the boardwalk, his medical bag in hand, and head toward him.

Good . . .

Sam slowed his pace almost to a stop and allowed the doctor to reach him. When the doctor looked at him and gave him a courteous nod, he saw the badge on Sam's chest. Before the doctor could acknowledge him, Sam fell in beside him and walked along the boardwalk.

"Dr. Milton, I'm Arizona Ranger Sam Burrack," Sam said. "I have a young man with a belly wound waiting at your house." As he spoke he shifted his eyes past a darkened alleyway across the street.

The old doctor grumbled and shook his head as the two of them walked on.

"Belly wounds, liquor poisoning, stabbing and cuttings," he said under his breath. "They don't need a doctor here, they need a battlefield hospital. . . ."

As the Ranger and Dr. Milton walked on toward the doctor's house, across the street in an alley the Cundiff brothers, Joe and Willie, sat with the horses in a dark corner and stared in silence. Neither spoke until the doctor and the Ranger were out sight. Then and only then did Joe Cundiff pull his rifle up from its saddle boot, check it and hold it propped up on his thigh. His thumb pulled the hammer back. Out of sight they heard a hound bellow out as the Ranger and the doctor approached it in the darkness.

"I'll be damned and go to hell," Willie Cundiff whispered beside his brother, his right hand wrapped around the butt of his holstered revolver, his left hand gripping his reins and his saddle horn. "We have run all this way to get him off our trail, and the son of a bitch is right here *waiting for us*?" He stared around at his brother in awe and amazement. "There is something just ain't natural about all that."

"I know," Joe whispered back in a defeated tone, his hand tight on his rifle. "It makes you wonder why even try."

"Don't go getting moody on me, *god*damn it," Willie said harshly. He drew his Colt, half cocked it and spun the cylinder making sure it was fully loaded with a round lying up under the hammer.

"I'm trying not to," Joe said. "But it ain't easy, after all we went through getting rid of him." He sat rigid, staring out of the alley in the direction the doctor and the Ranger had taken.

"Well . . . , we're taking a stand right here in Alto Cresta," said Willie. "We never should have run in the first place." He gave his brother a hard look.

"What . . . ?" said Joe. "It wasn't my idea to run."

"The hell it wasn't," said Willie. "I saw rabbit in your eyes the minute the shooting started."

"Hunh-uh," said Joe. "Don't even start blaming me. You said *run*; I ran." He gave a shrug.

Willie let out a tensed breath, considering everything.

"All right," he said. "It's of no matter now just whose idea it was," he said. "We both see now that we can't shake this devil loose. We've got to kill him."

Joe stared at him in silence for a moment.

"You meant just the two of us?" he said.

"That's exactly what I mean," said Willie. He started to nudge his horse forward.

Joe stopped him, reaching over, taking his horse by its bridle with his free hand.

"Wait," he said. "What about first we round up whoever's here and have them give us a hand? Everybody is gathering up. There's bound to be some of the gang here. Alls we've got to do is tell them—"

"Tell them what . . . ?" said Willie, jerking his horse away from Joe's grip. "Tell them how we had the Ranger four to one, but lit out, most likely got Bonsell and Cleary killed?" His words heated as he added, "Or tell them how we've been all this time running like a couple of cowards, trying to get away from him—here he was waiting for us the minute we hit town?" He nudged his horse forward. "No, thank you, brother. We're killing him. That's the end of it."

"Damn it, Willie," said Joe, nudging his horse along behind his brother. "I got an awfully bad feeling about this."

Chapter 14

In front of a tall up-reaching sequoia cactus standing diagonally across the street from the doctor's house, a skinny red hound the Cundiffs had heard barking a moment earlier stood with his head lowered, chewing eagerly. The hungry canine didn't even look up as the two brothers' horses walked past him.

"Must've caught himself a tasty barn rat," Joe said, looking over at the thin, bare-ribbed hound. "Looks like he could use a tasty rat or two."

"At least the bugle-mouthed bastard won't be announcing us coming," said Willie quietly. The two kept their horses at a slow walk, staring ahead at the doctor's large clapboard house.

"You figure he's in there, Willie?" Joe asked, his hand getting nervous and sweaty on his rifle stock.

"He was with the old town doctor here. Where else would they have gone?" He gestured a short nod along the vacant street ahead of them. Looking at the front of the house they saw a lamp burning dimly in a window.

"Yep," Joe agreed. "He's here for sure."

The two turned their horses to a hitch rail out front on the doctor's house.

"This time he's not going to be one jump ahead of us," Willie said. They stepped down from their horses and hitched them to the rail. "We've got him cold. Start shooting as soon as his feet hit the porch."

"Yeah, yeah, hurry up. Call him out," Joe said, starting to warm up excitedly to the prospect of having the Ranger where they wanted him. "I've got him, *I've got him!*"

"Well, well, look at you now," Willie said with a sly grin, taking his time now, looking confident. He held his Colt down his side, cocked and ready. He turned back to the house. "Ranger! Come out here!" he demanded. As he called out, he raised his Colt and took aim on the middle of the front door.

"What do you want, Willie Cundiff?" the Ranger's voice called out from the dark street behind them.

The Cundiffs stood frozen for a moment, trying to make sense of the Ranger being in the street behind them. Willie lowered his Colt as they turned and faced the lone figure standing diagonally across from them in front of the cactus, rifle in hand.

"Jesus . . . ," Willie said under his breath.

The red hound stood at the Ranger's left side. He licked his big tongue out across his flews and sniffed at Sam's hand. The Ranger scratched the dog's bony head and nudged him away.

"That's all I've got for you, pal," he said, speaking sidelong to the hound. Raising his tone he called out to the Cundiffs, "I asked, *What do you want, Willie?*"

Willie Cundiff swallowed hard; so did Joe standing close beside him.

"We're tired of you dogging us, Ranger," Willie called out. "It all stops right here."

Sam thought about it, realizing that these two must've thought his entire manhunt was centered on them.

"Willie, you should understand," Sam said. "I'm not just out to take down you Cundiffs. I'm out to take down all of the Golden Gang."

"Yeah, we understand all right, lawdog," said Joe, getting bolder. "We understand that you've been down our shirts ever since that day you caught up to us—"

"Listen to me, Joe," Sam said cutting him off. "This is the first I've seen or even thought of you two since that day."

"You're lying," Willie cut in sharply. "Don't be listening to him, Joe. We've got him worried." He stepped closer to the Ranger in the middle of the dirt street. "Not so sure of yourself, now, huh, Ranger?" he said to Sam.

The Ranger raised and cocked his rifle. What could he say? The two were convinced he'd been on their trail day and night. He saw no use in talking to them. He needed to make his move before they got spread out.

"And another thing, lawdog," Joe said, taking a bold step forward, his rifle up in both hands. "Us Cundiff boys have never had to—"

Sam first shot hit him dead center and sent him backward, leaving a black mist of blood in the dark purple night. As soon as he saw Joe fly backward, Sam levered up another round as he swung his Winchester to Joe's right and pulled the trigger as a shot from Willie's Colt whistled past the side of his head.

His second shot hit Willie Cundiff high in his shoulder and spun him spinning in a full circle. As the big outlaw tried to right himself steadily on his feet, Sam's second shot hit him squarely in his chest, sending him backward and flipping him over the hitch rail beside his nervous horse. The horse jerked sidelong, badly spooked but held by its reins. Beside the scared animal, Joe's horse reared against its reins and almost fell onto its side.

Sam levered a fresh round into his rifle chamber. He stooped and picked up both spent cartridges and dropped them into his duster pocket. He walked forward, around the hitch rail, his hand out toward the spooked horses. As the horses settled a little he loosened their reins and watched them turn and bolt away along the dark street. Then, he leaned his rifle against the hitch rail as the red hound came bounding over from the cactus and stood probing its muzzle all around the dead men.

"Get back now," Sam said to the curious canine. He dragged the two bodies closer together and leaned down and took them both by their collars and dragged them across the street and dropped them behind the big cactus.

Along the street, lamps and lanterns came to life in darkened windows. Sam looked up the street at the cantina, then turned and walked back and picked up his rifle. The hound who had watched him curiously raised its floppy muzzle and let out a loud, yodeling howl.

Stepping onto the front porch of the clapboard house, Sam saw the front door swing open. The old doctor stood looking at him as he walked inside.

"Anything I need to do out there?" the doctor asked, looking him up and down.

"No," Sam said flatly. "Turn out the light and keep the twins safe. I've got some more work to do here."

"*Work . . . ?*" The doctor gave him a bemused look.

The Ranger didn't offer to elaborate; he walked past him into the dark house.

Inside Chavez's Cantina, the five gunmen left at the bar all turned as one at the sound of gunfire and hurried out the front door. Chavez let out a tight breath, realizing that the whole day these men had slowed his business by more than half. *But what can you do?* he asked himself. Picking up a lantern from under the bar, he hurried around and followed the gunmen out front onto the boardwalk. Behind him, Joey Rose half stood, his face and chest covered with thick bandages. He mumbled something incoherently to Chavez, then collapsed back down in his chair.

Seeing townsmen hurrying along the street, women in housecoats, men pulling up their suspenders, Jake Cleary stepped down from the boardwalk, walked out into the street and gazed in the direction the gunfire had come from.

"It's all down in front of that big pipe-organ cactus," he said to the others.

"I expect we'd better go see what it was before all the space gets taken," Cutthroat Teddy Bonsell said with a sharp grin. He stepped out onto the street with Cleary and started walking. The others fell in with them, the five walking abreast at a saunter, not wanting to look too curious, or excited. They kept the same slow cool pace as the townsfolk hurried past them.

When they stopped eight yards away from the doctor's clapboard house, they saw townsmen and women milling in the street looking all around, confused. The street showed no sign of a shooting even though the faint smell of burned powder wafted in the night air.

"What the hell kind of shooting is it, nobody lying dead in the street?" Bonsell said, clearly disappointed.

"Must've been some drunk shooting off his guns," said a townsman. "We're getting lots of that of late." He gave the outlaws a sour look and turned and walked away.

"*Excuse* us all to hell," Bonsell called out as the man walked away.

The gathered crowd looked all around for a while, then appeared to lose interest and started drifting back to their warm beds. Chavez himself, holding the unlit lantern at his side, milled around with the gunmen for a moment longer, then started to turn and walk back to the cantina.

"Hold up a minute, barkeep," said Roy Mangett, looking down studying the dirt. "Fire that lantern up, hoss. I believe we've got something here."

Chavez struck a match, lit the lantern, and held it out over the dirt street.

"Give me that," said Mangett, grabbing the lantern from his hand. He stooped, one palm on his knee, and held the lantern closer to the dirt street.

"Well, help my time, what have we here?" he said. He moved the lantern back and forth slowly, seeing the drag marks reach from the empty hitch rail all the way across the street. "I sense some foul play afoot, after all." He grinned.

The other gunmen gathered around him and looked down at the long scrape marks in the dirt where Sam had pulled the dead gunmen over behind the sequoia. They followed Mangett over and around the cactus.

"Holy *Madre* . . . !" Chavez whispered, crossing himself deftly at the sight of the two bloody bodies sprawled in the dirt. The other men stood staring in silence.

Between the two bodies, the red hound stood with his four feet spread in a fighting stance. He gave a low, warning growl.

Holding the lantern out, Mangett stomped his foot loudly at the hound.

"Get the hell out of here, you cur!" he shouted. "They ain't your dinner!"

The gunmen advanced; the hound retreated grudgingly, its teeth and flews streaked with blood from where he'd been licking the dead men's open wounds.

"Jesus, Roy," said Bonsell as the hound slinked away. "It's the Cundiff brothers, Willie and Joe." He looked at Jake Cleary.

Cleary said, "The last we saw of them, they left us jackpotted for the Ranger."

"The Ranger, hunh?" said Mangett. He looked all around the dark street outside the circle of lantern light. "You figure the Ranger done this?"

"I would not figure against it," said Cleary. He also

looked all around, warily. Bonsell looked around too, also with a dark, suspicious expression. Beside them Dorsey took on the same look. His hand fell instinctively to the butt of his holstered revolver.

"Something wrong with you fellows?" Mangett asked. "Has something got you all spooked?"

"Spooked? *Naw . . . ,*" said Bonsell. The three gunmen shook their heads as one. Mangett and Weidel gave each other a look.

Bonsell turned back to the Cundiffs' bodies and cocked his head curiously.

"Poor sonsabitches. They both were always plagued with a cowardly soul," he said. He looked around again and lowered his voice. "Think that damned Ranger is lurking around here now?"

"I would not be surprised," said Mangett, holding the lantern down and turning it off to take himself out of the light.

"I hope he is," said Cleary. He jerked the big LeMat revolver from his waist and held it up with both hands. "I ain't shot a man with one of these big babies since the Civil." He grinned and wagged the heavy gun.

"It makes sense, the more I think of it," Mangett said. "He kills these two and hides their bodies. We don't find them right off, so we go on back to the cantina. We get all settled in—"

"That's his style all right," Bonsell cut in sharply. "If he's here he'll be coming to the cantina."

The men all looked at one another.

"Come on, hurry up," said Bonsell, breaking into a trot. Cleary and Dorsey fell into a trot alongside him.

"Wait!" shouted Mangett. But he and Weidel also started running, catching up to Bonsell.

"He thinks he'll catch us by surprise inside the cantina, he's got another think coming!" Bonsell called out over his shoulder.

Losing the cool, calm demeanor they'd had only moments earlier, the gunmen raced toward the cantina in the middle of the street as if in a footrace. Chavez stood watching in disbelief.

Before they had gone twenty yards, Mangett tried to grab Bonsell's arm and pull him to a halt. But before he could, he saw the Ranger step out of the shadows of the town apothecary, his Winchester to his shoulder.

"Hold it! There he is—!" Mangett cried out in total surprise. The Ranger's first shot hit him in his broad chest and sent him rolling sideways in the dirt.

The other gunmen, sliding to a halt, caught completely off guard and confused, broke toward whatever cover they could find. The Ranger saw what they were trying to do and wouldn't allow it. Before they could get to cover and reorganize he began firing. Systematically, he took quick aim and shot the outlaws down one after the other. First Roy Mangett, next Chris Weidel, followed by Ed Dorsey. He took aim on Cutthroat Teddy Bonsell, but at the last second he held his rifle instead toward a large cooperage barrel where Jake Cleary had ducked down and taken cover, the big LeMat nine-shot in hand.

Moving sidelong, the Ranger lowered the hot smoking Winchester and laid it in the dirt street. Instead of drawing his big Colt, he pulled the big LeMat he'd taken from Virgil Piney back in Poco Fuego.

"Listen up, both of you," Sam called out. "You're still my prisoners."

"But we got away," Bonsell called out. "Damned near got blown out of our skin!"

"It doesn't matter," Sam said, "you're still my prisoners. Step out and let me see your hands." He kept walking slowly, sideways, knowing that neither of these men were going to lay down their guns and give themselves up.

"You're out of your mind, Ranger!" Bonsell shouted from behind the front corner of a building, seeing the Ranger cut away a slice of his cover with every sidelong step. He looked around quickly and saw no other place to go. "Stop right there, Ranger! Or, I'll blow your head off."

The Ranger didn't stop until he had a good angle at both outlaws' positions from the middle of the street.

"Hold your fire, Cutthroat," Sam said. "I'll be taking you along with me as soon as I kill Jake Cleary."

"Like hell you will," Bonsell shouted. He ventured a step away from the corner of the building to take aim. As soon as he raised his Colt, the big LeMat bucked in the Ranger's hand. One of the high-charged .42 caliber lead balls nailed Bonsell in his shoulder and spun him along the side of the building five feet before dropping him on the ground.

"Uh-oh!" Jake Cleary called out. "Did I just hear a big Confederate horse pistol *talking dirty*?"

"That you did," Sam said, having already made it plain that he intended to kill Cleary. "I know you've got one too, Jake. I saw it in your waist back in front of the doctor's house." He held the big LeMat with both hands, feeling the four-and-a-half-pound weight of it right away.

"I've killed more men with one of these than I'd care to count, Ranger," Cleary said, still huddled down behind the big cooperage barrel. "I look forward to doing the same to you."

"Then step on out and let's let her buck," Sam said. "I'm only taking Cutthroat with me. No offense intended."

"None taken, Ranger," said Cleary, standing up slowly, seeing the big LeMat in Sam's hands, held out at arm's length. He grinned in the darkness. "Heavy, ain't it?" he said, gripping his own big LeMat, cocking it toward the Ranger.

"Too heavy," Sam said. He'd cleaned and reloaded the big cap and ball monster the night after he'd taken it from Piney. The .42 caliber loads he'd charged heavily, loading eight more grains of black powder in it than the gun makers called for. The twenty-gauge chamber he'd filled with loose buckshot and two .42 caliber lead balls.

Without another word, Cleary fired his LeMat. The ball whistled past the Ranger's head. As the black smoke drifted away from Cleary's shot, Sam squeezed his LeMat's trigger and saw the streak of fire reach out across the dark street like a dragon's breath. The big gun bucked hard in his hand. The ball nailed Cleary in his chest and slammed him backward against the front wall of the building. He slid down to the boardwalk as the second blue-orange ball streaked out and nailed him above his right eye. Blood and brain matter splattered the wall behind him. His chin tipped forward onto his chest and bobbed as if nodding in agreement.

The Ranger stood in a cloud of black powder smoke and looked at the big gruesome gun in his hand. *One hard-hitting, ugly French nightmare,* he told himself, turning the gun in his hand. *But what a shooter. . . .*

Around the corner of the building, Cutthroat Teddy Bonsell lay stunned in the dirt, grasping his bleeding shoulder. Sam walked over, the cloud of powder smoke seeming to follow him like a dark, angry spirit. He stopped and stood over Bonsell.

"Don't shoot me . . . with *that* thing no more," he said in a broken voice.

"I'm not going to shoot you again, Cutthroat," Sam said. He shoved the warm LeMat down behind his gun belt. "I told you, I'm taking you with me."

"Yeah?" said Bonsell. "What if I say I ain't going?"

"You'd be wrong," Sam said flatly.

"What if say I ain't even here?" Bonsell cackled with laughter in spite of his bleeding wound.

"I don't know how to even answer that," Sam said. He pulled the wounded outlaw to his feet as more townsfolk hurried back onto the street to see what was going on. Sam gave him a shove toward the doctor's house.

"Don't worry, folks," he called out to the gathering townsfolk. "I'm Arizona Ranger Sam Burrack. These are men who are wanted for crimes all over the territory."

Farther back on the street, he saw Lindsey Delmar

watching with a shocked look on her youthful face. She stood wrapped in a large wool blanket from the doctor's supply closet. As Sam approached her, she stepped back and looked at him as if seeing him for the first time.

"How's Toby?" he asked as he and his wounded prisoner walked past her.

"He's—he's all right, Ranger," she said, seeming to snap herself out of some stalled state of mind. Yes, this was the man who had saved her and her brother's lives, she reminded herself. She walked alongside the Ranger. Looking up at him, she ventured to ask in a quiet tone, "Are you all right?"

Sam looked at her and nodded his head.

"I'm back to work, Lindsey," he said. "This is what I do."

"I understand," she said, and she walked on beside him to the doctor's clapboard house.

PART 3

Chapter 15

——

Somewhere in the passing night the Garlets' trail lead them across the border onto the Mexican badlands. At a small water hole atop a short hill line above the desert floor, Prew helped his brother Tillman gather dried wood and mesquite brush and build a sheltered fire behind the largest boulder in a broken line of other such boulders standing like monuments in the rocky earth.

Prew cut open a tin of beans with his boot knife, raised the edge of the tin to his lips, poured in a mouthful of beans and juice, and passed it on. When it had made its rounds and back to him, Prew finished the beans and tossed the can aside. With a steaming tin cup in his hand, he sat on his blanket across the small fire from his two brothers. The three sipped fresh hot coffee in silence. Somewhere in the distant night a coyote yelped out to fellow denizens of the desert hills.

"I make it we'll be getting there tomorrow," he said, studying his brother's face as he spoke, looking for any sign of improvement.

"Good," said Tillman, sounding normal enough. He

paused for an uncomfortable moment, feeling Prew's eyes on him. Finally he ventured to ask, "Getting where?"

"To Kane's hideout, damn it," Prew said, feeling his hope slip a little. "Jesus, Till, are you no better at all?"

"I'm all right," Tillman said. "I just lost you for a minute there." He looked at Foz, then back at Prew. The Bluebird sat watching the brothers from a few feet away, out of the glow of firelight. "The fact is, I think I'm over the poisoning." He gave a short, proud smile and nodded. "Yep, I am, I'm sure of it."

"That's good, Till," said Prew. He looked at Foz. "What about you Brother Fozlo? Are you getting over it?"

Foz just stared darkly at him for a moment.

"You had no right or reason to say some of the things you said about me, Prew. Don't even think I'm going to forget about it."

Prew studied him closely as he spoke.

"We can talk about all this some other time and place, Foz," he said, keeping his words clear and deliberate. "Right now, before we get to Kane's, I want to know, are you feeling any—"

"Calling us idiots in front of the others," Foz said, cutting his brother off. His eyes shone like black, wet glass in the purple darkness. "You're lucky I don't have a gun. I'd kill you."

"Whoa, easy, Foz," said Tillman. "Prew didn't mean none of that; did you, Prew?"

Prew didn't answer. He sat in silence for a moment, staring at Foz, seeing a strange look of hatred mixed with madness in his younger brother's eyes.

Finally, without taking his eyes off Foz, he spoke to Tillman.

"Let me ask you something, Till," he said quietly. "Both of you drank about the same amount of that stuff. Is that right?"

"That's right," Tillman said. "The barkeep said he told us we drank it too fast—"

"Then how come you're getting over it and Fozlo here is still looking and acting like he's half out of his mind?"

"There you go again belittling me," Foz said. He started to rise from the ground. Tillman reached over and pressed him down by his shoulder.

"Easy, Foz," he said. In answer to Prew he shrugged and said, "I don't know. I expect it treats everybody different."

Prew stared at Foz.

"Is that it, Foz?" he said calmly. "It treats everybody different?"

"Yeah, I guess, if Till says so," Foz said, scowling at his older brother. "Are you accusing me of something?"

"You tell me," said Prew. Still staring, he reached around to his bulging saddlebags, opened one and pulled up the jug of mescal. He held the jug out in front of him and shook it. "My, my," he said in mock surprise. "It was full when I left Midland Settlement with it. Now it's half empty."

"And you're saying I drunk it," said Foz.

"Only if you tell me you didn't," said Prew, holding the jug, staring harder at Foz.

"Hey, wait a minute, Prew," Tillman cut in. "This is not the time to go turning against each other. Hell, who can say what—"

"Shut up, Till," said Foz. He sat returning Prew's stare, his eyes glassy, a string of drool hanging from his lower lip. "I drunk it, Prew, so what? Every damn time you wasn't looking I drunk some more. There, you satisfied?"

"Brothers, let's not let this thing turn ugly on us," Tillman warned. "Hell, ain't we all blood here?"

"How much have you drank, Foz?" Prew asked.

"I don't know," Foz said. "Whatever ain't there I reckon." He gave Prew a defiant look.

Prew stirred the jug around, gauging its contents.

"No wonder Till's getting better and you're not," he said. "What is it about this stuff that you can't leave it alone?"

"I don't know," Foz said. A wicked little grin came to his drawn hairless face. "But I love it. The harder it hits me the better I like it."

"Why?" Prew said, still stirring the jug around in his hand.

Tillman sat staring; so did the Bluebird.

"*Why* hell. Try it yourself, you want to know *why*," Foz said to Prew.

"What does it do for you that whiskey don't?" Prew asked.

Foz chuckled in a dark tone.

"Makes me see things!" he said in a lowered voice. "It's got me seeing things right now—unholy things! I see screaming devils riding terrible beasts, the likes of which could only rise from hell to earth!"

"Take it easy, Fozlo," said Tillman. He looked at Prew. "He's joshing you now, Brother; you know he is."

"Am I?" Foz said on a dead serious note. He looked back at Prew. "I'm not going to quit drinking it," he said. "I'll drink it until it kills me." He held a hand toward Prew over the low fire. "Give it to me. I druther die drinking it than live without it."

"Stop acting crazy, Fozlo," Tillman said quietly.

"Get your hand down, Foz," Prew said. He pulled the cork from the jug. "I expect it's time I see what all this is about."

The three sets of eyes around the fire watched Prew turn up a swig from the jug, lower it, and make a sour face.

"Holy Joseph . . . !" he said. "That tastes even worse than I thought it would."

"Give yourself a couple minutes," Foz said, reaching for the jug, "you won't be saying that."

Prew looked at the outreached hand as he thought of everything his brother had said, including making a threat on his life. He took a breath and let it out slowly, with a look of resolve.

"Help yourself, Foz," he said, passing the jug. "You too, Till." He looked back and forth between his brothers. "The quicker it's gone, the better for all of us." The Bluebird sat staring, his blanket drawn around him.

"That's what I say," said Foz, lifting the jug. He took a long swallow and passed it to Tillman, who studied the jug before deciding to take a short swallow. When he lowered the jug he also made a sour face and passed it to the Bluebird. The Mex-Indian took a long, gurgling drink, lowered the jug without so much as a blink and handed it full circle back to Prew.

The four men spent the next hour passing the jug around from hand to hand, until at length the Bluebird finished it off. Clearly, Prew and Tillman had drunk much less of the strong liquor than the Bluebird and Foz.

"And that's the end of it," Prew said with finality. He pushed himself to his feet and caroused aimlessly about the campsite. He felt buzzing inside his head, and twice he thought he'd seen shadows of someone, whose skin was the color of a frog, dart in and out of the shadows outside the firelight. But he shook it off, reminding himself of having seen things in the past when he'd spent an evening in an opium parlor. He looked down at Tillman.

"How do you feel now, Till?" he asked.

"I feel . . . just like I should," Tillman replied with a pleasant smile. Prew noted his eyelids were drooping as he spoke.

Prew looked over at Foz, then back to Tillman.

"You don't feel like killing me dead?"

"*Heee-eell*, no," Tillman said, his head bobbing. "I couldn't kill a fly right now, if it was talking bad about our ma."

Prew looked at the Bluebird, who sat the same as before, though the pupils of his eyes were larger, blacker, and shinier.

"How about you, Bird?" he asked. "You feeling all right? Not wanting to kill nobody?"

"Yes . . . even so," said the Bluebird, nodding his head.

Prew chuckled a little. He swatted at what he thought was a brightly colored moth circling his head, then reminded himself he was only imagining it. He laughed out loud, staggered a step and caught himself.

"Damn, it is strong stuff, I'll give it that," he said. He steadied himself on his feet and looked at Foz. "You still packing a mad-on for me, Fozlo?"

"No," said Foz, dreamily. "But if I had a gun I'd still kill you." He laughed out loud, pushing himself to his feet. Prew and Tillman looked at each other and laughed along with him. The Bluebird nodded and gave a trace of a tight smile, not hearing a word of it.

"I'll tell you something . . . ," said Foz. He staggered in place, caught himself and almost stumbled into the fire. Prew caught him by his arm and stopped him. But Foz rounded his arm away from Prew and turned and walked away to the edge of the water hole and stared into the shimmering moonlight on the water. The others watched as he sighed and turned away and walked to the edge of the hillside and looked down onto the sandy valley floor.

"I'm ready to *go*," he sang out, spreading his arms as if to take off flying. He leaned out dangerously on the rocky edge.

Behind him, Foz heard Tillman shout, "No! Please! Don't do it, Prew!"

"Prew . . . ?" said Foz, his eyes closed, smiling. "Hell, Till, I ain't Prew—"

Foz barely finished his words when the gun in Prew's hand bucked and a shot resounded. The tip of the barrel only an inch behind Foz's head, the blast sent an blue-orange fire exploding through the back of Foz's head and streaking out through the front, spreading a black mist of blood across the purple night.

At the sound of the shot in the quiet night, the horses reared and whinnied and fought against their tied reins. Foz's blaze-faced roan ripped its reins free and ran wildly all around the campsite. At the same time, Tillman had come to his feet and ran forward, screaming his younger brother's name. The Bluebird stood and walked along behind him trancelike, his blanket held closed at his chest.

"Foz! No! *Jesus no!*" Tillman shouted at the rocky edge of the hill. He stared down seeing no sign of his brother, only a steep, craggy hillside. Below it, silvery-white sand lay spread in every direction, glowing in the creamy, purple starlight.

"Easy, Till," said Prew, grabbing Tillman's arm and holding him back, as if he himself might plunge out into thin air. "I had to kill him," he said gently, evenly. "You saw how it was with him. He was gone on mescal, he wasn't coming back."

Tillman jerked free of the hand on his arm and stepped away from him.

"I didn't see that, Prew!" he shouted, his eyes shining large and black. "He was just talking, talking is all!"

"No, Brother," said Prew shaking his head. "I wish it was so, but it ain't. Twice he said he'd kill me if he had a gun. You saw the whole thing. You heard him."

"I heard him, Prew, but he didn't mean it! He was riding high on mescal—just like we are right now!" He backed farther away; the blaze-faced roan ran and whinnied and reared and pawed wildly at the air. "Look at you, Prew. The stuff has you loco as a cave bat right now; me too! You didn't have to kill him."

Prew stood staring calmly at Tillman, his Colt hanging smoking in his hand.

"Listen to me, Till," he said in a cool, rational tone of voice, taking a step closer. The Bluebird stood four feet behind Tillman, staring shiny-eyed across his shoulder at Prew. "It's true the mescal has my brain boiling a little some. But I've got it under control." He pointed a finger up as if poking a hole in the wide, starry sky. "I'm way up there, looking down on us and what we're doing here. This has all been made clear to me. I knew what I had to do. Can you understand that? Mescal ain't got me, I've got it."

"God almighty, Prew, listen to yourself," Tillman said. "You've gone flat-out crazy on that stuff! What now? Are you going to kill me too?"

"No," Prew said, still calm, thinking he had a good grip on his faltered faculties. "I've done all I had to do. Now, we've got to go on like nothing happened."

"I can't do that, Prew! Damn it, you killed Foz! Can't you realize what you've done?"

"We're through talking about it, Till," Prew said. "Now cut it out"—he slashed a hand across his face under his chin—"before one of us does something we regret. . . ." His words trailed to a halt as he watched the Bluebird step up closer behind Tillman. As if taking Prew's slashing gesture to heart, the Indian reached a big boot knife around under Tillman's chin and opened his throat with one long vicious slice. Dark, arterial blood spewed and cascaded down his chest in braided streams.

"You—you killed him!" Prew said, puzzled, as if struggling to sort through the lingering incidentals of a terrible dream.

The Bluebird stared at him, the bloody knife in hand. Tillman fell to his knees, then toppled over onto his face, his hands clutching against a river of blood. The Bluebird, shiny-eyed, his face tightly drawn under the powerful effects of the mescal, clenched his teeth and nodded his head.

"You signaled me," he said.

"Damn you, Injun!" Prew bellowed. "I didn't signal you to kill him!" He raised the smoking gun and aimed it at the Bluebird's chest.

The Bluebird looked confused by Prew's actions. He dropped his knife, let his blanket fall to the ground.

"Don't shoot," he said, stiffly. He pointed out at the rocky edge where Foz had fallen. "Brother Foz, no drink all the mescal."

Prew paused, stunned.

"What? He didn't . . . ?" His gun barrel slumped an inch. "He—he said he did. . . ."

The Bluebird shook his head.

"No, he did not drink it," he said. "I see the Golden Riders drink it. Say they go to jake—they go around cantina, drink mescal."

"Then"—Prew paused again—"then why did Foz say he drank it?" he asked.

"I don't know," said the Bluebird. "Mescal make him crazy, I think."

Prew shook his lowered head, then looked back up at the Bluebird.

"And why are you talking so much?" he asked. "All of a sudden you understand English?"

The Bluebird shut his lips clamlike and stared at Prew, seeing the big Colt move away from him and fall back to Prew's side.

"I shut up now," he said.

Chapter 16

———

The Bluebird was still up as the first rays of sunlight mantled the eastern hill line. The sound of Prew's gunshot had sparked his hearing for a while the way loud noises sometimes did. It was waning now, but while it lasted, it had been glorious. His hearing, coupled with the powerful effects of the loaded mescal, had brought his spirit to a level seldom found. He'd spent the night listening to any sounds, intricate or inane—sounds of night and of life on these dry desert badlands. He was there, a part of those things and their sounds once again, if only briefly.

He'd heard the sound of coyotes, of a lone and distant wolf. He'd heard the wings of flying creatures batting and dipping, stirring and muddling the veil of night's darkness without leaving their print. Their sounds had spun inside him a siren's message of willfulness and need, sounds of the spinal mindless procurement of life here in this arid wilderness whereupon every struggle, every hoof, paw and footprint led inevitably to the devout certainty of death's cold embrace.

Yes . . . even so . . .

He'd heard the soft scrape of a lizard's nails across a stone and its red eyes blinked as the lizard turned and skittered off along the far edge of the water hole.

During the night he'd relished and savored the crackle of the fire as it sought out what elements of life remained in the desert wasteland. He'd listened and watched as the once familiar sound of porous wood, long dried and dead, came to life for a short time as if summoned upon to its final purpose—its last waltz down on the hardpan belly of the earth. He'd heard the flames bow and rustle.

Sound moved through his heart as it never had before he'd lost it. And now he breathed deep, testing the reverberation of his warm breath back in his nasal cavity. It had been there throughout the night. Now it was gone. His breath was no longer audible to him. Inside his skull there was once again only flat, white silence.

And there it was. . . . He wiped a palm beneath his eye.

He sat at the rocky edge Fozlo Garlet had fallen from the night before when his brother's bullet split his brain— the same bullet that had given him back his hearing for a time. Yes, it had been a strange and puzzling night, he reminded himself, staring at the sunlight, getting his share of the sun's raging energy before it grew too bright and hot for him to stand. He'd decided he would call last night, *La noche de los hermanos blancos*—the night of the white brothers.

He didn't hear Prew Garlet struggle to his feet and look all around the campsite. He didn't hear the footsteps across the ground behind him. Yet, he was not startled when he felt Prew's hand take him by the shoulder. He turned and looked up at Prew's face. He knew he was being spoken to, but the words were too distant for him to understand.

"Goddamn it, Bird!" said Prew, looking down at the dark, flat stare. "What? Are you ignoring me now? You forgot how to speak English, *again*?"

The Bluebird only nodded in agreement and rose to his feet. He gestured toward the rekindled fire where a pot of fresh coffee sent a strong aroma wafting on the morning air.

"Hell, yes . . . ," Prew whispered painfully, raising a hand to the side of his head. As he turned toward the fire, he saw Foz's blaze-faced roan standing off the side, alone, tied to a rock spur. The big horse milled restlessly hoof to hoof, back and forth, whinnying, stirring dust. The other horses stood calmly where they'd been hitched all night. His own horse had been saddled, so had the Bluebird's, its saddlebags bulging with dynamite. Foz's and Tillman's saddles still lay in the dirt near the campfire.

"My God, no . . . ," Prew said under his breath, raising his other hand to his head as well. He staggered in place, then straightened and looked at the Bluebird. "I remember what happened, but only sort of." He looked all around, at the blood in the dirt, but he didn't see Tillman's body. All he saw were the marks of bootheels where the Bluebird had dragged the dead outlaw to the rocky edge and flung him over it.

"You . . . took care of everything?" he asked haltingly, looking at the Bluebird.

The Bluebird only nodded and followed him to the campfire. Prew looked at the ground a few feet away and caught a flash of Foz's roan lying dead in a pool of dark blood, its throat slit, a deep bloody gash revealing windpipe and tendons. *Jesus . . . !* So real was the image, he had to bat his eyes and shake it from his sight. He looked over at the big roan to assure himself, seeing it still milling, agitated and restless.

All right, he told himself, *that's enough of that. . . .* The mescal was still at work in his brain. But he wasn't going to give in to it.

Turning to the Bluebird as they walked on to the campfire, he asked, "Had you ever drank any stuff like that before?"

The Bluebird, seeing Prew's lips move, not able to make out the distant muffled sound of his voice, only gave his usual nod, and walked on.

"Hell, what am I asking, sure you have," Prew said.

At the fire the two sat down and poured hot coffee into tin cups and drank in silence until Prew heard the sound of horses drawing near them from along the hill trail. He picked up his rifle and checked it. Seeing him stand, looking across the campsite where the trail entered the water hole, the Bluebird also stood up and turned with Prew, gun in hand toward the sound of the horses. As they watched, two horses rode into sight and stopped. The riders sat staring for a moment. Finally one nudged his horse a step closer.

"Hello, the camp," he said. Then he called out, "Prew Garlet, is that you?"

Prew recognized the two outlaws, Lester Stevens

and Mason Gorn, from the old Mexican trade settlement. The Bluebird stood staring blankly.

"It's me all right," Prew said. "Howdy, Lester. Howdy, Mason. Last I saw you two, I recall you saying you had us all covered at the settlement if any lawmen came snooping."

"We did say that," said Stevens. "The fact is no lawman ever showed up snooping." He grinned. "I reckon our reputation must be growing."

"Are you going to call us in, or what?" Gorn said.

"Yep, come on in," said Prew, lowering his rifle. "We've got coffee boiled, if you brought a cup."

"We've got one," said Stevens, the two of them nudging their horses closer. At ten feet away, they stopped the animals, stepped down from their saddles and rummaged tin cups out of their saddlebags. "Had we known it was you up here, we'd have rode up last night. We heard shooting from half across the flats. For all we knew it was Apache bucks drunk on trade liquor, shooting at one another for practice—crazy as Apache are." He looked the Bluebird up and down and said, "No offense."

"He's not Apache," Prew said, seeing the Bluebird only staring at the two.

"Oh . . . ," said Stevens. "Anyways that's what we figured, so we didn't butt in." As he spoke the two walked forward, tin cups in hand. Looking all around they saw black dried blood on the dirt.

"Is everything okay here?" Gorn asked.

"It'll do," Prew said. He felt a tightness at the back of

his neck. Watching them, he caught a flash of them both dead on the ground, their horses turning and racing away. Knowing it was the mescal playing tricks on him, he squeezed his eyes shut, then flung them open wide. The two gunmen were still walking toward him. They stopped and turned to the fire. Gorn picked up the coffeepot and filled his cup.

"Dang, Prew, you look like you've been up chasing the moon all night," said Stevens. "Where's your brothers, anyway?"

"What's it to you, Stevens?" Prew said heatedly. As soon as he'd heard his voice turn angry, he regretted it, but it was too late.

"Hey, I'm just asking, is all," said Stevens, his attitude also changing, his smile falling away from his face. "Don't go getting high-hat on me."

"I didn't mean to get testy," Prew said. As soon as he'd said that he realized that too was a mistake. Once he'd spoken in anger he never should have come down from it. With men like Stevens and Gorn, it paid to stand your ground no matter what.

"Hear that?" said Gorn with a flat, unfriendly grin. "Prew's apologizing. I believe he's had himself a change of heart." He stood with his thumb hooked in his gun belt only inches away from his gun butt.

"Is that what you're doing, Prew Garlet?" said Stevens. "You apologizing for acting cross with me? Are you having a change of heart, or just a weakness of nerves?"

"Don't push it, Lester," Prew said. The Bluebird stood

watching, trying to make out what might be expected of him. After misunderstanding Prew's signal last night, he wanted to be sure of himself before he acted.

"What . . . ?" said Stevens, in a dark, serious tone. "Did you just say, *don't push it*?"

"Yeah, that's what I said," Prew replied.

He stared at Stevens, his hand also poised near his holstered Colt. As he stared, he caught another quick flash of the two gunmen lying dead in the dirt, their horses spooked, racing away in a rise of dust.

Damn . . . ! What was all this . . . ?

He forced himself to blink and try to clear his foggy mind. All right, now that things were back as they should be.

"Something's wrong with him, Lester," Gorn cut in. "Look at him. He acts like he's losing his mind."

Stevens didn't answer right away. He glanced at the drag marks in the dirt left by the Bluebird when he'd pulled Tillman over to the edge and tossed him out. As his eyes followed the marks so did he. He stopped at the edge and looked down and did a quick double take. Then he turned back to Prew and the Bluebird and with a nasty grin as he spoke to Gorn.

"Come over here, Mason, and take a look at this," he said.

Gorn stepped over warily, keeping his eyes on Prew and the Bluebird. At the edge beside Stevens, he stared down and was taken aback.

"Uh-oh," he said. "I see feet sticking out down there."

Stevens chuckled and cut back in.

"Has somebody been naughty here?" he said. "Prew,

am I wrong in thinking that you two have done something untoward?" He let his hand fall away from his
gun. "Because, if that's the case, it's no skin off—"

Prew's Colt came up, cocked and aimed. The shot
hit Stevens before he could even finish his sentence. He
spun with the impact and flopped to the ground face-
first. Beside him, Gorn started to make a move, but
Prew's Colt swung to him and fired before he cleared
his gun from its holster. He flipped backward, tried to
rise, but then collapsed in the dirt. Both of their horses,
spooked by the sudden gunfire, spun and bolted away.
Prew stood watching as though frozen in place, wondering what had prompted him to kill these two. It was
none of their business what had happened here the night
before, and it was likely Stevens had been on the verge
of telling him so. But it was too late now. He stood
watching as the Bluebird trotted off after the horses as
they slowed to a halt a few yards away.

Jesus . . .

He looked down at the smoking gun and turned it in
his hand as if in a trance. For a moment he had a hard
time realizing which image had been real and which one
had not. As the Bluebird ran back leading the two horses
and stood before him, Prew had to bat his eyes, close
them for a second and reopen them, testing himself.

The Bluebird stood with a trace of a tight grin on his
face, the reins to the dead outlaws' horses in hand. He
nodded at the two bodies on the ground.

"Throw them over the cliff?" he asked.

Prew stared at him for a moment, then nodded in
reply.

"Yes, get rid of them," he said. "Turn all these spare horses loose. We don't need any Golden Riders coming by and finding any of them."

"No . . . we don't need that," the Bluebird said, seeming to understand him perfectly. He started to turn away, to where Foz's, Tillman's and the other two dead gunmen's horses stood bunched together.

"Hey. Hold it, Bird," said Prew. When the Bluebird turned back to him, he asked, "How come you're understanding what I'm saying now?"

The Bluebird gave him a flat, blank stare.

"I hear things better around you," he said.

At the end of a winding hill trail Braxton Kane sat his dapple-gray horse between his two right-hand men, Dayton Short and Earl Faraday, two former guerilla riders from the Missouri-Kansas border wars. The two guerilla riders had thrown in with Kane and his Golden Riders when the law had gotten too hot on them everywhere except Colorado Territory. Most of his other men referred to Short and Faraday as Kane's Bulldogs. When Kane needed something special taken care of, these two were his top men to get the job done, no matter how bloody the work.

"Something bothering you, Boss?" Short asked, seeing how Kane studied the trail below with a concerned look on his face.

Kane didn't answer right away. He gave Short a grim look and waited, as if settling something in his mind.

"You men recall it ever taking this long to get everybody gathered in for a big job?" he said finally.

The two gunmen nudged their horses closer to the trail's edge on either side of him.

"Now that you mention it," said Short, "Earl was just saying the other day how it seems like it's taking your brother Cordy and some of the others a long time to get here." He grinned beneath a long, drooping black mustache. "I went so far as to say there ain't enough whores twixt here and Abilene to keep a man from one of our *big* jobs."

"So, you both think there's something holding them?" said Braxton.

"Well," said Faraday, "if they ain't here, there must be something holding them up. Usually by this time you've got yourself, twenty–thirty men here, easy enough."

"Not to mention Cordy and his rowdy pals," said Short. "You think me and Earl ought to ride out, see who's in El Ricon, see if we can find out what's keeping everybody?"

Kane sat silent again for a moment; the two gunmen gave each other a look.

"Yeah, I think so," Kane said, finally. "I've got a big job waiting for us—requires a good dynamite man. I sent for the best in the business. A Mex-Injun called the Bluebird. You ever heard of him?"

"The Bluebird?" said Faraday. "Sure I've heard of him. Like you said, he's supposed to be the best blowup man in the business. Learned his trade from the South American Suala Soto."

"That's him," said Kane. "I've got the Garlet boys bringing the Bluebird up here. Sniff around, see where the hell they are."

"You've got it, Boss," said Faraday.

"I've heard of the Bluebird too," Short cut in. "Always heard he's the best. I heard he blew up everything from Chihuahua to the Honduras for the Mexican-German mining companies." He grinned again, his face pale behind his black mustache. "I'd be honored to have him open a big ole safe for us, let me run my fingers through some fresh U.S. greenbacks."

"How about some bright yellow gold ingots?" Kane said quietly. He gave the two a secretive sidelong glance.

"I can live with that too," Short said. "I have never had a minute's trouble turning ingots into cash money."

"So, Boss," said Faraday, "when do you want us to head out, see if we can find out what's keeping everybody?"

Kane gave the two another sidelong look, then gazed back out across the Mexican hill line.

"Ain't you gone yet?" he said.

Chapter 17

El Ricon, the Mexican Badlands

It was dark the following evening when Short and Faraday, having traveled all day and most of the night before, rode into the small, dirty town and stepped down from their horses at a hitch rail out front of the Luna Loca cantina and brothel. Laughter, guitar and accordion led by the blare of a trumpet reached out and met them as the two stepped onto a plank boardwalk toward the blanket-draped doorway.

Firelight flickered from iron firepots filled with wood, refuse and fuel oil standing in front of the Luna Loca and along the half-empty street of the small mining community. Five yards away, two half-naked brothel girls stood smoking thin black cigars and sharing a bottle of rye with a drunken teamster. They disregarded the two newcomers and concentrated on their easier prey.

"Well, well, look who's here, pals," said a voice in the darkened shadows just out of the firelight as Short and Faraday walked closer.

Another voice replied as two more men stepped forward from the shadows into the flicker of the street fire.

"Dayton Short and Earl Faraday, as I live and breathe," the voice said.

"Howdy, Luke, howdy, Quince . . . Woods," said Short, he and Faraday both touching their hat brims, recognizing the three.

Luke Bolten, Jimmy Quince and Hank Woods touched their hat brims in return.

"We were talking about you two earlier tonight," said Luke Bolten, a tall, wiry gunman with a reputation for being fast with a six-gun. "Wondering if your man Braxton's got any gun work that might need doing."

Short and Faraday stopped and looked at the three figures lounging against the front of the adobe building. Short turned to Faraday with a look, then turned back to Bolten.

"I would ordinarily tell you to speak to Brax himself about gun work. But it turns out you might be getting here at just the right time."

"Oh, yeah?" said Bolten, his interest piquing. He and the other two stepped closer. "Something told me we might be hitting here at the right time. What have you got planned?"

"That would be for Braxton and us to know," Faraday said a little sharply. He eyed the big nickel-plated Russian revolver glinting in the firelight in Bolten's cross-draw holster.

"But the thing is," Short cut in, "we'll take you there, make sure he knows you're available."

"And we're all obliged for your help," Bolten said for

the three of them. "It is damn hard talking to Braxton when he's got something big planned."

"It won't be for you, not this time," said Faraday. "We're looking around for some men right now. But you fellows be ready to ride when we come back through here."

"Whoa, Short. We're ready to ride right now," said Bolten, not wanting to take a chance on the two leaving without them and not coming back. "What say we ride along with you wherever you're headed? You never know out here when you might need some guns backing you up."

Short considered it for a moment, then nodded.

"All right then, come with us," he said. "The first place we're headed is right through that blanket to get us some rye whiskey. Then we're headed up out of here."

Bolten grinned and looked at the other two gunmen.

"And you can rest easy, knowing that me and Quince and Woods here will have you both covered while you drink it," the outlaw said, only half joking.

"I feel better already," said Faraday as the five of them filed inside the Luna Loca and walked through the blaring music to the bar.

Seeing the five men walk to the bar, knowing that Short and Faraday rode with Braxton Kane, the bartender wasted no time standing a bottle of rye and shot glasses along the bar. He had already poured the rye when Short and the others stopped at the bar. Short gave him a nod.

"Obliged, Cooney," he said to the red-nosed bartender.

As he and the others raised their glasses, he asked Ned Cooney, "Has any of our hombres come through here today?"

"No," the bartender said, "just these fellows." He nodded at the three gunmen standing with Short and Faraday. "I figured them for Golden Riders soon as I laid eyes on them."

Short gave a chuckle.

"Hear that, hombres? He took you three for part of our bunch soon as he saw you."

The three gunmen only nodded, staring at the bartender. Looking nervous, Cooney swallowed a knot in his throat.

"Did I—did I do something wrong?" he said.

Short downed his drink and shook his head.

"No, Ned, you done good," he said. He wrapped a hand around the bottle to pour himself another shot.

The bartender looked relieved.

"Thank you kindly," he said. "I hope you mentioned me to Braxton Kane. I can be ready to ride *anywhere* he wants me to, *anytime* he wants me to."

"He knows that, Cooney," said Short with a stare. "I ain't forgot about you. Now why don't you get on away from here whilst me and my pals talk." As Short spoke the trumpet player blew out a long string of loud sharp notes.

"Damn . . . !" said Faraday with wince. He said to Cooney, "If you want to be useful how about raising your scattergun and shooting that fool's horn out of his mouth?"

The bartender looked trapped and worried.

"Well . . . I suppose I—that is, if he's bothering—" His words stuttered and halted, but even so his hand reached down under the bar.

"Easy, Cooney," said Short, "he's just joshing you."

The bartender let out a tense, tight breath.

"Now go on, let us talk," Short said.

As the bartender hurried away along the bar full of drinkers, Bolten chuckled and shook his head.

"Why'd you stop him? I believe he would've done it."

"So do I," said Short.

"It shows you how bad everybody wants to throw in with us Golden Riders," said Faraday.

"Finding gunmen has never been hard to do," Bolten came back quickly. He looked sidelong at Hank Woods and Jimmy Quince, then gave Faraday a narrowed look. "But finding three *good ones* like us is a whole different story."

"Alls I'm saying is—" said Faraday.

"Besides," said Bolten, cutting him off, "If gunmen are wanting to ride with you *that bad*, where are they?" He gestured around the smoke-filled cantina. "All I see is *you and us*"—he nodded down the bar toward Ned Cooney—"and some half-simple cork puller, ready to shotgun a horn player because he's too stupid to tell you was joshing with him."

Short reached over with the bottle of rye and filled Bolten's glass before Faraday could offer a comeback.

"Right you are, Luke," he said. "Pay Earl no mind. We've been letting him piss so close to the house he's starting to think he's smarter than the barn dwellers." He gave Faraday a glance, letting him know to shut up.

"The fact is we *should* have more men here right now than we do." As he spoke he looked at the others' glasses, making sure they were full. Then he set the bottle aside, picked up the cork and corked it. "What say we all drink up here and go find out why?"

When the five men left the Luna Loca they rode in purple-gray moonlight until well after midnight, seeing not a single campfire in any direction. Overhead, a deep rounded blanket of stars lay glittering across a velvet Mexican sky. As the trail sloped upward into a labyrinth of random stonework, black slices of shadow reached out and down from the tops of jagged hill lines. On the edge of a cliff, the five men bunched their horses close together. They looked out across a silver-streaked ocean of sand strewn with islands of stone, of tall saguaro cactus, their spiky arms raised as if being robbed.

"Maybe most of your Golden Riders won't risk a fire, the Apaches being what they are in Ole Mex, these days," said Luke Bolten.

Short and Faraday eyed Bolten in the grainy moonlight. Quince and Woods looked out on the desert floor, their hands crossed on their saddle horns. After a silence Faraday addressed Bolten quietly.

"I believe after riding with us a while," he said, "you'll find that Golden Riders don't fear *anything*, Apache or otherwise. Them with *fear* are best advised to seek other means of employment."

A silence ensued, then Bolten turned slightly facing Faraday who sat right beside him.

"Let me ask you something, Earl," Bolten replied

quietly, recalling Faraday's attitude back at the Luna Loca cantina. "Are you the hardheaded sumbitch whose ass I'm going to have to trounce soundly to make a place for myself among this bunch?" He'd pulled off his riding glove as he spoke.

"I just might be," Faraday said, coming back quickly. "Slide that saddle from under you, we'll find out." He spun his reins around his saddle horn, ready to leap to the ground.

But Bolten reached over, jammed his first two fingers up Faraday's large nose and crooked them forward, hard. Faraday shrieked, bucked and flopped. He tried to reach for his gun, but Bolten had him. Every move Faraday tried to make, Bolten jerked his head farther forward and down, twisted it askew until the hapless outlaw's face lay over above Bolten's lap.

"Jesus, *turn him loose*, Bolten!" shouted Short, his hand on his gun butt. But upon seeing Woods and Quince also gripping their side arms, he pulled his hand away.

"*Naw*, he's all right," Bolten said confidently. He twisted Faraday's head a little more, roughly. Faraday's thrashing and threatening rage turned into a sob, a plea for mercy. The former border guerilla eased his big Smith & Wesson Russian from its holster, held it up and cocked it. Knocking Faraday's hat out of the way with the gun barrel, he shoved the tip of the barrel straight down into Faraday's ear.

"Take 'er easy now, hoss," he said down to Faraday. "You've just seen how fast I can turn ugly."

"Damn it, *Luke*!" said Short. "*Let him go!* We're too noisy up here."

Bolten took his time.

"Woods?" he said. "If I shoot him from here, am I risking a bullet in my leg?"

"Yep," Woods said without having to look any closer. "Either that, or you're going to ruin a good horse."

"That's what I thought," Bolten said. He lifted Faraday's face toward his, jerked his fingers out of his nostrils and gave his nose a solid thump with his palm. Faraday's head snapped back. Before he could recover, Bolten reached down expertly and flipped his Colt up from its holster even as Faraday's hand grappled for it. "*Hunh-uh*, now," he chuckled in dark warning. "Everything you do will likely put you in more pain than you already are."

"Son of a bitch . . ." Faraday said hoarsely to no one in particular, bowing forward, his nose bleeding into his cupped hand. His hat hung sidelong from his head by its string.

Bolten gave a smug grin to Woods and Quince and reached over, took the hat and straightened it atop Faraday's head.

"Surprising as hell, wasn't it?" he said to Faraday. He patted the outlaw's slumped shoulders, then looked at Short. "Will that do it? That's how I use to do things before I got civilized."

Short only stared at him for a moment. Then, before he started to speak, he heard a sound from farther along the trail and turned in his saddle toward it.

"Whoa, what was that?" he asked in a hushed tone. The gunmen sat quiet, listening intently.

"I heard it," Quince whispered.

"So did I," said Woods. Faraday was too absorbed with his bleeding, throbbing nose to notice anything.

"It's no critter," said Bolten. "It sounds like a person—a person in pain." He gave Faraday a sidelong glance. "What say you, Earl?" he taunted.

"Come on, follow me," said Short, unwrapping Faraday's reins from his saddle horn and holding on to them. Turning his horse, taking the lead back from Bolten, he pulled Faraday's horse alongside him. They nudged their horses away from the cliff at a quick walk, single file. As they moved like ghosts along the trail Short heard the sound again. This time they all heard it.

"Yep, that's no critter," Bolten confirmed. He booted his horse up alongside Faraday's, reached over and stuck the bleeding gunman's unloaded Colt down into his holster. "Don't be aiming this at things that aim back," he whispered in a condescending tone. He rode side by side with Faraday and Short until they slowed their horses to a halt and sat watching a lone figure struggling and groaning, dragging itself along the trail toward them on its belly.

"My God . . . ," Earl Faraday managed to say with a stuffed nasal twang. "Somebody's lost all their legs. . . ."

Bolten gave Faraday a sidelong look and shook his head. Before Short could get collected and step down from his saddle, Bolten pitched his reins to Woods who'd sidled up to him. "Everybody sit tight, I've got this," he said. Short sat staring, smoldering, holding Faraday's reins in his hands.

Down from his saddle and walking forward, Bolten

held his nickel-plated Russian out and cocked down his side. As he moved forward, Short stepped down from his saddle, pitching Faraday's reins to him. The others stepped down too and walked forward, spreading out on the narrow trail.

"Say now, ole pal, where you headed?" Bolten asked half cordially. He planted a boot firmly down in the dirt only inches from the crawling man's face. He held the Russian cocked and pointed at the man's bloody head.

"Thank—thank God. You found me . . . ," the man rasped, dropping his jaw onto the rocky dirt.

"Yeah . . . ?" Bolten cocked his head a little. "You might want to thank us instead, if you're wanting a ride out of here."

"Help me . . . ," the man said in a waning voice.

"Damn, he's one of ours," said Short, stepping in beside Bolten, rolling the man's head with the sole of his boot and taking a better look.

"One of ours, sure enough?" Bolten said in a bemused tone. He shook his head at the bleeding man on the ground, then back along the dark trail.

"What . . . ?" said Short, catching a critical edge to Bolten's question.

"Oh, nothing . . . ," Bolten said. He slid the barrel of his Big Russian behind his duster lapel and down into this cross-draw holster. Seeing Short stare at him for a reply he said, "To be honest, so far your bunch ain't exactly impressing the hell out of me." He only uncocked the Russian after he'd seated it in its leather. "That one's got his nose broken, this one appears to be shy of transportation. No wonder they haven't showed up—" He gazed out along the dark trail, the wide sand flats below. "They could all be wandering around lost out there."

Chapter 18

In the low rising morning sunlight, the Ranger and Cutthroat Teddy Bonsell eased their horses around a turn on the high trail and stopped at the charred remnants of a campsite. Across the campsite, a line of buzzards stood along the rocky edge. The big scavengers divided their attention between the bodies of three dead men lying on the rocks below, and on one of their own species flopping on the ground a few feet away, its head stuck tightly inside an empty bean tin. The big buzzard appeared exhausted in its struggle, as if having spent the night in such a state of blind captivity.

"Holy Moses . . . ," Bonsell whispered. "I know I still ain't seeing things exactly right," he said sidelong to Sam, not taking his eyes nor his fascination off the head-locked buzzard, "but *please* tell me there's a buzzard over there wearing a tin can over his head."

"Yes, I see him too," Sam said. "It's not so much that he's *wearing* it. I think he got nosy and it grabbed him and won't turn loose."

"That helps me a little," said Bonsell, still staring at the big, flopping bird, "but not a whole lot."

"Get down from your horse," Sam said. "Let's see what we can do."

"Do about *what*?" Bonsell asked, swinging his leg over, stepping down from his saddle.

Sam didn't answer. Instead he swung down from his horse and gathered both horses' reins.

"Wait. You're not stopping to help a buzzard, are you?" Bonsell asked, amazed.

"I've helped worse," Sam said, leading the horses as the two walked closer to the stuck bird. Growing nervous, the buzzards along the edge gave up their roost and flew away with a powerful batting of wings.

"All right, I understand," said Bonsell, as if having a change of heart. "I don't like seeing an animal suffer myself. Go ahead, I'll stay back here out of your way."

"Staying beside me would be best for you," the Ranger said, stopping and reining the horses to a low rock stuck in the ground.

"Best for me how?" Bonsell asked.

"It'll keep you from feeling a bullet hit you when you try to make a run for those rocks," Sam said calmly. He nodded toward a stand of rock on the far side of the campsite.

Bonsell was taken aback.

"Make run for it, on foot? *Hunh-uh*, Ranger," said Bonsell. "I'd have to be crazy making a run for it out here, no horse, no gun, a bloody shoulder wound trying to heal?" He gestured at the bandage under his bloodstained shirt.

"That *would* be crazy, wouldn't it?" the Ranger said.

"Yep, it for sure would," said Bonsell, his eyes still bloodshot and sunk in his forehead.

"Keep telling yourself that while you sit here with only one boot on."

"One boot on?" Bonsell looked down making sure he wasn't missing some footwear. Then it came to him what the Ranger was saying. "Aw hell, are you joshing me?"

"Have I *ever*?" the Ranger asked, his voice getting a little sharper.

"All right," said Bonsell, "here goes." He sat down in the dirt and took a boot and held it up. Sam took it and pitched it a few feet away.

"Stay sitting there, and watch," he said to the outlaw. "We get this bird straightened out, we'll see why his cousins are so interested in the rocks down there."

On the ground ten feet from them, the buzzard had stopped flopping and batting the dirt, its greasy-looking talons stopped scratching at the bean tin. Sam saw its heartbeat pulsing hard all the way down in its belly. Sam made his few footsteps silently, knowing the bird was not fooled, but also knowing that as worn out as it was, he might get close enough to grab its talons out from under it before it could stop him. *And then what . . . ?* He wasn't sure, but he'd know in a minute, he told himself.

Bonsell watched him swipe a hand out and around, catching the tired buzzard's legs in his gloved hand and quickly upending the odorous fowl.

"I can't believe this . . . ," Bonsell said under his breath. He watched the exhausted bird still try to flap its wings as the Ranger held it upside down for a minute. Then he stooped onto one knee and laid the bird out in way that seemed to settle it.

"Tell him you mean him no harm, Ranger," Bonsell called out cynically. "Tell him you're only here to help him."

Sam gave the gunman a sharp look. He huddled over the bird, twisted the tin back and forth gently, examining the bird's neck closely.

"Cut the other end out of it," Bonsell called out. "Shove it on down, he can wear it around his neck."

"Shut up, Teddy," Sam called out, keeping his voice down. Holding the bird, he lifted the can as he turned it back and forth, careful of the sharp, inner edge.

"I'll be dipped," Bonsell said in surprise, seeing the tin can come loose and the big buzzard's head snap at the Ranger's gloved hands. "You did it, Burrack! You set that gut-plucker free!" He stood on one boot and his sock foot. "If I ever see a buzzard caught in a tin can, I'll know to send for—"

"Sit down, Teddy," the Ranger warned, his free hand going to his holstered Colt. Bonsell dropped like a rock.

Sam pitched the bird aside on the ground as it clawed and bit at him. Instead of flying away as Sam thought it would, the bird hurried away, one wing dragging the dirt, and huddled and gasped for air. Sam dropped the can, crushed it flat under his bootheel and walked back toward Bonsell.

"Ranger, I've never seen anybody befriend a buzzard," he chuckled.

"I'm better at catching buzzards than I am at setting them free," Sam said flatly.

"That's real funny, Ranger," said Bonsell on a sour note, catching Sam's meaning.

"On your feet, Teddy . . . Get your boot on," said Sam, reaching down, untying the horses from the rock. Overhead, buzzards circled in large numbers, begrudging two humans the use of their abandoned roost. Sam led the horses over to the rocky edge and looked. Behind him, Bonsell had straggled back putting on his boot. As he walked closer, Sam pointed along the edge ten feet away.

"Stay that far off my side, Teddy," he said.

"Afraid I'll push you over it, Ranger?" Bonsell asked boldly.

"No," said Sam. "I'm afraid you'll try to end up down there with them." He gestured down at three bodies lying in the rocks below. A half-dozen buzzards stood on the dead men's backs, their feasting, pulling and plucking beaks causing the bodies to jerk and move as if still alive.

"Recognize any of them?" Sam asked, watching the twitching, writhing corpses. Along the steep hillside four saddles lay strewn about in the rocks.

"I might recognize that one," Bonsell said with sarcasm, "if he had a little more face left."

Sam only nodded and watched with a grim expression.

"Poor sonsabitches," said Bonsell in a hushed tone. "See? That's why I never helped that buzzard."

"A buzzard didn't kill those three men," the Ranger replied quietly. "The birds just showed up for the feed."

"They're still buzzards, Ranger," Bonsell said. "If I had my way I'd kill every one of them on earth."

The Ranger looked up at the sky full of slow circling scavengers.

"You're ambitious, Teddy, I'll give you that," he said.

"I've seen enough of this," Bonsell said, taking a step back from the edge.

"Me too," Sam said.

The two turned from the grisly scene below. Sam led the horses with him as he looked all around on the ground. He stopped and looked at the long, red smear of dark blood in the dirt. All around he saw horses' hooves leading off along the trail, the drag marks wiping some of them out.

Someone badly wounded, following riders on horse-back . . . ?

"Come on, Teddy," he said, "we've got one crawling away." He handed Bonsell the reins to his horse; the two led their animals less than a half mile along the rugged trail when the dragging marks and the dried blood came to a halt among boot prints and horse tracks. Sam noted some of the horse tracks were not as recent as others. *Two separate sets of riders,* he decided.

"Looks like you've reached a dead end, Ranger," Bonsell said smugly, watching the Ranger stoop down over the dark dried spots of blood in the dirt. Sam touched a gloved finger to one of the heavier drops. He stood up and studied a smear on his fingertip.

Still a little wet . . .

"We've got tracks to follow now, Teddy," he replied finally, wiping his gloved fingertips together. "When we run out of tracks to follow, I'm counting on you telling me which way to go."

"Count all you want, Ranger," Bonsell said. "When you're through *counting*, you still won't hear me tell you a damned thing."

"I hope you don't say much now that you'll be embarrassed when the time comes to change your mind, Teddy," Sam said.

"Keep watching, Ranger," Bonsell said with a crooked determined grin. "Tell me when you see I'm about to change my mind. You have no idea where Braxton Kane and the men hide out. If you did it would only get you killed."

"In the saddle, Teddy," the Ranger said. "You'll tell me when the time's right." He paused, then said, "I'm counting on you."

"Like hell I'll tell you," Bonsell sneered. As he spoke the two swung up into their saddles. The Ranger turned his horse back along the trail they'd come, away from the tracks in the dirt. Bonsell nudged his horse over beside him.

"Wait, Ranger. Which way we going?" he asked.

"Back through the campsite to the main trail," Sam said.

"These prints will lead us back to the main trail, just at a different place," Bonsell offered.

"I know," said Sam, "but it's a higher trail we were on. I like being up where I can see everything. We'll pick up these tracks again where the trails connect."

Bonsell shook his head.

"I can't see backtracking, even if it's just a half mile," he said.

"You don't have to see it, Teddy," Sam replied. "I see it for you. That's why I'm here, remember?"

They rode on in silence through the campsite toward the main trail. As they passed the place where Sam had freed the buzzard from the tin can, they saw no sign of the big bird, only a small, dark feather where the bird had lifted up and batted away after regaining the strength to do so.

"Looks like your feathered pal is gone, Ranger," Bonsell said. He gave a cruel grin. "I hope the two of you meet again somewhere, *real soon*."

"If I don't meet him, maybe you will," Sam replied, his coppery dun moving along at a walk. "If you see him first tell him I said hello."

Dayton Short, Earl Faraday and Hank Woods sat their horses atop a ridge overlooking the main trail. Short didn't like the way Woods kept himself back a few feet from him and Faraday, as if to keep an eye on them. But this wasn't the time or place to say anything. Bringing these three along with them had been a mistake, he'd decided. But it was a mistake he'd have to live with until they got back to Kane's hideout.

"Here they come," Faraday said beside him beneath his big swollen nose. He nodded out toward the trail, his voice sounding thick and nasal. On the trail, they saw Bolten and Jimmy Quince riding along toward them at a brisk gait. Faraday adjusted himself in his saddle and nodded back over his shoulder. "When is somebody else going to do this?"

Behind Faraday's saddle sat Lester Stevens, the man they'd found crawling along the trail. Stevens was still unconscious, lying against Faraday's back, his wrists tied around Faraday's waist to keep him from falling off.

"I don't know," said Short, a little testily. "You lost the card draw. You're stuck with him for now."

"Damn it." Faraday spit. "I was hoping these two would've killed somebody and brought back a horse for this one." Stevens lay against him as limp as a dead man. Quince had donated the dirty shirt that they'd tied around Steven's gunshot wound as a bandage.

They sat watching as Bolten and Quince rode up around a large boulder and joined them.

"Nobody back there, hunh?" Short asked Bolten.

"Oh, there's somebody back there—two of them in fact," said Bolten. "But whoever they are, they turned back before they got down under our gun sights."

"Lawmen . . . ," Short deduced, studying the trail in dark contemplation. "A posse, maybe?"

"Lawmen's a possibility," Bolten said. "But it's not a posse. Two men out front of a posse wouldn't have turned back. Finding prints that fresh, they would sit still, waited for the others and come on like bloodhounds." He looked around the rugged hill country. "These two might be why your pals haven't been showing up. Nothing like a shiny badge to send a squirrel up a tree."

"Golden Riders ain't squirrels, Bolten. We eat lawmen for breakfast," Faraday said in a thick nasal twang.

"Run on back there and *eat them*, then, if you're hungry," Bolten challenged. He turned his horse back down toward the trail. "We're going to follow the other horse tracks *we* found."

"Wait up," said Short. "We're going when and where *I say*," he said stiffly.

"Suit yourself," said Bolten, still moving his horse toward the trail, Woods and Quince falling in beside him. "Show us a better direction and we'll take it."

"Damn it . . . ," Short growled under his breath, knowing Bolten was right. He booted his horse forward almost at a run and quickly moved around in front of the other three on the trail. Faraday stayed at the rear of the riders, the wounded gunman leaning heavily on his back.

Chapter 19

———

Prew Garlet and the Bluebird had ridden a full day and made it as far as a dry creek bed at the edge of the sand flats. With the mescal still boiling in his head, and the memory of his brothers' deaths becoming more clear and real in his fevered brain, Prew flung himself from his saddle and grabbed on to a stand of brush. For over an hour he'd wretched and gagged like a poisoned dog. The Bluebird sat off to the side on the slope of the dry creek bed and watched with a stoic expression.

When Prew had finished and slumped over onto his side, the Bluebird stood up, walked over and dragged him out of the sun. He washed Prew's face with canteen water and left him lying faceup, staring at the blue, distant sky. Prew watched the world twist out of shape and swirl and spin. He pictured Foz landing on the rocks below the campsite. He pictured Tillman with his throat sliced open, falling to the ground.

"Just . . . shoot me," he murmured to the Bluebird, out of his head. But the Bluebird only saw his lips moving. He had no idea what he was saying. He only nodded in reply, rose up and walked to the horses. He took down their sad-dlebags, saddles and bedrolls. Then he made a camp where they stayed for over two days and a night, until Prew appeared over his bout with the loaded mescal.

On the third morning, after three cups of strong cof-fee and a modest breakfast of warmed elk jerky and hard soda crackers, the two gathered their gear and supplies, and prepared their horses for the trail.

"I'll tell you something, Bird," Prew said as he tight-ened his horse's cinch and tested his saddle with both hands. "I have never in my life drank *anything* like that." He stepped back from his horse and dropped a stirrup down its side. "And I'll tell you something else, I'll never drink nothing like it again."

Standing a few feet away, not seeing Prew's face, the Bluebird had no idea he was even being spoken to. He stood staring at a single rider who had slipped in close without being seen and stepped down from his saddle and stood facing the two from across the creek bed.

"Hello, the camp," Luke Bolten called out, now that he realized the Indian saw him.

Prew spun around in the direction of the voice, his hand going to his holstered Colt. The Bluebird only continued staring.

"Easy now, ole pard," Bolten said to Prew. "I'm bet-ting you and me are on the same trail." He eyed the Mex-Indian, already supposing him to be the Bluebird.

Prew held his hand firm on his gun butt.

"Oh? And what trail might that be, pilgrim?" he asked, a suspicious look on his drawn face.

"Allow me to be as blunt as a missing thumb," said Bolten, a flat smile on his face. "I'm betting you're a couple of Golden Riders." He held up a hand in a show of peace. "If that be the case, we're sent to see what's taking you so long."

Prew let his hand fall from his gun butt, but didn't answer, not just yet.

"All right then. . . ." Bolten gestured his raised hand toward the other riders just out of sight in a stand of rock and brush, and waved them in.

Seeing Dayton Short and Earl Faraday riding ahead of the other two riders, Prew relaxed and watched the riders come in closer and start down the far side of the creek bed. Then he tensed as he saw Lester Stevens flopping unconscious against Faraday's back. As they crossed the creek bed, he watched closely, knowing he'd have to determine quickly what they might know about how Stevens got the bullet hole in him.

"Prew Garlet!" Dayton Short called out as he slid his horse to a halt in a sidelong spray of dust. The others reined down all around him. "I am damn glad to lay eyes on you." He looked around, saw the Bluebird and touched his hat brim toward him. "I was getting concerned the same thing happened to you that happened to this poor sumbitch." He gestured toward Stevens.

Prew looked at the wounded outlaw flopping against Earl Faraday.

"That's Lester," said Prew, looking surprised. "What happened to him anyway?"

"That's what we'd like to know," Bolten cut in, leading his horse up the side of the creek bank in the dust the others had raised with their horses. "I'm Luke Bolten, this is Hank Woods and Jimmy Quince." He motioned at the other two gunmen, then said, "Do you know there're two riders back there tracking you along this trail?"

"No, I don't," said Prew. "Obliged you telling us about them. I'd hate to make it this close to Kane's place and get ambushed." He gestured at the Mex-Indian. "This is the Bluebird. Kane sent me to escort him back."

"Howdy, Bird," said Bolten.

"He don't speak English so good sometimes," said Prew.

"Sometimes, hunh?" said Bolten. "You mean other times he speaks it all right?"

"That's right," said Prew. "I don't know if he speaks Spanish any better. I've tried both."

Bolten turned to the Bluebird and rattled a few curse words at him in Spanish.

"Whoa," said Prew taking a step back in case the Bluebird jerked up his gun and started firing.

"Stay out of this, Garlet," said Bolten. He laughed as the Bluebird nodded his head in agreement. Then he said in English, "You are one stinking flea-bitten bastard, Mr. Bluebird." He sat grinning. The Bluebird returned his grin and nodded vigorously.

Prew looked puzzled.

"This Mex-Injun couldn't hear a bear fart if it aimed at his face," Bolten laughed.

"What?" said Prew, looking around at the Bluebird.

"He's deaf, damn it," Bolten said in a louder voice.

"You don't know that," Short said in a sharp tone.

"Yes, I do," Bolten said confidently. "If he could

hear what I said, we'd be shooting holes into each other right now."

"It makes sense, now that I think about it," Prew said. "He used to handle explosives for the mining companies."

"There you have it," said Bolten. "His hearing got blasted away a long time ago." He grinned at Prew and Short and said, "I'm going to check my horse's hooves now. If there's anything else you need me to figure out for you, maybe we could do it over some coffee?"

The outlaws watched him walk away leading his horse. Woods and Quince stepped down from their horses and followed.

"Pay him no mind," Faraday said to Prew under his breath. "We don't know if they'll be riding with us or not." He looked at Short and said, "Can we get Stevens off me for a while."

Prew and Short helped untie Stevens' wrists and lowered him from behind Faraday's saddle. They carried him into the thin shade of a twisted ironwood tree and laid him in the dirt under its branches.

"Where's your brothers anyway?" Short asked, leaning down beside Stevens with a canteen.

"I don't know," said Prew. "We've had lots of trouble getting up here. I don't mind saying, I'm a little concerned. My brothers are always up for a big job like the one we've got coming."

"It's not just your brothers, Prew," Short said. "I can name a half dozen men or more shoulda been here by now. Something's afoot. I'm thinking a lawman is dogging us."

Prew ventured, "You figure that's what happened to ole Lester here?"

"I don't know," said Short. "But we'll damn sure find out if we can keep him alive long enough to tell us."

"I think we should ride back and shoot whoever it is back there," said Faraday. He held Stevens' head up enough for Short to pour water onto the wounded man's parched lips. "Wait a minute," he added, looking at Stevens' face, wobbling his head back and forth in his hands. "We're wasting water on a dead man." He dropped Stevens' head and stood up, wiping his hands on his trousers. "I've been toting a stinking corpse all this time."

Prew breathed a sigh of relief.

Short stood up. "We're going back to Kane as fast as we can. See what he's got in mind." He capped the canteen and looked around at Prew. "What do you think, Prew? Want to ride back and look for your brothers, or get on up to Kane, head out for this big job he's got?"

"Let's get on to Braxton Kane's," he said. "I've got a feeling I can't do much for my brothers." He glanced up at the Bluebird who stood watching them with caged eyes.

The Ranger spotted the new flock of buzzards circling in the sky as he and his prisoner rode the last mile down onto the edge of the sand flats. They stopped for a minute and Sam looked up at the big birds, then back over his shoulder in the direction of the last grizzly feast they'd discovered over the edge of the high trail.

"I could have left you behind, Teddy, if all I had to do was follow the buzzards," he said to Bonsell.

Bonsell didn't answer. He sat watching the buzzards circling high up and ahead of them for a moment, then nudged his horse forward beside the Ranger and the two men rode on.

A half an hour later they had reached the dry creek bank and saw the body of the dead outlaw dragged to the side and left for the scavengers. Two big birds already stood atop the dead man's belly. Three more stood lined along the other side of the creek bed.

"Look at them, Ranger," said Bonsell, the two of them stepping their horses down into the dry bed and across to where the body lay spread-eagle in the afternoon sun. The two buzzards on Stevens' chest stopped their pecking and stood red-beaked, looking at the two approaching horsemen. "They're so used to you, they don't even bother to move when you ride up. Must be they know a good friend when they see one."

"That's enough out of you," Sam said.

But Bonsell wasn't finished. He gave an ugly grin.

"Must be you and them are all one big happy family," he said.

Sam didn't answer. He stepped his dun closer until finally the two big birds rose up reluctantly and batted their big wings skyward. The other three held their ground on the creek bed edge and stared curiously.

"You know him?" Sam asked.

"Never seen him before in my—" Bonsell's words stopped as Sam's Colt came sidelong and rapped him on the side of his head hard enough to make him wobble in his saddle. "Jesus, Ranger," Bonsell said in pain, yanking his hat off and cupping a hand on the whelp the gun barrel raised. "There was no call for that."

"I told you I'm counting on you, Teddy," Sam said evenly to the pained outlaw, sliding his Colt back into its leather. "Imagine how disappointed I am when you let me down that way."

"It don't seem fair, a lawman gets to rough a man around this way," Bonsell said.

"I sympathize with you," Sam said. "But it makes up some for having to chase you curs down, hear all your sharp-mouthing. Now, let's try again, see if you've just learned anything. Do you know this man, Teddy?" he repeated.

"Ranger, I told you, I never seen this—" His words stopped short again, this time when he saw Sam's hand go back to his holstered Colt. "Okay, yes! I do know him," he said quickly. "His name is Lester Stevens."

"One of your Golden regulars, is he?" Sam asked, letting his hand drop away from his Colt.

"I wouldn't say he's a *regular*, so much as I'd say he rides with us sometimes when—" He saw the Ranger's hand go back to the gun butt. "All right, yes! I suppose you could say he's a regular. Damn, why are you asking if you already know?"

Sam's hand slipped away from the Colt again.

"I don't already know the answer, Teddy," he said. "But I do know when you're lying. See how that works? See why it's important that you not lie to me, just the two of us out here . . . us and the buzzards *that is*." He gave Bonsell a flat, sidelong stare.

"Hell, that's crazy talk, Ranger!" Bonsell said. "That just sounds like an excuse to bust a man's head any time you damn well please."

"No," Sam said, "not just anytime I please, Teddy, else I'd be busting your head every three minutes. But I believe we've come to a place where you need to know that if you don't tell me the truth every time you open your mouth, I'll get tired of fooling with you and feed you to these buzzards."

"You need me, Ranger," Bonsell said smugly.

"Not if you're not helping," Sam replied. "I can drop you and follow the tracks as far as they'll take me. I don't want deadweight hanging behind me." He turned his eyes upward for a second, then looked straight ahead. "You let me know right now if I'm not going to be able to count on you, Teddy. I'll keep us both from wasting each other's time."

A quiet and sudden change in the Ranger's tone and demeanor caused Cutthroat Teddy Bonsell to look at him in a new light. He just stared at him as they stopped their horses and stepped down beside Lester Stevens' body. He wasn't sure if it was the lingering effects of the mescal, or if the Ranger was purposely playing with his mind. But something told him that here in this desolate stretch of Mexican desert, unarmed, was not a good place to agitate a lawman widely known for his ability to kill.

"Ranger, I—I was just joshing you back there about the buzzards and all," he said in earnest. "I didn't mean nothing by it."

"I understand, Teddy," Sam replied. "I have as much

a sense of humor as the next man." He nodded at the body on the dirt. With his hand on his Colt he looked at Bonsell closely and said, "This man being a regular, those other bodies we found by the high trail, I take it we're getting closer to the Golden Riders' hideout?"

"Yeah . . . ," Bonsell said in a meek, submissive voice. "We're getting closer. We've got a turnoff less than twenty miles ahead."

Sam nodded, looking down at the body in the dirt, dust caked in Stevens' open eyes.

"You want to drag your friend over and throw some rocks on him, that'd be all right," he said quietly.

Bonsell considered it for a moment.

"Naw," he said, "we rode together some, we weren't what you'd call friends, pals, nothing like that." He gazed off in the direction of the horse tracks leading away along the dusty, desert floor. "We've got a blow coming. I'd just as soon get on . . . get this over with."

They turned to their horses, stepped up in their saddles and left the creek bed. They rode on in silence beneath a darkening sky and a rise of hot desert wind.

PART 4

Chapter 20

A storm had blown in hard from the southwest by the time Short and Faraday led the rest of the outlaws through a winding rock pass and out onto a stretch of rocky flatlands. In the open doorway of an abandoned stone and adobe building Braxton Kane stood watching as the riders rode the last fifty yards toward him. On Kane's left beside the open door stood a rifleman named Buford Barnes. On his right stood the bartender from the Luna Loca, Ned Cooney. Cooney held a shotgun at port arms.

"It's about damn time some of you gunnies started showing up here," Kane said, eyeing the men as they stopped at a hitch rail. He looked at Prew and said, "Where's your brothers? Where's everybody else? What the hell's going on?"

"It's been a hard trip, Brax," Prew said as he and the men stepped down from their saddles. "I wouldn't count on my brothers showing up at all. I've got a feeling they've all three met a bad end."

"Too bad," Braxton Kane said gruffly. "I'm damned sorry to hear it. I liked those hombres."

"We had a bank job go wrong, they went to jail," said

Prew. "The Bluebird blew half the town down getting them out." He paused, then said, "Now, I've got some even worse news for you, Brax." He hesitated, then said flat out, "Ranger Sam Burrack killed your brother, Cordy."

"What the hell are you saying?" Kane looked angry, as if it were all a lie.

"I hate to bring this news to you," said Prew. "But I heard it from Cutthroat Teddy Bonsell and Jake Cleary. They were with him when it happened. The Ranger killed Cordy and stuck Bonsell and Cleary in jail in Midland. The Bluebird and I blasted them out, blew about half the damned town down. We split up with Bonsell and Cleary, left them with Mangett, Weidel and Joey Rose in Alto Cresta. Joey Rose was cut all to hell, I doubt he's coming. The others were supposed to catch up to us after they took care of anybody trailing us. But they never came along." He offered a wary look.

The men stood in silence. Braxton Kane pounded his fist quietly on the hitch rail.

"Samuel by-God Burrack . . . ," he growled. "I'll kill him if it's the last thing I do on earth." He looked off for a moment, his eyes squeezed shut. When he opened them, he let out a tight breath and tried to continue as if Prew had never mentioned his brother's death. He looked at Luke Bolten, Hank Woods and Jimmy Quince.

"Good to see you men riding with us again," he said.

Bolten stepped forward.

"When we heard your men weren't showing up, we offered to ride along with these two and see why," he said. "If you've got a big job, you can count on us."

"Obliged, Bolten," said Kane. "You three come along

at the right time. I'm going to make all of us rich." He patted the gunman on his shoulder. He stepped over along the hitch rail and stood looking at the Bluebird. "I'm damn glad to see you," he said to the Mex-Indian. "Are you ready to blow something up for me, fill your sack with gold, Mr. Bird?"

The Bluebird nodded, not hearing a word.

"You must've wasted no time getting here, Cooney," Short said to the tall bartender.

"He didn't," said Kane, speaking for Cooney. "He came here straightaway, right after you fellows left the Luna Loca. Since we were getting short of hands, I took him on. If the others show up, there's still enough for everybody. This is a big job."

Cooney grinned, and kept quiet.

Kane looked off at the sight of rain moving across the stretch of flatlands toward them.

"We're going get wet here in about a minute," he said, estimating the distance of the rain and the strength of the wind shoving it closer. "Let's get inside. Barnes," he said to the rifleman, "you and Cooney get these horses in the barn. Get them watered and grained. Then get on back here. We've got to talk about this gold that I can't wait to get my hands on." He rubbed his hands together in anticipation as he talked.

Inside a long bunkhouse built especially for the riders when they gathered together to plan their ventures, the men pitched their saddlebags at the foot of a row of narrow-framed beds. When they'd finished washing the trail from their faces and hands and dusted down their clothes and hats, they formed a half circle around Braxton Kane to listen.

Outside, the storm had moved in and settled low overhead. Thunder exploded like cannon fire, so loud and close that Kane had stopped and waited for it to settle. With each solid, seemingly earth-splitting clap of thunder, the Bluebird raised his eyes toward the ceiling. A faint smile of contentment moved across his tightly set lips.

Finally the storm grumbled past them and Kane walked in front of the men.

"All right, hombres, here it is," he said. "Barnes and the new man, Cooney, is staying here guarding the place. So, it looks like there's going to be eight of us. I had figured on more, but we'll have to go with what we've got. This is a onetime opportunity. We can't wait for anybody else to show up." He looked all around. "We can't wait for them, and we can't let nothing slow us down until this job is over. Even avenging my brother's death has to wait. When you see how much this job is worth, you'll understand why."

He paced back and forth in front of a glowing hearth, iron poker in hand as he continued speaking. The men watched and listened in rapt silence.

"The German consulate in Matamoros has transacted a large purchase of U.S. gold ingots from the mint in Denver City. The U.S. Army is guarding the shipment by rail all the way to the northern Mexico border. They'll be using the mint's steel-plated safe car."

A low groan started to rise among the men. But Kane raised a hand stopping them. He paused and grinned.

"But from the border, even though they're using the U.S. mint car, the Mexican *federales* will take over guarding the shipment." His grin widened at the thought.

"*Muchas gracias*, Mexico!" Bolten called out with a laugh.

Dayton Short looked disgruntled by Kane and the others laughing along with Bolten.

"Brax, if you're talking about the border crossing at Sonoyta, there's no rail spur there."

"Not at Sonoyta, there never was," Kane said, the men's laughter fell away at Bolten's quip and they got serious again. "But owing to this big shipment there is a brand-new spur not far from there. That's where they'll make the change. There'll be a six-car train headed out of there with just enough guards to not spark too much interest." He grinned again. "They figured ole boys like us will be sniffing like hounds at anything heavily guarded, coming along a brand-new stretch of rail coming out of that direction. One of those cars will be the mint car. It'll be disguised. We'll have to see which car it is. . . ."

Kane looked around at the fervent faces, letting the interest build. Then he gave a shrug. "But I don't mind doing that much for a shipment of gold . . . do you, men?"

The men nodded and murmured in agreement.

But Short looked concerned.

"Has anybody *seen* this new rail spur, Brax?" he asked.

"Yes," Brax said pointedly. "I have. I saw it seven months ago when they started laying track, and I went back and saw it two weeks ago, through a telescope, just to make sure my inside information was reliable." He nodded. "The rail stretched as far as I could see."

The men murmured again in agreement with Kane.

"Somewhere," he continued, "they're going to have to unload the mint car onto wagons to take it on to Matamoros." He looked back and forth at the faces; then he stopped when he glanced at the Bluebird. "But before they get the chance, Mr. Bird here is going to blow that car wide open. We're going to kill a few *federales*, unload it ourselves, and cut out—bringing the gold right back here."

"There's something you need to know about the Bluebird," Short said in a cautioning tone.

"Yeah . . . ?" Kane gave him a look, annoyed with Short throwing cold water on his plans. "What is it, Dayton, Gawd-damn it."

"Brax, the Mex-Injun is deaf," said Short. "I wouldn't say it if it wasn't true."

Kane looked taken aback, but only for a moment.

"We'll see about that," he said, sounding more and more put out with Short. "Why don't I just ask the man himself?" He turned to the Bluebird and said, "Bird, can you hear me?"

The Bluebird studied his face a moment and nodded.

"I hear you," he said in a deep, gruff voice.

"I'll be damned," said Short with a dejected look, as Kane's eyes turned to him with a sour stare. "Brax, I swear, he's deaf. Ask Prew, ask Bolten!"

"Damn it, man," said Kane, "I just asked *him*. If he couldn't hear me, I expect he wouldn't have answered!" Anger rose in his voice as he spoke. But he turned to

Prew and Bolten and asked, "What the hell is Short talking about?"

Prew looked at the Bluebird, then back at Kane.

"I think maybe Bluebird doesn't hear exactly right all the time," he said. "But he seems to be fine now."

When Kane's eyes turned from Prew to Luke Bolten, Bolten shrugged and gave a half grin.

"Short's acting a little finicky if you ask me," he said. "I did say that a man who spent a lot of time working around mine explosions might have some trouble hearing everything going on around him—"

"You said he's deaf, damn it!" Short barked. His hand almost went to his gun butt. But he caught himself and stopped. Bolten chuckled, looked down and shook his head at Short's near eruption.

"Enough of this!" Kane shouted, whacking the iron poker on the plank floor. "Bird . . . ," he said swinging back toward the stoic Mexican-Indian. "If I point at something and tell you to blow the hell out of it, can you do it, or not?"

"I do it," said the Bluebird, nodding.

"There you have it," Kane said with finality, staring hard at Short. "I think Bolten's right, you're getting finicky on us. Unless you've other things worrying the living hell out of you, let's talk about who's going to be doing what on this job."

Short gritted his teeth and kept his mouth shut as the outlaw leader continued.

The Ranger and Cutthroat Teddy Bonsell, having ridden wide of El Ricon, had taken shelter beneath a cliff overhang in a short hill line just above the flatlands. They'd made it up the sloping rock hillside to the overhang only seconds ahead of a wind-driven deluge and a bombardment of thunder. With the nervous horses standing behind them, they sat in the dirt, reins in hand for an hour watching long twists of lightning reach down from a boiling, black sky.

"El Ricon is the last of the towns in this hill chain," said Bonsell. "It's all desert flats and hill from here to Kane's."

Good, Sam told himself, listening.

"With this blow wiping out the tracks, maybe you'll need me a little more than you thought you would," Bonsell said, testing his position with the Ranger. But the Ranger wasn't giving Bonsell an inch of ground.

"Are we going to have to go through all this again, Teddy?" he asked quietly. As he spoke he reached down and slipped his Colt from its holster and turned it in his hand as if inspecting it.

Bonsell got the message.

"No, we don't," Bonsell said quickly. "I was just thinking out loud, is all."

"I see," the Ranger said. He held the Colt a moment longer as if considering whether or not to holster it. Finally, he sighed to himself and lowered it back into its leather. "How much farther do you say we are from Braxton Kane's hideout?" he asked. He'd been measuring their distance based on the twenty-mile estimate Bonsell had given him earlier; but he wanted to see if Bonsell was keeping track himself. Bonsell came back without hesitation.

"Less than five miles, Ranger," he said, looking Sam in the eyes. "We'd gone about fifteen before this blow set in." He gestured his eyes out through the sidelong rain toward the trail they'd ridden along the flatlands. "A mile and half farther, you can see the trail leading up to it."

Sam nodded; it sounded reasonable.

"If you don't mind saying, Ranger," Bonsell ventured, "how are you going to go ride there and face as many men as Kane's going to have all around him?"

"I'm not," Sam said. He just stared at Bonsell.

"You're not . . . ?" Bonsell asked. He gave a slight chuff. "Then just what is it we're doing going up there?"

"We're not," Sam said. "Leastwise, not for a while."

"All right," said Bonsell, with a slight shrug, "you don't want to tell me."

Sam considered it. Knowing it wasn't information Bonsell could use one way or the other he said, "You said they're gathering for a job. That means they'll be coming out soon enough, headed for that job. I'd rather meet the Golden Riders out here on my ground, instead of up there on theirs."

"No offense, Ranger," Bonsell said, "but it won't matter. Either way, you face up to them, they're going to kill you."

Sam looked at him intently.

"That would work out good for you, wouldn't it?" he said.

"Yes, it would," said Bonsell; he shrugged again. "No point in me denying it."

"The fact is," Sam said. "I'm not going to face off

against them. I'm going to follow them to this big job. See if we can't all get better acquainted once we get there."

Bonsell stared at him for a moment, bemused at the idea.

"I'm starting to think you're crazy, Ranger," he said. "I heard it before, now I'm starting to believe it."

"We'll just have to wait and see, Cutthroat Teddy," Sam replied quietly. "A lawman's only crazy if his plans fail."

"If it fails, do I get to ride away, Burrack?" Teddy asked boldly.

"If my plan fails," Sam replied in an even tone, "who's going to stop you?"

Chapter 21

It was turning dark by the time the storm had blown itself out across the Mexican badlands. The heavy rain left the thirsty desert making sucking sounds in every direction as it drew the water down deep into the dry earth. The Ranger made coffee with water he'd caught in a coffeepot he'd placed beneath a steady stream of runoff from the cliff overhang. He strained most of the hillside silt from the water through a clean spare bandanna he pulled from the bottom of his saddlebags.

After a meal of coffee and jerked elk, Sam and Bonsell pitched their saddles and bedrolls on either side of the small fire for the night. As a precaution, Sam handcuffed one of Bonsell's wrists to his saddle stirrup, as he had been doing each night before they turned in. Even with the outlaw cuffed, Sam kept his sleep to a thin level, able to snap himself awake at the slightest sound, the faintest movement around him.

Bonsell had learned the Ranger's sleeping habits the first night out, having snapped a twig of mesquite and seeing Sam's Colt come up from under his blanket, pointed and cocked. From that point on, the wily outlaw had resolved himself to his captivity, at least for the time being. All Bonsell had managed to do was keep the Ranger on alert, which would get him nowhere. It was better if the Ranger eased his guard down a little. Bonsell knew an opportunity would present itself. When it came he could make his move. Until then he had to relax, wait for it, recognize it and be ready to pounce on that opportunity the very second he saw it arrive.

With the small fire banked against being seen either along the low hill line or out across the sand flats, they slept under the overhang, outlaw and lawman, each in what small and tenuous space they'd claimed for themselves on the hard belly of the earth.

During the night, his Winchester leaning against a rock beside his saddle, Sam's eyes opened at the faintest sound of something on the hillside trail above them, back in the direction of El Ricon. Awake, he lay listening, his eyes moving across Bonsell's sleeping face, his Colt ready to take on anything the night presented. Yet, after a long silence, the whole of his senses probing and searching the darkness all around him, he heard nothing else foreign to the night; and he let his eyes close again and went lightly back to sleep.

Before dawn the two awakened, first the Ranger, then the prisoner. Bonsell sat up smelling the aroma of fresh coffee boiling in the pot over a thin fire. He looked over at the Ranger who sat staring at him, a tin cup steaming in his gloved hand.

"What is this big job Kane has lined up?" he asked flatly, assuming Bonsell would know.

"Nice try, Ranger . . . ," Bonsell said, still waking

up, pushing a cuffed hand back through his dark, tangled hair. "But Kane never tells a man more than he needs to know until the time comes."

"You said he sent for the Bluebird," the Ranger said, "so we know it has to be something hard to get to. Not something he can goad somebody into giving up from a money drawer or a strongbox."

"Yep, I'd say that's a fair guess," said Bonsell. He jiggled his cuffed hand; Sam half rose, stepped around, unlocked the cuffs and sat back down.

Rubbing his wrist, Bonsell reached out, filled his waiting tin cup and sat back. He blew on the coffee and sipped it. Sam watched and waited. He'd learned that Teddy Bonsell always let something slip, said more by accident than he intended to without being pushed or pressured.

"Tell me about the jail break again," Sam said, sipping his coffee.

"Again . . . ?" Bonsell sighed into his steaming cup. "I didn't leave nothing out about it, Ranger."

"I just like hearing it," Sam said, watching, listening.

"I bet you do like hearing it," Bonsell said with sarcasm. "All us Golden Riders getting blown out of our eyebrows."

"Why do you think the Bluebird used such a high charge?" Sam asked, ignoring Bonsell's remark. "It doesn't take near that much to rip out a jail window. He blew one man out into the street, bars and all. Half of Midland Siding is having to be rebuilt or repaired."

"Putting blame where blame's due," said Bonsell, "a lot of that explosion came from the mercantile store's firing powder."

"Still," the Ranger continued, "the explosion wouldn't have reached the mercantile if the Bluebird hadn't used so much to blow the jail window."

"You've got me there, Ranger," said Bonsell. "I know he nearly killed us all. I still have ringing in my head if I turn a certain way."

"You figure the Bluebird always carries that much dynamite?" Sam asked, trying to get a lead on what Kane had in mind for the Mexican-Indian to do.

"A man who makes his own dynamite can carry as much as he wants to, I expect," said Bonsell.

"You've got a point . . . ," Sam replied, but he wasn't buying it. Nobody carried dynamite unless they needed it, especially a man who knew its strength, who'd spent his life witnessing its powerful devastation.

Changing the subject from the Bluebird, Sam looked all around the rugged, desolate terrain.

"Braxton Kane found him a nice safe hole to crawl into, I'll give him that," he said.

Bonsell gave him a short, nasty grin, unable to keep his contempt for the law hidden for too long at a time.

"You're going to give him more than that when he gets you in his sights," he said. "Killing Cordy Kane was the worst mistake you ever made."

Sam ignored his remark and tried to keep him focused on some kind of revealing conversation.

"How far do the Golden Riders go to pull a robbery?" he asked quietly.

"As far as Braxton Kane wants them to go," said Bonsell. "High Montana, except there ain't nothing there—deep Mexico, if it's gold, and if there's enough of it to make it worth the ride."

"Montana's got gold, too," Sam said, listening for anything he might need. "Better grade of gold at that."

"Yeah, I guess so." Bonsell shrugged. "I was just making a point." He paused, then said out of the blue, "Kane's been spending lots of time around Sonoyta, up around the crossing? See, if I was a lawman, I'd be smart enough to figure he might be up to something there." He tapped his head to indicate his ingeniousness. "But that's just me." He grinned at his cleverness.

Sam's mind piqued up at his words, but he kept his demeanor calm, unmoved.

"Naw, I don't think so," he said coolly. "There's nothing there."

"Ha, that shows what you know," Bonsell said. "Cordy and I rode up there right before we got you stuck on our trail."

"Yeah? So what?" Sam said.

"So, I heard him and Cordy through an open window when we got back. He was giving Cordy the devil for taking me with him. Cordy lied, told him he didn't take me all way there with him. Said we split off and met again later in El Ricon."

Sam worked the information across his mind.

"Still," Sam said, "there's nothing in Sonoyta that would need a dynamite man carrying as much as the Bluebird is carrying. Sonoyta means nothing." He shook his head.

Bonsell gave him a sour look. Sam could tell the

cocksure outlaw didn't like his ideas being disputed, especially by a sworn enemy, a lawman.

"Maybe not now," Bonsell said, "but there's a rail spur going on south of there. Once it's up and going, it'll cause Sonoyta to spring up like Abilene. 'Course you might be too shortsighted to see it."

"Yep, I expect so, Teddy," Sam said, getting the picture, wondering why the Mexican government or anyone else would build a rail spur south of Sonoyta. "Get your coffee finished, Teddy. We're going to ride up closer to Kane's place, take ourselves a look." He pushed himself up, dusted the seat of his trousers and slung coffee grounds from his tin cup.

Sonoyta, huh . . . ?

He'd keep it mind, Sam told himself, picking up his rifle and saddle and turning to the horses.

With no tracks left to follow across the sand flats, the Ranger kept to the low, rocky hillside, Bonsell riding in front of him. The two took a longer trail circling above the wet sand flats and came to the same place they would have had they crossed the low desert floor. Following a trail upward a half mile, Bonsell stopped and held his horse out of sight just below the crest of a hill.

"Right over this edge, we'll start seeing Kane's place as we get closer," he said.

"Then let's go," Sam said.

"The thing is, they'll be able to see us too if we ain't careful," said Bonsell. "If they see us now, they'll kill you, and just as likely kill me for bringing you here."

"Then you'd best see to it we *are* careful," Sam said.

"If he's got rifle guards out, we'll never get past them, Ranger," Bonsell said, having a change of heart now that they were down to the killing edge of the game. "Don't you understand what I'm saying here? They'll kill us both!"

Sam saw the raw fear in his eyes now that they'd reached their destination.

"I understand what you're saying. Let's go," he ordered Bonsell quietly. "Whatever made you think you'd live forever?" He reached out and slapped Bonsell's horse on its rump.

The horse bolted upward; Bonsell's lower lip trembled in fear and anger.

"That's a hell of thing to say, Ranger—!" he shouted over his shoulder, yanking back on his horse's reins even as it bounded up over the crest of the hill. Coming over the crest right behind him, the Ranger sidled close and slapped the horse's rump again to keep Bonsell from pulling it back.

"Keep moving, Teddy!" the Ranger shouted.

"Damn it to hell, Ranger! *Stop slapping my horse!*" Bonsell shouted. "What's *wrong with you*?" But Sam would have none of it. A third time he slapped the horse's rump. The horse almost reared against Bonsell's tight-handed reins.

"Take us to cover, Teddy," he shouted at Bonsell.

Seeing the Ranger was not going to let up, Bonsell lessened his grip on the reins and let the horse settle onto all fours and dart forward. He looked at the big stone, timber and adobe house in the distance and even gave his horse a hard bat of his boots.

Sam followed right at his side as the two raced to a stand of rock and trees thirty yards away. As the horses moved into the cover and the two men brought them to a sliding halt, Sam turned and looked at Bonsell.

"Looks like his rifle guards must've taken the day off," he said.

"It's a good thing for us if they did," Bonsell said, still a little out of breath. "You would have gotten us both killed otherwise."

"Nobody's fired a shot, Teddy," Sam said. "For all we know there's nobody here."

"Brax Kane would never leave this place unguarded," said Bonsell. "It might be they're just waiting for us to get closer, then open up on us."

"It might be," Sam said, not convinced. He looked all around on the ground and found the tracks of two horses that had to have been made after the storm. He thought about the sound he thought he'd heard in the night up along the hill trail from the direction of El Ricon. His eyes followed the prints from where they came into sight from brush and rock and led straight toward the big house.

More Golden Riders showing up . . . ? he asked himself.

Before he could pursue the question any further, rifle shots exploded from the direction of the house. A second later return fire erupted from a stand of wild grass less than fifty yards from the house's front door. A horse cried out in the grass as a bullet struck it. Sam saw it just as it fell out of sight, whinnying pitifully. *A familiar-looking horse . . . ?* He saw rifle smoke rise from behind a tree and saw glass break in the one of the house's front windows.

"Looks like we've rode into a gun battle, Teddy," Sam said, watching the gunfire from around the edge of a rock.

"Let them have it," Bonsell said, "so long as it ain't pointed in my direction."

"*Hunh-uh,*" said Sam. "Get ready to ride. I think they're in the grass on my side."

"You think they are? But you don't know for sure?" Bonsell asked.

"That's all we got for now," said Sam. "Are you going to ride on your own, or do I have to keep smacking your horse's rump all the way?"

"You're going to get us shot!" said Bonsell. As they spoke, bullets whizzed back and forth between the outlaw hideout and the guns blazing in the grass.

"No, I'm not," Sam said hurriedly, "not if you do like I say. I saw a barn twenty yards on the right side of the house. We're making a run for it. Stay in front of me and keep your horse at a run. There's a good chance we'll make it."

"A *good chance*?" said Bonsell. "You're crazy! I need better odds than a *good chance*!"

Sam drew his hand back as if ready to swat Bonsell's horse on the rump.

"I don't have time to argue with you, Teddy," he said in a determined voice.

"Damn it, Ranger! Stop *doing that*!" Bonsell shouted. He turned in his saddle and batted his boots to his horse's sides. "If I make it to the barn, I'm not going no farther. I swear I'm not!"

As soon as they rode out from behind the rocks, rifle fire from the house turned its attention away from the grass and in their direction. Sam fired his Colt as he rode, Bonsell lying low in his saddle only a few feet ahead of him. From the grass, the gunfire pounded steadily on the house, providing Sam and Bonsell cover until they directed their horses inside the open doors of the barn and leaped down from their saddles.

"Ha! That wasn't so bad," Bonsell said, now that the rifle fire couldn't reach them. "As far as I'm concerned—"

"I'm going in," Sam said, cutting Bonsell off. He reloaded his Colt as he spoke. Outside, the firing continued heavily back and forth.

Sam saw a determined look come to Bonsell's eyes.

"Go on ahead, Ranger, shoot them curs!" he said. "I'll stick right here and see to it our horses are safe."

"Obliged, Teddy," Sam said. Then he reached out from behind his back with his handcuffs and snapped one around Bonsell's wrist. "You can watch about the horses from over here." He dragged the outlaw to a stall door and snapped the other cuff around an iron hinge.

"Ranger, you can't leave me here handcuffed! What if they kill you? What happens to me?"

"Then you'll have to tell a good story, how I made you bring me here," Sam said. He grabbed his rifle from his saddle boot and ran out the barn door in a crouch toward the side of the house, catching the riflemen on their blind side as they fired into the grass and trees.

Chapter 22

————

The gunfire from the trees and grass kept the gunmen busy in the front of the house while Sam ran in a crouch and took cover at the side wall, out of sight. Seeing him trying to take position, the gunfire from the grass grew even heavier. Sam ran alongside the house, found a half-filled rain barrel and rolled it on its bottom edge over to the window standing ten feet above the ground.

As the gunfire thumped into the front of the house and zipped along past him, he leaned his rifle against the wall, placed a short plank across the top of the barrel and climbed atop it.

Here goes. . . .

Gripping the ledge of the open window, he climbed up and rolled over the ledge and crashed onto a landing on a staircase. Hearing his entrance, two gunmen turned toward him from the front window, their rifles already firing.

Sam flattened on the landing and stuck his Colt out between two ballasts and returned fire. His rapid shots hit one man twice in the chest and sent him flying backward through the window onto the front porch. The

other man threw a jammed rifle aside and grabbed for
a shotgun leaning against a chair. But before he got the
shotgun leveled to fire, another shot from Sam's Colt
sent him stumbling backward against the wall. He slid
down as the shotgun fell from his hands.

The Ranger stood and walked down the stairs, one
step at a time with caution. He heard the back door
slam shut behind a pounding of boots across the back
porch. With only one round left in his smoking Colt, he
shoved the gun into its holster and drew the big clumsy
LeMat from where it stood in his waist. A long strip of
rawhide ran through a lanyard on its butt and looped up
around Sam's neck.

"Don't—Don't shoot, *please* . . . !" the wounded man
leaning against the wall pleaded, seeing the big gun in
the Ranger's hand.

"Don't make me," Sam replied, stepping closer, the
big LeMat out and cocked, already feeling heavy in his
hand. Out front in the tall grass the shooting had waned
to a halt. "How many of you are here?" he demanded.

Gripping his bloody chest, the wounded man tossed
a glance toward the front window.

"Barnes and me, now," he said. He gestured to the
rear of the house and added, "Those . . . two jackrab-
bits . . . couldn't stick."

"So I noticed," Sam said, hearing boots pound
around the side of the house and take off across open
ground. He kicked the shotgun aside and leaned enough
to look out the front window. He saw Joey Rose, his
face covered with gauze like a mummy, and John Garlet running, guns blazing in their hands. Garlet ran

shirtless, covered in bandage and gauze from his waist up. His right arm was thickly plastered and held up shoulder-level, a diagonal iron rod running up from his hip, supporting his elbow.

Sam watched them run twenty yards before a concentrated volley of gunfire cut them both down.

"Hey . . . ," said the wounded man, tugging a bloody hand at Sam's trouser leg. "I'm dying here . . . ain't I?" he said, his voice sounding weak, starting to wheeze in his bleeding chest.

"I believe you are," Sam said evenly. He stooped and started to untie a bandanna from around the man's neck, to hold against the flow of blood. But the man shook his head weakly. "No need in a bandage," he wheezed. His dimming eyes went to the big LeMat in Sam's hand. "Obliged . . . you not shooting me with that."

"Think nothing of it," Sam said quietly. He lowered the LeMat, feeling the weight of it hang on the rawhide strip.

Seeing the gun not pointed at him, the wounded man looked relieved.

"I was . . . making good . . . tending bar . . . then *this*," he said. His head lolled to one side, bobbed once and lay there, his dead eyes staring aimlessly across the room.

"We make our choices . . . ," Sam said quietly, knowing the man wasn't listening. He stood up, shoved the LeMat back down in his waist and raised his Colt from its holster and began reloading.

"Ranger Burrack," a voice called out from the direction of the tall grass.

Hearing a familiar voice, Sam stepped over and

stood in the open front window. He raised a hand and waved it back and forth slowly. He gave a slight smile and shook his head to himself, seeing Sheriff Schaffer and the Delmar twins walking toward the house from the grass and tree line. Lindsey helped the limping sheriff move along, both her hands supporting his forearm. Sam could see a wide strip of cloth circling Schaffer's leg just above his knee.

Her brother, Toby, helped John Garlet hobble through the grass, Garlet's unbandaged arm looped over his shoulder. Garlet's bandaged and plastered arm stuck out from his shoulder like an outrigger on a boat. Sam saw fresh blood running from under the thick gauze surrounding Garlet's head.

Sam watched the four draw closer, curious to hear their story.

"I can't tell you happy we are to see you, Ranger," Sheriff Schaffer called out.

"Same here," Sam replied, although curiously. He stepped over the low window ledge and onto the front porch. He met them at the steps and helped Lindsey walk Schaffer over to a chair and sat down. Toby lowered John Garlet into a chair beside him. John Garlet stared up at Sam with a peculiar idiotlike grin.

"I know you," said the grinning outlaw.

"Keep quiet, Garlet," said Toby, carefully removing the gauze to check a bullet graze on the outlaw's head.

"I've got a prisoner in the barn," Sam said, looking from one face to another, then settling on the sheriff, "but I've got to ask, what brings you up here, Sheriff?"

"Chasing these Golden skunks, same as you, Ranger,"

Schaffer said. "I've never seen nothing like them. You shoot one, and two more pop up in his place!"

"It's tough, a gang this big," Sam said.

"Don't I know it," said Schaffer. "I started out chasing this lunatic when he escaped from the doctor's office. He met up with Joey Rose along the way—Rose being the one lying out there dead, I'm pleased to say. They both ran up here, so, here *we* are. I took a bullet in the leg two days ago. But it's a clean enough wound." He grinned and gestured a nod toward Lindsey. "Can't complain though . . . it gets me attention from this lovely young lady."

Lindsey smiled and looked down.

"Hush now, Sheriff," she said modestly.

"So did I," John Garlet mindlessly cut in, grinning, eager to be a part of the conversation.

Ignoring the outlaw, Sam gave Toby a questioning look.

"I couldn't just sit still and watch the sheriff go out here alone," the young man said. "I asked myself what would Ranger Burrack do in a situation like this." He shrugged. "So, here I am."

"But I did it because it's my job, Toby," Sam said in a cautioning tone.

"And it might be *mine* too, someday," Toby replied.

"You've been a good influence on my brother, Ranger Burrack," Lindsey said. "And I admit, on myself as well." She blushed a little. "I don't know if he was being brave or being foolish, but I wasn't about to let him go alone. So here *I am*, too."

"Was that the big buckskin I saw go down out there?" Sam asked, already dreading the answer.

"Yes, it was," Lindsey said. "But he's all right," she added quickly. "Toby pulled him down out of the gunfire. He just has a graze along his rump. We've named him Easy. I hope you don't mind."

"No, I don't mind. . . ." Sam took a relieved breath upon hearing the horse was alive. "All right," he said. "I'm going to go get my prisoner."

"I'm going to *hang myself*," John Garlet called out as Sam turned to walk away.

Sam looked around at Sheriff Schaffer, who shook his head and said, "It's that loaded mescal, Ranger. It affects everybody different. This one has babbled about hanging himself so long, I'd pay him to do it."

"Hear me, Ranger? I'm . . . going to . . . *ha-ang myself.*" Garlet spoke melodiously, as if singing the words to a song.

"Good luck . . . ," Sam said to him over his shoulder.

When Sam returned to the house with Bonsell, the others had gone inside, Toby keeping watch at the front window in case any more riders arrived. Now that there were other people around, Sam had cuffed Bonsell's hands in front of him. On their way to the house, the cuffed outlaw looked down at his wrists and frowned.

"You have no cause to do this, Burrack," he said. "I have done nothing to warrant such treatment."

"We'll be leaving here shortly, Bonsell," Sam said, the two of them walking on. "Keep behaving yourself. I'll take them off along the trail a-ways."

"Keep behaving myself . . . ," Bonsell chuffed under his breath. "You think you're talking to a child?"

"No," said Sam, "I think you're a full-grown man. So act like it. If you were a child, I might hesitate busting your head with a gun barrel." He stopped Bonsell at the porch steps and gave him a pointed stare. "Do we understand each other?" he asked.

"Yeah," Bonsell said with sarcasm, "we understand."

The two walked up the porch steps and in through the open front door. Toby Delmar turned from the open window, looked Bonsell up and down critically, then turned to Sam.

"Now that you're here, do you suppose I can go fetch the horses and look at Easy's bullet graze?"

"Go ahead," Sam said.

"Lindsey found some food in a pantry," Toby said, turning toward the front door. "She's fixing us up something to eat."

"Sounds good," Sam said. He nodded the twin on, out the door toward the grass and tree line where they had left their horses. As Toby trotted away toward the tall grass, Sam looked at the two dead bodies lying where they'd fallen, one leaning against the wall, the other sprawled on the porch right outside the large front window.

"What a mess," Bonsell said, looking down at the bloody bodies.

"You know these two?" Sam asked.

"Yep," said Bonsell. "Take these cuffs off, and I'll tell you who they are."

"I told you when I'd take the cuffs off," Sam replied. "Tell me who they are, else I'll leave you cuffed until tomorrow."

Bonsell blew out a breath in exasperation.

"There's just no dickering with you, is there?" he said.

"Not a whole lot," Sam said.

"That one is Buford Barnes," he said pointing to the body on the front porch. "He's Brax Kane's houseman, all-around guard and personal assassin."

"I've heard of Buford Barnes," Sam said. "To tell you the truth, I thought he'd been dead for years. I haven't seen any paperwork on him anywhere."

"No, he was alive and kicking," said Bonsell, "just laid up here, taking it easy, killing anybody the Kane brothers pointed him at."

"Well," said Sam with finality, "he's dead now."

"Yes, I'd say he is," Bonsell replied, giving Sam a sarcastic look. "Too bad though. He's known as a hard-killing dog. I'd have given anything to see you face off with him one-on-one."

"I just did," Sam said flatly, returning his look.

Bonsell looked away and grumbled under his breath.

"This one?" Sam asked, nodding at the one leaned against the front wall.

"That's *Stupid* Ned Cooney," said Bonsell. "The last time I was up here, he was tending bar in El Ricon. Struck me he'd kill his ma for a chance to join the Golden Riders."

"Looks like he got his chance," Sam said, remembering Cooney's last words of regret. "Come on, let's get that one off the porch, carry them both out back."

"Not with these cuffs on," said Bonsell.

Sam just looked at him and motioned him toward the front window.

"All right, then. Damn it," Bonsell said walking over, stepping out the window ahead of the Ranger.

"Say Buford Barnes and Kane were real close?" he said.

"Like hounds in a hailstorm," said Bonsell.

"You figure Barnes knew where Kane and his men were headed?" Sam asked.

"If anybody did, Barnes did," said Bonsell. "Kane told him everything."

The two reached down. Bonsell took the dead outlaw by his bootheels; the Ranger took the front of Barnes' bloody shirt in both hands.

"So, it appears you've killed the man who could have told you everything you wanted to know, Ranger." Bonsell grinned as they raised the body, carried it down the front steps and around the house.

"I thought you had it figured they were headed toward a new rail spur near Sonoyta?" Sam said.

"I thought it, for a while," said Bonsell. "But now I've changed my mind. That was foolish thinking on my part."

Sam studied his eyes as they laid Barnes' body on the ground and walked back for the hapless bartender.

"I've changed my mind too," Sam said, looking down at all the fresh hoofprints in the dirt that led off in the direction of Sonoyta. "Now that you're thinking they're *not*, I'm thinking they *are* headed there."

Chapter 23

In the afternoon, the Ranger and Bonsell climbed back into their saddles, ready for the trail. The twins and Sheriff Schaffer stood at the hitch rail to see them off. John Garlet sat in a chair on the front porch, barefoot, an ankle shackled to a support post. He babbled and laughed under his breath as if engaged in conversation with a room full of people. Sam looked up at the bandaged outlaw.

"Do you expect he'll ever be right?" he asked Schaffer.

"I doubt it," said the sheriff. "I believe he's as good now as he'll ever get." He sighed and added, "I don't know if mescal made him crazy, or if the crazy was already there and all the mescal, peyote, cocaine and God-knows-what-else did was let it seep out."

Sam watched the babbling outlaw look out at him with a blank grin and wave his plaster-casted fingertips.

"Ah . . . don't worry about him, Ranger," Schaffer said. "He ain't in so bad a shape for a man who poisoned himself blind drunk and got himself blown up—rode a jail cell door near a hundred feet before lighting in the dirt."

"I expect you're right," Sam said. He turned and looked at the twins standing near Schaffer. Seeing the Ranger's concerned expression, Schaffer tipped his hat up and looked up at him.

"And don't worry about me and these young folks either," the sheriff said. "We've got this covered. I'll get that poor idiot out of sight, in case any Golden Riders show up." He gestured off toward Sonoyta. "Take care of your business out there."

Sam nodded and looked down at him.

"I will, Sheriff," he said.

"I still say I ought to ride along with you, Ranger," Toby said, standing a few feet away beside his sister. He smiled. "What better way for me to get experience as a lawman?"

"Hush, Toby," Lindsey said, hitting her brother half-heartedly on his arm. "You've got no business traipsing off chasing outlaws. We've got to get back and get Dan and our wagon."

Toby ignored his sister and looked back up at Sam.

"I mean it, Ranger," he said. "First chance I get I'm casting my lot as a lawman."

Sam looked at Schaffer.

"See if you can talk some sense into him, Sheriff," he said, only half joking.

"Why, Ranger?" Schaffer said clasping his hand down on Toby's shoulder. "He's a strong, brave lad. Somebody's got to pin themselves to a badge once fellows like you and I are too old to trim our whiskers."

"I suppose you're right," Sam said. He touched his hat brim toward the twins, then the sheriff.

"Blah-blah. What a mess of pig slop," Bonsell said between Sam and himself as they backed their horses away from the hitch rail and turned them to the trail. " 'First chance I get I'm casting my lot as a lawman,' " he mimicked the young twin, his cuffed hands on his saddle horn.

"Shut up, Bonsell, if you ever want to get rid of those handcuffs," Sam said.

The outlaw fell silent, realizing he'd just touched upon a raw nerve, making fun of the twins and the old town sheriff. He smiled to himself with satisfaction.

Nudging his coppery dun forward, the Ranger led them along, following the new tracks that could have been made only after the storm had washed all other tracks away. After a mile and a half, he brought the dun to a halt; Bonsell stopped his horse beside him. Sam turned in his saddle, the handcuff key in hand and motioned for the outlaw to hold out his wrists. Bonsell complied.

As Sam loosened the cuffs and withdrew them, Bonsell rubbed his wrists and gave a thin smile.

"I didn't mean to get under your bark back there, Ranger," he said.

"Sure you did," the Ranger said flatly, putting the cuffs away behind his back.

"But you have to admit, folks like those two and the old sheriff are hard to listen to, them and their goody-goody ways," Bonsell ventured.

"Not for me, they're not," Sam said in defense of Sheriff Schaffer and the orphaned twins. "I'll take *their* kind over *your* kind any day."

"Ha!" said Bonsell. "I don't believe that. Look where you live your life, Ranger. You're more at home in my world than you are in theirs. I know you are. I can see it in you. You like it where you live, and how you live—"

"You don't see anything, Teddy," said Sam. "That's why you're here, having to wait for somebody to turn a key for you." He paused, then said, "You don't know nothing about me. All you need to know is when we get close to Kane and his men, if you give us away, try to run out, I'll kill you before you get ten feet."

Bonsell shut up quickly again and turned facing the hoofprints and the trail ahead.

They rode on, neither of them speaking for the rest of the afternoon. Yet, as they reached the place where the hoofprints turned upward off the sand flats trail onto a rocky hillside, Sam stopped and drew his Winchester from its boot. He checked the rifle and held it ready.

"What's the deal, Ranger?" Bonsell said. "Are you getting fainthearted on me?"

"This whole trek, Kane's had men waiting at every stop and turn," Sam said. "I don't expect it to be different now."

"If you're scared," said Bonsell, "maybe you'd best give me a gun and let me lead us."

"No gun, Teddy," Sam said sternly. "But I'll take you up on leading us, only because if anybody's waiting up there I'll have my hands full. I don't want you behind me." He gestured Bonsell forward with his rifle barrel.

"Now, you see? That's the kind of talk that would hurt most people's feelings, Ranger," Bonsell said, nudging his horse forward, ahead of Sam onto the upward path. "But I have come to overlook it, knowing how you are—"

Sam saw Bonsell fly backward from his saddle just as a rifle shot resounded from up among a tall stand of rock on the sloping hillside. As if in reflex, Sam threw the butt of his Winchester to his shoulder and fired three shots in rapid succession at a drift of rifle smoke. With nothing but the smoke as a target he hadn't expected to hit anything. But his cover fire bought him and the dun a few precious seconds to get off the path and in among the rocks while the shooter ducked down.

It worked. By the time the ambusher had collected himself and fired again, the Ranger was down from his saddle, had pushed the dun farther out of the way, and raced out in a crouch and dragged Bonsell back into cover. A shot nipped the earth behind his bootheel as he and the wounded outlaw fell among the rocks. Bonsell's horse raced away along the hillside.

"My . . . horse," Bonsell said, choking on blood.

"Lie still, Teddy," Sam said; another rifle shot ricocheted off the large rock.

"Lie still . . . ?" Bonsell said through bloodstained teeth. "Look at me . . ." He spread his bloody hands showing Sam his gaping chest wound, and gave a pained grin. "You . . . can't tell me . . . what to do no more. . . ." His head fell to the side even as the Ranger tried to stop the blood by wadding the front of Bonsell's shirt and pressing it to the wound. Another shot rang out from up the hillside.

The Ranger leaned the dead outlaw against the large rock, stood and picked up his rifle. He gathered the dun's reins and hitched the nervous horse to a stand of brush. Then he unlooped his canteen strap from his saddle horn, calmly sat down at the edge of the large rock and waited, knowing there was no cover worth trying for up the side of the hill.

Hun-uh, not with rifle sights on his chest. . . . He'd seen how well the ambusher could shoot.

Looking out at the evening shadows growing long across the hillside and the sand flats below, he realized darkness would be his best way out of here. The ambusher wouldn't give up his advantage and come down and face him in the open—it would be foolish. It would be just as foolish for the shooter to wait up there and let darkness even the odds between them. Besides, Sam told himself, no outlaw would want to waste their time here, taking a chance on getting shot while the rest of the gang rode on to gather up the spoils of their trade. *No way. . . .*

He looked over at Cutthroat Teddy Bonsell, sitting dead in the dirt, leaning against the rock in a pool of blood. He uncapped his canteen, took a long sip of water and leaned back against the rock, and waited.

Fifteen miles from the new rail spur outside of Sonoyta, Mexico, Braxton Kane and his men sat in the morning sunlight atop a high bluff overlooking the wide badlands below. Woods and the Bluebird sat in the seat of an empty freight, Bluebird with a satchel full of dynamite slung over his shoulder. He held an unlit cigar between his fingers. In another wagon Jimmy Quince sat in the driver's seat hunched down in his trail duster, a rifle propped against the seat alongside him.

From the other side of the tall bluff, Prew called out to Kane as he spotted the lone rider racing up the trail toward them.

"Here comes Dayton Short," he called out.

"It's about damn time," Kane said to the riders gathered around him. "I expected him last night." He didn't bother looking around toward the approaching rider. Instead he gazed back out, down onto the badlands floor. He studied the glint of steel rails running straight, dark and shiny on a cleared path through stands of mesquite, prickly pear and short twisted fire barrel cactus standing rigid in the wavering heat.

"I feel lucky today . . . ," he murmured to himself.

"Here he is, Kane," said Luke Bolten, standing down beside his horse a few feet from Braxton Kane. "Want me to see what took him so long?"

Braxton gave Bolten a long look, knowing the dislike festering between the two men.

"No," he said finally. "I can speak for myself, Bolten."

"I know you can, Boss," said Bolten. "I'm getting overanxious, wanting to do my part here."

Kane turned away from him and stepped down from his saddle. He met Short and grabbed his horse by its bridle as Short slid it to halt.

"Why you riding so hard, Dayton?" Kane asked as Short leaped down from his saddle, his rifle in hand.

"I rode like this all night, afraid I might miss out on everything," Short said catching his breath. He jerked his hat from atop his head and slapped sand and dust from his clothes.

"Is our back trail clear?" Kane asked. "We're going to be riding it hard in a little while."

"Yes it's clear, *now*," said Short. "Just like we thought, that Ranger was following us." He took an open canteen that Prew Garlet handed him, swigged a mouthful of tepid water, swished it and spat it out. He gave Kane a firm stare. "Cutthroat Teddy Bonsell was riding with him. Notice I'm saying *was* riding with him." He handed the canteen away. "I put a slug straight through his blood-pumper."

"Cutthroat Teddy, helping lead a lawmen to us . . . ," Kane mused quietly. He shook his head. "What the hell is this world turning into?" He collected himself and said to Short, "You killed him too then?"

"Yes I did—I mean no—I mean I don't know, Brax," Short said.

Kane just stared at him.

"What I mean is, he's gone," Short lied. "As soon as I cut ole Teddy down, all I saw was the Ranger's back-side. He was getting out of there." As he told it, he looked all around with a grin, making sure everybody heard him. "I expect that Ranger thought himself tough until he found himself in the sights of a Golden Rider."

The men nodded and murmured in agreement.

"*Ha . . . !* You must be getting squirrelly, Short," Luke Bolten cut in. "I've never heard of Burrack hightailing it from anything or anybody."

"Calling me a liar?" Short bristled. His rifle started to swing up in his hands.

Kane grabbed the rifle barrel and shoved it down before Bolten could answer.

"I've never heard of Burrack hightailing either, Date," he said. "I hate thinking what he might have done if Bonsell took him through the hideout."

"I do too. . . ." Short took a breath and simmered; he let his rifle hang at his side. "You've both heard of him hightailing now," he said. He gestured back at the trail he'd ridden in on. "Either I hit him and he died on the run, or he's hightailed it and ain't coming back for more." He stared at Bolten as he concluded, "You don't see him dogging me, do you?"

"You'd better hope you ain't lying to me, Short," said Kane. As he spoke he and the others felt the first faint rumble of steel wheels in the rocky ground beneath their boots. "If you are, you know I'm going to kill you." He gave a look around at the men. "Then we'll be cutting your share of this gold up between us."

"I'm not lying, Boss," Short said with a sincere expression. Under their boots the rumble of the steel wheels grew more intense.

"All right, then. We'll find out more about it later." He grinned and turned and motioned the men up onto their saddles. "Right now, we've got to go catch ourselves a train."

The men turned excited. The ones already mounted pulled bandannas up over the bridge of their noses. The ones still afoot hurriedly jumped up atop their horses and gathered their reins.

In the empty freight wagon beside the Bluebird, Woods

reached out and pushed the brake handle forward, unsetting it. He turned and grinned at the Bluebird.

"You ready to blow something up, Bird?" he said.

"I am," said the Bluebird with a nod, only half understanding what Woods had said. As Woods slapped the reins to the wagon horses' backs, the Bluebird struck a match and lit the big cigar, keeping it away from the long length of fuse coiled around his shoulder.

Chapter 24

The Ranger lay on a twenty-foot-wide jut of stone, above the sandy lower slope of a hillside. He'd ridden up off the sand flats only moments ago, after following the ambusher's tracks all night. At dawn he'd seen he was close enough for the fleeing ambusher to spot his dust if the hard-riding outlaw had slowed long enough to look around. He wanted the ambusher to lead him straight to the Golden Gang, so he pulled back a little rather than take the chance of being discovered and pulled away on a wild-goose chase.

This would do. . . .

He waited, ten minutes, maybe longer, he told himself. But that was all right. He would see the ambusher again as he rode back into sight. If he lost him for a while, that would be all right too. He still had his horse's fresh tracks laid out before him. He stared out through the telescope toward a place where the worn trail led around a wide rocky abutment that stood sunken back against a shorter line of hills. Waiting for the ambusher to reappear, he scanned the length of the

new rails running out from Sonoyta. He slowly scanned
the lay of the broken hills both short and tall, and—

Whoa . . . ! What's that?

He homed the telescope onto the dust roiling up from
behind one of the lower hills. Just in time he caught
sight of the riders and the two empty freight wagons riding down onto the flats in a hard run. Far to his left he
saw black locomotive smoke streaming along atop
another rise of low hills, going straight to the riders.

Train robbery . . . !

He started to spring to his feet. He saw he wasn't
close enough to stop the robbery or even warn the train.
But with any luck he could start picking off the Golden
Gang as they made their getaway. But before he'd risen
all the way from the rock, the hard stab of a blunt rifle
butt nailed him between his shoulder blades and set
him back down. The blow sent his telescope flying
from his hand, down over the front edge of the rock and
tumbling down the sloping hillside.

"I hope you move again, gringo," said a voice behind
him, "so I can hit you some more."

Sam didn't try to rise again. But he did turn his head
enough to see the dusty, sweat-stained uniform of a
federale corporal standing crouched over him, a long
French rifle in his hands.

Still struggling to catch his breath after the rifle
blow, Sam spoke over his shoulder.

"I'm glad to see you, Corporal," he said. "I'm Arizona Ranger Sam Burrack. I've caught a robbery about
to take place—"

His words stopped short as another rifle blow struck him in the same spot, this one not as hard, not hard enough.

"Do not talk unless you are told to," the soldier said harshly.

"That is enough, Corporal Sererro," said another voice, this one sounding of higher authority. "Get him on his feet."

"Hands in the air, gringo!" the corporal demanded. Sam ventured a look around as the corporal grabbed his shoulder and pulled him up off the rock surface. Across the flat-topped rock, Sam saw a tall, lean captain standing with a big French revolver in his hand. On either side of him stood three troopers, all six with their rifles up, cocked and aimed.

The captain gave a trace of a smile beneath a thin, black mustache, eyeing the Ranger badge on Sam's chest. The six-point metal star stood pinned to his vest, half obscured by the lapel of his duster.

"Tell me my dusty friend," he said in good border English, looking Sam up and down, "why does an Arizona Ranger take such an interest in our new railroad enterprise?"

"I just spotted a robbery getting ready to bust loose down there," Sam said, with urgency in his voice.

The captain only stared at him, as if in disbelief for a second. He looked out past Sam's shoulder and into the distance, his view falling short in the wavering heat.

"That does not tell me why an Arizona Ranger is here, watching our train," the captain said.

Sam saw something deeper in the captain's eyes. These soldiers had not happened upon him by chance. They were out here for a reason.

"I'm tracking some outlaws," Sam said, trying to hurry. "I'm allowed to do so under the Matamoros agreement—"

"I know about the Matamoros agreement, Ranger," said the captain, cutting him off. "What do you know about this train you were watching?" As he spoke he pulled a French telescope from inside his dusty tunic and stretched it out and looked through it.

"I don't know nothing about your train, Captain," Sam said quickly, "Except that if this bunch is robbing it, it must be carrying a rich load—something that's going to take two freight wagons to haul away."

"*Capitán* Ameile, I can see smoke from the train," the corporal said as the captain continued looking through his telescope, searching for the riders and the wagon.

Sam saw the expression change on the captain's face as he stopped scanning with the telescope and homed in on the riders and the wagons.

"*Ae-ah . . . !*" he said with a start. "You tell the truth, Ranger." He jerked the telescope from his eyes and collapsed it quickly and shoved it inside his tunic. He stared at Sam, urgency now in his eyes as well. "It is gold, Ranger! The train carries gold! More gold than you or I can imagine! That is why I patrol out here today, to keep watch on the gold." He waved his men's rifles down.

Sam leaned and looked down off the rock behind the captain. He saw a dozen more men on horseback.

"You must come with us for now, Ranger," the captain said. "I must see proof that you are not a part of the robbers."

"I understand, Captain," Sam said. He knew better than to waste precious minutes arguing. When the time was right, he'd split away from the captain and the *federales* and do whatever he had to do to get his sights back on Kane and his Golden Riders.

The short six-car train moved along at a rapid clacking twenty miles per hour across the stretch of sand flat between the rocky lines of hills both low and high. Sitting atop the third car behind the engine, a guard sat scanning the terrain, wearing a pair of wide glass goggles against the wafting black smoke spiraling up and twisting back above the top of his head. He caught sight of the riders moving out toward the train from a narrow pass between two stands of tall canyon rock.

The guard stood up in a crouch and hurriedly began thumping his rifle butt soundly on the roof of the rail car beneath him. Having given the inside guards his warning, he turned to run along the catwalk on top of the car and duck down out of sight. But before he could disappear a rifle shot hit him high up in his left side at heart level. He crumbled off his feet and rolled limply off the other side of the roof.

"Good shooting, Bolten!" Kane shouted as the men's horses raced forward at a full run, the empty freight wagons falling behind, unable to keep up with them. "Kill them! Kill them all!" he yelled, racing on.

A heavy volley of rifle and pistol fire exploded among

the riders as wooden window covers raised and windows swung open. Along the sides of two of the cars, seven soldiers stood up with French rifles and returned fire. But the men on the swaying lurching train with the awkward long-barreled single-shot French rifles were no match for experienced horseback shooters carrying Winchester repeaters and deadly six-guns. They fell from sight one by one, either shot down or dropping for cover.

Out front of the moving train, Prew Garlet's horse raced out from a line of rocks and swung along the engine as it passed. Prew steadied his horse at a fast pace, leaned over, grasped his left hand firmly around an iron climbing rung and swung up out of his saddle, his Colt raised in his right hand. He waited until he knew the engineer and the fireman would see his rider-less horse veering away from the train. When they did, the fireman leaned out the window and aimed a shotgun down at Prew.

Prew's Colt resounded before the fireman could pull the shotgun's trigger. He flew sidelong out the window in a spray of blood. Prew had to duck as the discarded shotgun bounced against the side of the metal car and spun away.

Fifty yards back, Kane and the men saw Prew slip though the engine's side window. Kane smiled to himself behind his bandanna as the train began slowing down.

"Watch the Mexicans, men," he ordered his riders as they too slowed alongside the bullet-riddled rail car. "Make sure none of these chicken-soldiers decide to be a hero on us."

"I'm thinking they're all dead," Bolten called out as the train slowed even more, down to a slow crawl.

"If they're not already, see to it they are before I send in the Bird," said Kane. The train had come to a stop thirty yards past an earthen ramp created for wagon crossings.

"You got it, Boss," said Bolten, riding up beside the rail car, his nickel-plated Russian smoking in his hand. He jerked his bandanna down from his face and grinned. "I *looove* how I live," he beamed. He stood up in the saddle and pulled himself in through the open car window.

Kane looked back, judging the distance to the earthen ramp behind the train.

Faraday and Short stood up in their saddles and climbed in right behind them. Kane looked concerned until several shots resounded from inside the rail car. Bolten gave a dark chuckle and called out, "They're dead now, Boss."

Kane smiled. He turned to the freight wagons just now catching up, the Bluebird bouncing on the seat beside Woods, his lit cigar in his mouth. Jimmy Quince was in the other wagon right behind them.

"Get in and get 'er blown, Bird," he called out. "She's all ours." He swung down from his saddle and hitched his horse to the rear of the wagon. He saw Prew shove the engineer away and motioned the frightened man out across the sand flats. As the man took off running, Prew walked back from the idling engine.

"How's it all looking so far, Boss?" Prew asked in a

weak voice. Sweat streamed down his pale face. His eyes looked hollow, blank, confused.

"So far it's looking as slick as socks on a rooster," Kane said with a grin, stepping over toward the door Bolten had opened for the others. His smile went away, seeing Prew's face more closely. "What the hell's wrong with you?" he asked.

"Nothing," Prew said. "I drank some bad loaded mescal a while ago. I'm still having trouble shaking it. It keeps coming and going. I see things. I saw you get off your horse . . . it looked like three or four more of you got off behind yourself." He rubbed his head, realizing how crazy he sounded.

Kane just stared at him for a moment. Finally he burst out laughing and said, "Jesus! Remind me to find some of that stuff after we get done and safe somewhere."

"It's not something you want to do, Brax." Prew shook his sweaty head. "I—I think I'm losing my mind sometimes. There's no end to this stuff."

"Listen to me," Kane said, pulling Prew to the side away from the open door. His voice lowered. "Once we're done here, you keep the Bluebird in hand, and don't let him out of your sight. He looks up to you." He glanced all around. "Everybody else is going their own way. But it's going to be you, him, and me making our getaway together."

Prew knew better than to question Kane at a time like this.

"All right, Brax, I'm with you."

"Watch your heads!" Bolten shouted from the open door on the other side of the car where he and the men had jumped out and taken cover. Prew and Kane ducked down on their side of the car just as an explosion ripped upward through the roof

"Whooo-ieee!" Bolten blurted out, jumping up into the car ahead of everyone. He pulled the squeaking safe door open. "Kane, you've got to come look at all this gold!"

Kane grinned at Prew as they stood up dusting themselves off.

"Well, now, let's go see what we've got here," he said, delighting in his newfound fortune.

Bounding up into the car, they looked through the smoke as the men on the other wagon climbed back in on the opposite side.

"My, *oh my*! Ain't it a beautiful sight . . . ," Kane said in awe, staring at the smoky insides of the built-in safe covering the front half of the rail car. Pallets of gold ingots lay in a row, the ingots stacked over waist high, glistening even in the dark swirl of dynamite residue.

"And it's all ours!" Bolten said, excited.

As if snapping out of a trance, Kane shoved his Colt into its holster and turned to the men.

"All right, hombres, get those wagons to both doors and load them up high and tight!"

"When do we split the gold up?" Short asked.

"Don't worry about that right now!" Kane snapped, glaring at the Short. "You'll get your share."

The men leaned their rifles against the wall and holstered their revolvers. Woods turned his wagon and pulled alongside one door. The men started filling the wagons as Quince pulled his wagon around and aligned it up to the other door. The men worked feverishly for the next twenty minutes loading the gold onto the wagons from both doors. When the last of the gold was scooped up and carried out, Kane snatched an ingot from a pile in Woods' arms and sliced it with his boot knife. He examined the fresh cut and smiled.

"Perfect!" he said, pitching the ingot out to Woods who had stepped onto the wagon and laid down his load. Woods caught it and dropped it onto one of the stacks. "Get the tarpaulins over these loads and let's get going." He looked around at the men. "Short, you and Woods are switching places. Bird, Short, Prew and I are going with this wagon." He pointed to the wagon on his right, the one Woods had been driving. The wagon sat closest to the trail leading to the narrow pass between the two close-standing walls of canyon rock. "Bolten, Faraday, Woods and Quince, you four stay with that one." He pointed at the other wagon, the one that would have to go back thirty yards behind the train and use the earthen crossing ramp. "Is everybody all right with that?" The tone of his voice left no room for disagreement, neither did his hand lying on his holstered gun butt.

Bolten and Short gave each other a spiteful look, each knowing that Kane had split them up because of the bad blood between them.

"Sounds good to me," Bolten said.

Kane looked at Faraday, his nose still purple and swollen from what Bolten had done to him.

"Yeah, I'm all right with it," Faraday said grudgingly.

Kane looked at Quince.

"I'm a rich man; what do I care?" the outlaw said with a grin.

"That's the spirit," said Kane. He looked at the four. "I'm going on ahead with this wagon while you fellows cover us with rifles as far as the pass—in case anybody comes up on our trail."

"There's *nobody* on our trail," Bolten said with confidence.

"I was told there'd be a *federale* patrol scouting ahead of the train," Kane said. "If there's not, so much the better. But if there is, we're going to be ready for them. Once our wagon gets into the pass, we'll give your wagon rifle cover from the rocks until you've joined us." He looked all around again, then settled his gaze onto Bolten. "You four sit tight here until you know we've taken position in the rocks. You see anybody riding up on our trail, turn the rifles on them."

Chapter 25

As soon as the Ranger and the *federales* had heard the heavy gunfire in the distance along the new rail spur, the captain had led his cavalry patrol forward at a run. When they'd rounded a turn in a sandy rise and the idling train came into sight, Sam, riding near the captain's side, looked over and spotted the first wagon rolling out of sight into the narrow pass over a thousand yards away. The captain saw it too. Ahead of them, they both observed the second wagon sitting beside the train.

"Captain," the Ranger shouted above the loud rumble of horses' hooves, "let me go. They're getting away." He gestured his rifle barrel toward the distant pass.

The captain didn't answer for a moment, the two of them pounding on toward the train. But as they gained ground and shots zipped past them from both the train and the narrow pass, the captain waved his corporal and two more riders in closer to him and shouted, "Corporal, go with the Ranger." He motioned the three soldiers toward the shots coming from the pass where puffs of gray smoke rose up in the resounding gunfire.

The corporal and the men looked surprised, but veered their horses away from the hard-pounding patrol and joined the Ranger toward the narrow pass. Watching from atop a rock inside the pass, his rifle in hand, Braxton Kane saw the riders split away from the patrol and head in his direction.

"Damn it, they know we're here," said Kane to Short, Prew and the Bluebird standing beside him. The three stood with smoking rifles in hand. "I know they saw us before we got out of sight, else I would have never starting shooting at them." Along the flatlands gunfire exploded back and forth between the train and the charging *federales*.

"We'll never outrun them up here," Short said, "not with this wagon, not with all this gold. I had a feeling this was all a bad deal from the get-go."

"Did you really?" said Kane, turning to him, his Colt out and cocked an inch from Short's chest. "I think *you've* been a bad deal from the get-go. You've pissed all over my plan since the day I told you about it."

"Easy, Brax, I—"

Short didn't get his words out of his mouth. The Colt bucked in Kane's hand and sent him flying backward off the rock. The Bluebird and Prew stared down at his bloody broken body on the sandy ground below.

"Anybody else think this was a *bad deal* from the get-go?" Kane asked, the Colt smoking in his hand. He cocked it for another shot.

The two shook their heads.

"All right then," said Kane, the gunfire still exploding, the four riders getting closer. "Bluebird, take the rest of that homespun dynamite and blow that rock pass all to hell." He grinned at Prew and tapped himself on his forehead. "See? While you and your brothers washed your brains out with mescal, I was already figuring *possibilities*."

"Good thinking, Boss," Prew said. He pointed out onto the flatlands as the Bluebird hurried away and climbed out among the rocks at the narrow mouth of the pass. "One of those riders is not a soldier. These *federales* don't wear trail dusters and gray sombreros."

"Don't I know it," said Kane. Again the grin. "But surprise, *surprise*," he added. "Guess who does. . . ."

"Ranger Sam Burrack," Prew said flatly.

"Yep, that's him coming to call," said Kane. "Looks like I get to take vengeance without even going looking for him. I just wish I could see his face when all that rock comes falling down on him. But I'll settle for riding away with all this gold, while pieces of him splatter all over the desert floor."

At the wagon beside the train, Woods stopped firing out the window long enough to call out to Bolten who stood firing out the open door window across the rail car from him.

"Kane and his rifles have stopped covering for us, Luke!" he shouted. "They must be holding fire until we get started toward the pass!"

"I hope you're right," Bolten said. "If they don't we're dead, this many Mexes riding us down." He turned and continued firing. In the loaded wagon, Quince looked up from his smoking rifle.

"If we wait much longer, we'll never make it to the pass before they ride right up our shirttails!"

Bolten glanced over toward the pass, then out at the charging horsemen gaining ground.

"You're right, Jimmy, let's get the hell out of here."

Even as rifle shots zipped past them, the four spilled out of the rail car shooting. Quince jumped into the driver's seat of the wagon and turned it back toward the crossing ramp as the other three gunmen pulled their horses out from between rail cars and leaped into their saddles. They raced along the side of the rail train behind the wagon and across the ramp. With *federales* pounding closer, they headed toward the narrow pass, seeing the four riders headed in the same direction, far ahead of them. As he looked, he saw the figure in the gray sombrero and flapping duster tails veer away hard and sharp from the other three.

"What the hell is Kane waiting for!" Bolten shouted, neither seeing nor hearing any cover fire from the pass. As he shouted he saw Faraday rise out of his saddle and fall away in a spray of blood. He glanced around quickly at the wagon, making sure Quince was still driving it toward the pass. Yet, even as he looked he knew they would never make it unless Kane and his three men started covering them. And even then the odds looked bad for them. *Jesus . . . !* All this gold . . .

"Kane, damn you, *you son of a—*"

His words were drowned out as the desert beneath him seemed to lift in the air and slam down hard. Shattered rock, dirt and debris blasted him from his saddle and sent him rolling through more sand, through short, spiky briars and barrel cactus. Behind him, Quince flew up out of the driver's seat of the wagon and sailed away in the cloud of smoke and dust that churned and billowed behind the explosion. Without Quince slapping the reins to the horses' backs, the wagon slowed immediately but not before rolling over Luke Bolten as he tried to struggle to his feet.

In the dust and smoke, Woods staggered in place, his hands raised, having been thrown from his horse as the animal lost its footing in the powerful blast.

"I know, I know, I'm under arrest," he called out to the mounted *federales* who looked like ghost riders appearing through the swirling smoke. Half dazed, he staggered forward toward the Mexican captain. "See . . . ?" He wiggled his raised fingers. *"Mí, Americano,* under *arresto, sí?"* he said, as if the captain would not understand a word of English.

"No, you are not under arrest, you fool," the captain said, his voice even and calm.

"Ah . . ." said Woods, with a smile. "In that case—" But before he could take another step, a dozen rifle shots resounded and cut him to shreds.

Even before the blast had gone off, Braxton Kane and Prew had gotten in the wagon and ridden away while the Bluebird went about his job. The Mexican-Indian had taken his time getting the dynamite placed where it would deliver the most damage to the two large stands of canyon rock standing like sentinels at the mouth of the narrow pass.

When the blast did come, Kane only smiled sidelong

at Prew Garlet and kept the wagon rolling, their three horses' reins hitched to the freight wagon's tailgate. Prew turned in the seat and looked back.

"We'd better wait here for him. I think we've gone far enough," he said. When he saw Kane wasn't stopping he said, "You can't leave him back there afoot."

"He's a Mex-Injun, he'll do just fine on foot."

"I can't let you do this," said Prew.

"You can't stop me," said Kane. Before Prew could reach for his gun, Kane turned and jammed his cocked Colt into his chest. "I've gone about as far as I care to with you and him both. In fact, I wish I had gone on and killed you back when you told me you were still *seeing things* from drinking mescal." He shook his head slowly. "What makes you think I could rely on a man who puts poison like that in his head?"

"Brax, come on," Prew said, looking down at the Colt. "I'm over all that. I'm not seeing things anymore."

"Not seeing things anymore...." Kane mused. "The fact that you even have to say something like that is enough for me." He squeezed a shot into Prew's chest. Then he grabbed him before he could fall away, and squeezed another shot right beside it. Beneath him, the wagon jerked as the team of horses almost spooked and took off running. But Kane settled the animals with a firm hand on the reins. He quickly set the brake, stepped down and looked back along the trail for any sign of the Bluebird. When he didn't see him, he turned to the team of horses and went to work. He was no fool. He knew there was no way he'd get away from the *federales* with a freight wagon load of gold.

He unhitched the team of horses and untied the three saddled horses from behind the wagon. He hurriedly emptied the saddlebags from the horses' backs and filled them with gold ingots. It wasn't as much as he would have gotten had everything gone as planned; but it was still enough to get him where we wanted to go and keep him living high for the rest of his life.

He smiled to himself as he loaded the horse and got ready for the trail. Hell, he told himself, he might go deeper into Mexico, see if he could find some of that loaded mescal he'd heard so much about. Of course he wouldn't make a fool of himself like the Garlets and the other idiots who'd tried the stuff, *hunh-uh*, he had better sense than that, he thought, swinging up into the saddle.

The way he had it figured, with the pass closed he had about an hour or more start before the *federales* got up around the hillside and over to where he'd be. He nudged his horse forward, leaving the remaining gold lying in the wagon with Prew's body, in the Mexican sun. Too bad, but that's how it worked out. . . .

He booted his horse forward and rode upward along the hill trail at an easy clip, the horses loaded with gold on a long lead rope behind him. When he looked back now and then, he saw no sign of the Bluebird, or of any *federales*, or any of his own men. He didn't stop or let up on the horses' pace until he'd ridden a little over an hour. Then he stopped only long enough to pick up the canteen hanging looped on his saddle horn, uncapping it and raising it to his lips.

He'd swallowed a long tepid mouthful of water and

started to lower the canteen. But he froze at the sound of a horse's hoof scrape the hard dirt in the middle of the trail ahead of him. He looked up and saw the dark outline of the rider, the duster, the sombrero.

"Braxton Kane . . . ," the Ranger called out, sitting his horse crosswise on the thin dusty trail. "I'm Arizona Ranger Samuel Burrack—"

Kane didn't let him get his words from his mouth. He raised his Colt and started shooting. On his fourth shot he felt a hot, sharp pain race through his chest. He felt himself fall backward off his saddle. For a split second he felt his fingers claw at the bulging saddlebags—*his gold!*—as he slid from the horse's rump to the ground.

Sam rode the coppery black-point dun over and caught Kane's horses and the lead rope before the horses could bolt past him. He settled the horses and stepped down from the dun. He led the dun and the other horses over and looked down at Kane who lay gasping on the rocky ground.

"You—You . . . taking me in?" Kane rasped. Blood ran from his lips, through his trembling fingers clenching his chest.

"I'd hate to," Sam said, coolly. He held the Colt out at arm's length, cocked, smoking, ready to fire again.

Kane looked down at the gaping wound in his chest. He glanced over at the saddlebags full of gold, shook his head, and looked back up at the Ranger.

"Don't . . . then," he wheezed. He closed his eyes, tight.

The string of horses almost spooked again as the

second blast from the Ranger's Colt resounded out across the Mexican hills, the desert, the sand flats below.

"You've sure been a long day's work, Braxton Kane," he said down to the limp body lying dead in the dirt, knowing Kane couldn't hear him. He looked all around. He saw the dust still drifting back there, still rising and swirling, lazily now, wafting up from the desert floor. "But now we're all done here." He looked out in the direction of the *federales*, then at the horses. "Cover your ears, boys," he said, raising his Colt and firing four signal shots straight up in the air.

The string of horses jerked at the rope. Kane's horses and his own coppery dun only twitched their ears and tossed their heads a little. The dun chuffed and stuck his nose out. The Ranger ran a gloved hand down its muzzle, patted it.

"Tough guys, huh?" he said to the two hard-seasoned trail horses. Then he led all the horses over and hitched them to a scrub piñon out of the sun and he laid himself down in the shade of a rock. There might be other Golden Riders running loose, but he'd gotten the leader, and that was the main thing. The others he'd get to in time. Since the Bluebird wasn't up here, he'd either blown himself up or gotten away.

So be it. See you soon, Bluebird, he told himself, and he leaned back and closed his eyes and waited for the *federales*. After all, this was their job. He was just there . . . well, helping out, is all.

Mesa Grande, Arizona Territory

Sheriff David "Bronco Dave" Winters worked the ram-rod on the barrel of his cap and ball Army Colt and seated the final lead ball into the cylinder. Once the gun was loaded he kept its hammer at half cock and shoved a fingertip of pasty cornmeal batter down over the front opening of each chamber. The cornmeal paste, once dried, served to keep a loose spark from igniting all the other chambers at once, causing a dangerous chain-fire and making the gun blow up in his hand. With the ball of his thumb he pressed a firing cap onto each of the gun's six iron nipples.

This being the seventh cylinder he'd loaded, he left it in the gun, spun it and lowered the gun's hammer between two chambers for safety. Then he lay the big gun aside. Hearing a dark chuckle coming from an occupied jail cell, he looked up and saw the bushy-headed pris-oner, Sherman Geary, standing with his hands wrapped around the bars, grinning at him. Geary's eyes looked huge behind a pair of thick eyeglasses.

"Holy Joe and Mary, Sheriff," Geary said. "That's *forty-two shots* you've made up. Are you expecting a war to break out in Mesa Grande? Who are you scared of?"

Sheriff Winters eyed the prisoner, his bruised forehead, his swollen right jaw. Then he turned his gaze to his battered desk. Six extra cylinders he'd just finished loading stood shiny and black, with the same daub of cornmeal batter drying in their chambers.

Scared? Ha. . . .

"There's a saying, Sherman," the sheriff said. " 'I'd rather *have it* and not need it, than to need it and not *have it*.' "

"Yeah? Well here's another saying for you, *Bronco Dave*," said Geary, taking on a darker tone. " 'Let a man out of his cell, and he'll whop you worse than you've ever been whopped in your life.' "

"Never heard that one," the sheriff said, going along with him.

"You've heard it now," said Geary. "Let me out, I'll show you how an ass-whopping works." His eyes loomed large and swirly.

The sheriff gave a half smile and shook his head.

"Sherman, Sherman," he said in a patient tone. "If I had a dollar for every time you got drunk and tried to *whop* me, I wouldn't need this job." He paused, then said with a level gaze, "How's the welt across the back of your head coming along?"

Geary's hand went to the back of his sore head.

"You never hurt me none, if that's what you're thinking."

"That's too bad," said the sheriff. "I'll remind myself to swing a little harder next time."

Seeing the sheriff start to stand up from his desk to go make his rounds, Geary shook his cell bars with both hands.

"Come on, let me out of here. I'm sober now. Look at me," he said.

"I don't have to look. I can tell when you're sober," the sheriff said. "When you stop talking about fighting me, you'll be sober. Right now you're still drunk. I don't want you falling off your horse and breaking your neck on the way home."

"Damn it," Geary grumbled, turning away from the bars. "I swear to God, if I don't whop you senseless there ain't a dog in Georgia."

The sheriff just shook his head, used to it.

On the corner of his desk lay a rawhide bandoleer with six empty compartments for the extra cylinders he'd loaded. He picked up each cylinder one at a time, inspected it and placed it into its respective compartment and closed the flap and snapped it shut.

There. . . .

He hefted the bandoleer full of cylinders in his hand, looking at them. If he found himself needing a fast reload, here they were, loaded, capped, ready to fire. He would unpin the barrel from the gun's frame, slide off the empty smoking cylinder, slide on a loaded one, replace the barrel, set the pin, and he'd be back in the fight. He could do the whole thing in less than thirty seconds if he had to. Twice in his life he'd *had to*, he reminded himself. He caught a glimpse of those times, dead men, both white and Apache lying all around him, the battle still raging. . . .

He hoped he'd never *have to* again, he told himself, rising from the chair. He picked up the Colt lying on his desk, holstered it and carried the heavy bandoleer to the gun rack and hung it from a peg.

"Geary, can you eat something?" he asked the prisoner. "It might help sober you up."

The prisoner didn't answer. Instead, he cursed and flopped down onto his cot.

"You need to send that ole smoke wagon to the Colt factory," he called out to Winters. "They'll convert it to a *modern-day* gun for you for seven dollars—send you a box of bullets to boot. No real lawman carries a cap and ball. It's an embarrassment. Makes you look like from the days off—"

"Suit yourself," said Winters, cutting Geary short. "I'll bring you some food anyway, if your jaw's not too sore to chew."

"Don't worry about my jaw," Geary snapped back. "Worry about your own when I get out of here."

Sheriff Winters stepped away from the gun rack and picked up the loaded repeater rifle leaning against his battered desk.

"Any fool needing forty-two pistol shots is in worse trouble than he knows," Geary called out.

"You might be right about that, Sherman," the sheriff replied, levering a round into the rifle chamber. He smiled thinly. "But that's why God made the Winchester." He added a warning, "Don't be smoking while

I'm gone, Sherman. Town can't afford to build a new jail. I'd hate to throw you in the smokehouse next time you get your bark on."

Geary didn't answer.

With the rifle hanging in his left hand, Winters took his Stetson and the cell key from a peg beside the door. He snapped the large brass key ring at his waist and placed the Stetson atop his head. He adjusted the hat brim to the time of day and opened the door into a white glare of sunlight. But before he could step all the way out and close the door behind himself a bullet slammed into his chest, flung him backward back into his office and over the top of his desk.

His rifle flew from his hand; he left a bloody smear across the desk, clearing it of paperwork and incidentals, and landed broken and unconscious against a row of cell bars as the sound of the shot still roared along the street.

"Lord God!" Geary shouted. Springing up from his cot, he leaped over to where the sheriff lay sprawled against the cell bars. He adjusted his glasses quickly as if not believing his eyes. Flattened down on the floor lest another shot ring out, he reached through the bars and shook the downed sheriff by his shoulders.

"Sheriff! Wake up!" he shouted. Rolling the sheriff onto his side, Geary saw the gaping hole in his chest, the pool of blood forming and spreading on the dusty floor beneath him. "Don't you die, Sheriff, damn it! Don't you die!" he shouted, seeing frothy blood rise and fall in the sheriff's open lips.

"Hel-help me . . . ," the sheriff murmured in a waning whisper.

Help you . . . ? Geary looked at the blood pouring from the sheriff's chest. Then he shot a glance toward the open door, seeing people gathering in the street looking all around.

"Lie still, Sheriff," he said, even though the wounded lawman wasn't moving. Geary ran his right arm through the bars and took the cell key from the sheriff's belt. "I'm out of here sooner than you thought."

GRITTY WESTERN ACTION FROM
USA TODAY BESTSELLING AUTHOR
RALPH COTTON

Available wherever books are sold or at
penguin.com

Penguin Group (USA) Online

What will you be reading tomorrow?

Tom Clancy, W.E.B. Griffin, Nora Roberts,
Catherine Coulter, Sylvia Day, Ken Follett,
Kathryn Stockett, John Green, Harlan Coben,
Elizabeth Gilbert, J. R. Ward, Nick Hornby,
Khaled Hosseini, Sue Monk Kidd, John Sandford,
Clive Cussler, Laurell K. Hamilton, Maya Banks,
Charlaine Harris, Christine Feehan, James McBride,
Sue Grafton, Liane Moriarty, Jojo Moyes, Jim Butcher...

You'll find them all at
penguin.com
facebook.com/PenguinGroupUSA
twitter.com/PenguinUSA

*Read excerpts and newsletters, find tour schedules
and reading group guides, and enter contests.*

Subscribe to Penguin newsletters and get an
exclusive inside look at exciting new titles and the
authors you love long before everyone else.

PENGUIN GROUP (USA)

penguin.com

s0151